Best of D.H. Lawrence

D.H. Lawrence (1856-1930) was an English poet, novelist, playwright and critic who wrote his first novel, *The White Peacock*, in 1911, and was best known for his works *The Rainbow, Women in Love, Lady Chatterley's Lover* and *Sons and Lovers*. Due to his description of sexual proclivities in his novels and plays, he was a highly controversial figure of the early twentieth century and was subjected to censorship, persecution and misinterpretation of his work throughout his life. E.M. Forster has called him 'the greatest imaginative novelist of our generation'.

Best of D.H. Lawrence

D.H. Lawrence

RUPA

Published by
Rupa Publications India Pvt. Ltd 2003
7/16, Ansari Road, Daryaganj
New Delhi 110002

Sales centres:
Allahabad Bengaluru Chennai
Hyderabad Jaipur Kathmandu
Kolkata Mumbai

Edition copyright © Rupa Publications India Pvt. Ltd 2003

This is a work of fiction. Names, characters, places and incidents are
either the product of the author's imagination or are used fictitiously
and any resemblance to any actual person, living or dead, events or
locales is entirely coincidental.

All rights reserved.
No part of this publication may be reproduced, transmitted,
or stored in a retrieval system, in any form or by any means, electronic,
mechanical, photocopying, recording or otherwise, without the prior
permission of the publisher.

ISBN: 978-81-291-0114-3

Fifth impression 2017

10 9 8 7 6 5

The moral right of the author has been asserted.

Printed at Rekha Printers Pvt. Ltd., New Delhi

This book is sold subject to the condition that it shall not,
by way of trade or otherwise, be lent, resold, hired out, or otherwise
circulated, without the publisher's prior consent, in any form of binding
or cover other than that in which it is published.

CONTENTS

New Eve and Old Adam	1
The Prussian Officer	33
The Horse-dealer's Daughter	63
Fanny and Annie	85
The Woman who rode away	105
Things	153
Odour of Chrysanthemums	166
Second Best	192
Samson and Delilah	203
Sun	224

BEST OF
D.H. LAWRENCE

NEW EVE AND OLD ADAM

I

'AFTER all,' she said, with a little laugh, 'I can't see it was so wonderful of you to hurry home to me, if you are so cross when you do come.'

'You would rather I stayed away?' he asked.

'I wouldn't mind.'

'You would rather I had stayed a day or two in Paris—or a night or two.'

She burst into a jeering 'pouf!' of laugher.

'You!' she cried. 'You and Parisian Nights' Entertainment! What a fool you would look.'

'Still', he said, 'I could try.'

'You *would*!' she mocked. 'You would go dribbling up to a woman. "Please take me—my wife is so unkind to me!"'

He drank his tea in silence. They had been married a year. They had married quickly, for love. And during the last three months there had gone on almost continuously that battle between them which so many married people fight, without knowing why. Now it had begun again. He felt the physical sickness rising in him. Somewhere down in his belly the big, feverish pulse began to beat, where was the inflamed place caused by the conflict between them.

She was a beautiful woman of about thirty, fair, luxuriant, with proud shoulders and a face borne up by a fierce, native vitality. Her green eyes had a curiously puzzled contraction just now. She sat leaning on the table against the tea-tray, absorbed. It was as if she battled with herself in him. Her green dress reflected in the silver, against the red of the firelight. Leaning abstractedly forward, she pulled some primroses from the bowl, and threaded them at intervals in the plait which bound round her head in the peasant fashion. So, with her little starred fillet of flowers, there was something of the Gretchen about her. But her eyes retained the curious half-smile.

Suddenly, her face lowered gloomily. She sank her beautiful arms, laying them on the table. Then she sat almost sullenly, as if she would not give in. He was looking away out of the window. With a quick movement she glanced down at her hands. She took off her wedding-ring, reached to the bowl for a long flower-stalk, and shook the ring glittering round and round upon it, regarding the spinning gold, and spinning it as if she would spurn it. Yet there was something about her of a fretful, naughty child as she did so.

The man sat by the fire, tired, but tense. His body seemed so utterly still because of the tension in which it was held. His limbs, thin and vigorous, lay braced like a listening thing, always vivid for action, yet held perfectly still. His face was set and expressionless. The wife was all the time, in spite of herself, conscious of him, as if the cheek that was turned towards him had a sense which perceived him. They were both rendered elemental, like impersonal forces, by the battle and the suffering.

She rose and went to the window. Their flat was the fourth, the top storey of a large house. Above the high-ridged, handsome red roof opposite was an assembly of telegraph wires, a square, squat framework, towards which hosts of wires sped from four directions, arriving in darkly-stretched lines out of the white sky. High up, at a great height, a seagull sailed. There was a noise of traffic from the town beyond.

Then, from behind the ridge of the house-roof opposite a man climbed up into the tower of wires, belted himself amid the netted sky, and began to work, absorbedly. Another man, half-hidden by the roofridge, stretched up to him with a wire. The man in the sky reached down to receive it. The other, having delivered, sank out of sight. The solitary man worked absorbedly. Then he seemed drawn away from his task. He looked round almost furtively, from his lonely height, the space pressing on him. His eyes met those of the beautiful woman who stood in her afternoon-gown, with flowers in her hair, at the window.

'I like you,' she said, in her normal voice.

Her husband, in the room with her, looked round slowly and asked:

'Whom do you like?'

Receiving no answer, he resumed his tense stillness.

She remained watching at the window, above the small, quiet street of large houses. The man, suspended there in the sky, looked across at her and she at him. The city was far below. Her eyes and his met across the lofty space. Then, crouching together again into his forgetfulness, he hid himself in his work. He would not look again. Presently he climbed down, and the tower of wires was empty against the sky.

The woman glanced at the little park at the end of the clear, grey street. The diminished, dark-blue form of a soldier was seen passing between the green stretches of grass, his spurs giving the faintest glitter to his walk.

Then she turned hesitating from the window, as if drawn by her husband. He was sitting still motionless, and detached from her, hard; held absolutely away from her by his will. She wavered, then went and crouched on the hearth-rug at his feet, laying her head on his knee.

'Don't be horrid with me!' she pleaded, in a caressing, languid, impersonal voice. He shut his teeth hard, and his lips parted slightly with pain.

'You know you love me,' she continued, in the same heavy, sing-song way. He breathed hard, but kept still.

'Don't you?' she said, slowly, and she put her arms round his waist, under his coat, drawing him to her. It was as if flames of fire were running under his skin.

'I have never denied it,' he said woodenly.

'Yes,' she pleaded, in the same heavy, toneless voice. 'Yes. You are always trying to deny it.' She was rubbing her cheek against his knee, softly. Then she gave a little laugh, and shook her head. 'But it's no good.' She looked up at him. There was a curious light in his eyes, of subtle victory. 'It's no good, my love, is it?'

His heart ran hot. He knew it was no good trying to deny he loved her. But he saw her eyes, and his will remained set and hard. She looked away into the fire.

'You hate it that you have to love me,' she said, in a pensive voice through which the triumph flickered faintly. 'You hate it that you love me—and it is petty and mean of you. You hate it that you had to hurry back to me from Paris.'

Her voice had become again quite impersonal, as if she were talking to herself.

'At any rate,' he said, 'it is your triumph.'

She gave a sudden, bitter-contemptuous laugh.

'Ha!' she said. 'What is triumph to me, you fool! You

can have your triumph. I should be only too glad to give it you.'

'And I to take it.'

'Then take it,' she cried, in hostility. 'I offer it you often enough.'

'But you never mean to part with it.'

'It is a lie. It is you, you, who are too paltry to take a woman. How often do I fling myself at you—'

'Then don't–don't.'

'Ha!–and if I don't–I get nothing out of you. Self! self! that is all you are.'

His face remained set and expressionless. She looked up at him. Suddenly she drew him to her again, and hid her face against him.

'Don't kick me off, Pietro, when I come to you,' she pleaded.

'You *don't* come to me,' he answered stubbornly.

She lifted her head a few inches away from him and seemed to listen, or to think.

'What do I do, then?' she asked, for the first time quietly.

'You treat me as if I were a piece of cake, for you to eat when you wanted.'

She rose from him with a mocking cry of scorn, that yet had something hollow in its sound.

'Treat you like a piece of cake, do I!' she cried. 'I, who have done all I have for you!'

There was a knock, and the maid entered with a telegram. He tore it open.

'No answer,' he said, and the maid softly closed the door.

'I suppose it is for you,' he said, bitingly, rising and handing her the slip of paper. She read it, laughed, then read it again, aloud:

' "Meet me Marble Arch 7.30–theatre–Richard." Who is Richard? ' she asked, looking at her husband rather interested. He shook his head.

'Nobody of mine,' he said. 'Who is he?'

'I haven't the faintest notion,' she said, flippantly.

'But,' and his eyes went bullying, 'you *must* know.'

She suddenly became quiet, and jeering, took up his challenge.

'Why must I know?' she asked.

'Because it isn't for me, therefore it must be for you.'

'And couldn't it be for anybody else?' she sneered.

' "Moest, 14 Merrilies Street," ' he read, decisively.

For a second she was puzzled into earnestness.

'Pah, you fool,' she said, turning aside. 'Think of your own friends,' and she flung the telegram away.

'It is not for me,' he said, stiffly and finally.

'Then it is for the man in the moon–I should think *his* name is Moest,' she added, with a pouf of laughter against him.

'Do you mean to say you know nothing about it?' he asked.

'Do you mean to say,' she mocked, mouthing the words, and sneering; 'Yes, I do mean to say, poor little man.'

He suddenly went hard with disgust.

'Then I simply don't believe you,' he said coldly.

'Oh–don't you believe me!' she jeered, mocking the touch of sententiousness in his voice. 'What a calamity. The poor man doesn't believe!'

'It couldn't possibly be any acquaintance of mine,' he said slowly.

'Then hold your tongue!' she cried harshly. 'I've heard

enough of it.'

He was silent, and soon she went out of the room. In a few minutes he heard her in the drawing-room, improvising furiously. It was a sound that maddened him: something yearning, striving, and something perverse, that counteracted the yearning. Her music was always working up towards a certain culmination, but never reaching it, falling away in a jangle. How he hated it. He lit a cigarette, and went across to the sideboard for a whisky and soda. Then she began to sing. She had a good voice, but she could not keep time. As a rule it made his heart warm with tenderness for her, hearing her ramble through the songs in her own fashion, making Brahms sound so different by altering his time. But to-day he hated her for it. Why the devil couldn't she submit to the natural laws of the stuff!

In about fifteen minutes she entered, laughing. She laughed as she closed the door, and as she came to him where he sat.

'Oh,' she said, 'you silly thing, you silly thing! Aren't you a stupid clown?'

She crouched between his knees and put her arms round him. She was smiling into his face, her green eyes looking into his, were bright and wide. But somewhere in them, as he looked back, was a little twist that could not come loose to him, a little cast, that was like an aversion from him, a strain of hate for him. The hot waves of blood flushed over his body, and his heart seemed to dissolve under her caresses. But at last, after many months, he knew her well enough. He knew that curious little strain in her eyes, which was waiting for him to submit to her, and then would spurn him again. He resisted her while ever it was there.

'Why don't you let yourself love me?' she asked, pleading, but a touch of mockery in her voice. His jaw set hard.

'Is it because you are afraid?'

He heard the slight sneer.

'Of what?' he asked.

'Afraid to trust yourself?'

There was silence. It made him furious that she could sit there caressing him and yet sneer at him.

'What *have* I done with myself?' he asked.

'Carefully saved yourself from giving all to me, for fear you might lose something.'

'Why should I lose anything?' he asked.

And they were both silent. She rose at last and went away from him to get a cigarette. The silver box flashed red with firelight in her hands. She struck a match, bungled, threw the stick aside, lit another.

'What did you come running back for?' she asked, insolently, talking with half-shut lips because of the cigarette. 'I told you I wanted peace. I've had none for a year. And for the last three months you've done nothing but try to destroy me.'

'You have not gone frail on it,' he answered sarcastically.

'Nevertheless,' she said, 'I am ill inside me. I am sick of you—sick. You make an eternal demand, and you give nothing back. You leave one empty.' She puffed the cigarette in feminine fashion, then suddenly she struck her forehead with a wild gesture. 'I have a ghastly, empty feeling in my head,' she said. 'I feel I simply *must* have rest—I must.'

The rage went through his veins like flame.

'From your labours?' he asked, sarcastically,

suppressing himself.

'From you—from *you*?' she cried, thrusting forward her head at him.

'You, who use a woman's soul up, with your rotten life. I suppose it is partly your health, and you can't help it,' she added, more mildly. 'But I simply can't stick it—I simply can't, and that is all.'

She shook her cigarette carelessly in the direction of the fire. The ash fell on the beautiful Asiatic rug. She glanced at it, but did not trouble. He sat, hard with rage.

'May I ask how I use you up, as you say?' he asked.

She was silent a moment, trying to get her feeling into words. Then she shook her hand at him passionately, and took the cigarette from her mouth.

'By—by following me about—by not leaving me *alone*. You give me no peace—*I* don't know what you do, but it is something ghastly.'

Again, the hard stroke of rage went down his mind.

'It is very vague,' he said.

'I know,' she cried. 'I can't put it into words—but there it is. You—you don't love. I pour myself out to you and then—there's nothing there—you simply aren't there.'

He was silent for some time. His jaw set hard with fury and hate.

'We have come to the incomprehensible,' he said. 'And now, what about Richard?'

It had grown nearly dark in the room. She sat silent for a moment. Then she took the cigarette from her mouth and looked at it.

'I'm going to meet him,' her voice, mocking, answered out of the twilight.

His head went molten, and he could scarcely breathe.

'Who is he?' he asked, though he did not believe the

affair to be anything at all, even if there were a Richard.

'I'll introduce him to you when I know him a little better,' she said. He waited.

'But who is he?'

'I tell you, I'll introduce him to you later.'

There was a pause.

'Shall I come with you?'

'It would be like you,' she answered, with a sneer.

The maid came in, softly, to draw the curtains and turn on the light. The husband and wife sat silent.

'I suppose,' he said, when the door was closed again, 'you are wanting a Richard for a rest?'

She took his sarcasm simply as a statement.

'I am,' she said. 'A simple, warm man who would love me without all these reservations and difficulties. That is just what I do want.'

'Well, you have your own independence,' he said.

'Ha,' she laughed. 'You needn't tell me that. It would take more than you to rob me of my independence.'

'I meant your own income,' he answered quietly, while his heart was plunging with bitterness and rage.

'Well,' she said, 'I will go and dress.'

He remained without moving, in his chair. The pain of this was almost too much. For some moments the great, inflamed pulse struck through his body. It died gradually down, and he went dull. He had not wanted to separate from her at this point of their union; they would probably, if they parted in such a crisis, never come together again. But if she insisted, well then, it would have to be. He would go away for a month. He could easily make business in Italy. And when he came back, they could patch up some sort of domestic arrangement, as most other folk had to do.

He felt full and heavy inside, and without the energy for anything. The thought of having to pack and take a train to Milan appalled him; it would mean such an effort of will. But it would have to be done, and so he must do it. It was no use his waiting at home. He might stay in town a night, at his brother-in-law's, and go away the next day. It were better to give her a little time to come to herself. She was really impulsive. And he did not really want to go away from her.

He was still sitting thinking, when she came downstairs. She was in costume and furs and toque. There was a radiant, half-wistful, half-perverse look about her. She was a beautiful woman, her bright, fair face set among the black furs.

'Will you give me some money?' she said. 'There isn't any.'

He took two sovereigns, which she put in her little black purse. She would go without a word of reconciliation. It made his heart set hard again.

'You would like me to go away for a moment?' he said, calmly.

'Yes,' she answered, stubbornly.

'All right, then, I will. I must stop in town for to-morrow, but I will sleep at Edmund's.'

'You could do that, couldn't you?' she said, accepting his suggestion, a little bit hesitating.

'If you want me to.'

'I'm so *tired*!' she lamented.

But there was exasperation and hate in the last word, too.

'Very well,' he answered.

She finished buttoning her glove.

'You'll go, then?' she said suddenly, brightly, turning

to depart. 'Good-bye.'

He hated her for the flippant insult of her leave-taking.

'I shall be at Edmund's to-morrow,' he said.

'You will write to me from Italy, won't you?'

He would not answer the unnecessary question.

'Have you taken the dead primroses out of your hair?' he asked.

'I haven't,' she said.

And she unpinned her hat.

'Richard *would* think me cracked,' she said, picking out the crumpled, creamy fragments. She strewed the withered flowers carelessly on the table, set her hat straight.

'Do you *want* me to go?' he asked, again, rather yearning.

She knitted her brows. It irked her to resist the appeal. Yet she had in her breast a hard, repellent feeling for him. She had loved him, too. She had loved him dearly. And he had not seemed to realise her. So that now she *did* want to be free of him for a while. Yet the love, the passion she had had for him clung about her. But she did want, first and primarily, to be free of him again.

'Yes,' she said, half pleading.

'Very well,' he answered.

She came across to him, and put her arms round his neck. Her hatpin caught his head, but he moved, and she did not notice.

'You don't mind very much, do you, my love?' she said caressingly.

'I mind all the world, and all I am,' he said.

She rose from him, fretted, miserable, and yet determined.

'I *must* have some rest,' she repeated.

He knew that cry. She had had it, on occasions, for

two months now. He had cursed her, and refused either to go away or to let her go. Now he knew it was no use.

'All right,' he said. 'Go and get it from Richard.'

'Yes.' She hesitated. 'Good-bye,' she called, and was gone.

He heard her cab whirr away. He had no idea whether she was gone—but probably to Madge, her friend.

He went upstairs to pack. Their bedroom made him suffer. She used to say, at first, that she would give up anything rather than her sleeping with him. And still they were always together. A kind of blind helplessness drove them to one another, even when, after he had taken her, they only felt more apart than ever. It had seemed to her that he had been mechanical and barren with her. She felt a horrible feeling of aversion from him, inside her, even while physically she still desired him. His body had always a kind of fascination for her. But had hers for him? He seemed, often, just to have served her, or to have obeyed some impersonal instinct for which she was the only outlet, in his loving her. So at last she rose against him, to cast him off. He seemed to follow her so, to draw her life into his. It made her feel she would go mad. For he seemed to do it just blindly, without having any notion of her herself. It was as if she were sucked out of herself by some non-human force. As for him, he seemed only like an instrument for his work, his business, not like a person at all. Sometimes she thought he was a big fountain pen which was always sucking at her blood for ink.

He could not understand anything of this. He loved her—he could not bear to be away from her. He tried to realise her and to give her what she wanted. But he could not understand. He could not understand her accusations against him. Physically, he knew, she loved him, or had loved him, and was satisfied by him. He also knew that she would have loved another man nearly as well. And for the rest, he was only himself. He could not understand what she said about his using her and giving her nothing in return. Perhaps he did not think of her, as a separate person from himself, sufficiently. But then he did not see, he could not see that she had any real personal life, separate from himself. He tried to think of her in every possible way, and to give her what she wanted. But it was no good; she was never at peace. And lately there had been growing a breach between them. They had never come together without his realising it, afterwards. Now he must submit, and go away.

And her quilted dressing-gown–it was a little bit torn, like most of her things–and her pearl-backed mirror, with one of the pieces of pearl missing–all her untidy, flimsy, lovable things hurt him as he went about the bedroom, and made his heart go hard with hate, in the midst of his love.

II

Instead of going to his brother-in-law's, he went to a hotel for the night. It was not till he stood in the lift, with the attendant at his side, that he began to realise that he was only a mile or so away from his own home, and yet farther away than any miles could make him. It was about nine o'clock. He hated his bedroom. It was comfortable, and not ostentatious; its only fault was the neutrality necessary to a hotel apartment. He looked round. There was one semi-erotic Florentine picture of a lady with cat's eyes, over the bed. It was not bad. The only other ornament on the walls was the notice of hours and prices of meals and rooms. The couch sat correctly before the correct little table, on which the writing-sachet and ink-stand stood mechanically. Down below, the quiet street was half illuminated, the people passed sparsely, like stunted shadows. And of all times of the night, it was a quarter-past nine. He thought he would go to bed. Then he looked at the white-and-glazed doors which shut him off from the bath. He would bath, to pass the time away. In the bath-closet everything was so comfortable and white and warm—too warm; the level, unvarying heat of the atmosphere, from which there was no escape anywhere, seemed so hideously hotel-like; this central-heating forced a unity into the great building, making it more than ever like an enormous box with incubating cells. He loathed it. But at any rate the bath-closet was human, white and business-like and luxurious.

He was trying, with the voluptuous warm water, and the exciting thrill of the shower-bath, to bring back the life into his dazed body. Since she had begun to hate him, he had gradually lost that physical pride and pleasure in his own physique which the first months of married life had given him. His body had gone meaningless to him again, almost as if it were not there. It had wakened up, there had been the physical glow and satisfaction about his movements of a creature which rejoices in itself; a glow which comes on a man who loves and is loved passionately and successfully. Now this was going again. All the life was accumulating in his mental consciousness, and his body felt like a piece of waste. He was not aware of this. It was instinct which made him want to bathe. But that, too, was a failure. He went under the shower-spray with his mind occupied by business, or some care of affairs, taking the tingling water almost without knowing it stepping out mechanically, as a man going through a barren routine. He was dry again, and looking out of the window, without having experienced anything during the last hour.

Then he remembered that she did not know his address. He scribbled a note and rang to have it posted.

As soon as he had turned out the light, and there was nothing left for his mental consciousness to flourish amongst, it dropped, and it was dark inside him as without. It was his blood, and the elemental male in it, that now rose from him; unknown instincts suffocated him, and he could not bear it, that he was shut in this great, warm building. He wanted to be outside, with space springing from him. But, again, the reasonable being in him knew it was ridiculous, and he remained staring at the dark, having the horrible sensation of a roof low down over him; whilst that dark, unknown being, which lived below all his consciousness in the eternal gloom of his blood, heaved and raged blindly against him.

It was not his thoughts that represented him. They spun like straws or the iridescence of oil on a dark stream. He thought of her, sketchilly, spending an evening of light amusement with the symbolical Richard. That did not mean much to him. He did not really speculate about Richard. He had the dark, powerful sense of her, how she wanted to get away from him and from the deep, underneath intimacy which had gradually come between them, back to the easy, everyday life where one knows nothing of the underneath, so that it takes its way apart from the consciousness. She did not want to have the deeper part of herself in direct contact with or under the influence of any other intrinsic being. She wanted, in the deepest sense, to be free of him. She could not bear the close, basic intimacy into which she had been drawn. She wanted her life for herself. It was true, her strongest desire had been previously to know the contact through the whole of her being, down to the very bottom. Now it troubled her. She wanted to disengage his roots. Above, in the open, she would live. But she must live perfectly free of herself, and not, at her source, be connected with anybody. She was using this symbolical Richard as a spade to dig him away from her. And he felt like a thing whose roots are all straining on their hold, and whose elemental life, that blind source, surges backwards and forwards darkly, in a chaos, like something which is threatened with spilling out of its own vessel.

This tremendous swaying of the most elemental part of him continued through the hours, accomplishing his being, whilst superficially he thought of the journey, of the Italian he would speak, how he had left his coat in the train, and the rascally official interpreter had tried to give him twenty lire for a sovereign—how the man in the hat-shop in the Strand had given him the wrong change—of the new shape in hats, and the new felt—and so on. Underneath it all, like the sea under a pleasure pier, his elemental, physical soul was heaving in great waves through his blood and his tissue, the sob, the silent lift, the slightly-washing fall away again. So his blood, out of whose darkness everything rose, being moved to its depth by her revulsion, heaved and swung towards its own rest, surging blindly to its own re-settling.

Without knowing it, he suffered that night almost more than he had ever suffered during his life. But it was all below his consciousness. It was his life itself at storm, not his mind and his will engaged at all.

In the morning he got up, thin and quiet, without much

movement anywhere, only with some of the clearing afterstorm. His body felt like a clean, empty shell. His mind was limpidly clear. He went through the business of the toilet with a certain accuracy, and at breakfast, in the restaurant, there was about him that air of neutral correctness which makes men seem so unreal.

At lunch, there was a telegram for him. It was like her to telegraph.

'Come to tea, my dear love.'

As he read it, there was a great heave of resistance in him. But then he faltered. With his consciousness, he remembered how impulsive and eager she was when she dashed off her telegram, and he relaxed. It went without saying that he would go.

III

When he stood in the lift going up to his own flat, he was almost blind with the hurt of it all. They had loved each other so much in his first home. The parlour-maid opened to him, and he smiled at her affectionately. In the golden-brown and cream-coloured hall—Paula would have nothing heavy or sombre about her—a bush of rose-coloured azaleas shone, and a little tub of lilies twinkled naïvely.

She did not come out to meet him.

'Tea is in the drawing-room,' the maid said, and he went in while she was hanging up his coat. It was a big room, with a sense of space, and a spread of whity carpet almost the colour of unpolished marble—and grey and pink border; of pink roses on big white cushions, pretty Dresden china, and deep chintz-covered chairs and sofas which looked as if they were used freely. It was a room where one could roll in soft, fresh-comfort, a room which had not much breakable in it, and which seemed, in the dusky spring evening, fuller of light than the streets outside.

Paula rose, looking queenly and rather radiant, as she held out her hand. A young man whom Peter scarcely noticed rose on the other side of the hearth.

'I expected you an hour ago,' she said, looking into her husband's eyes. But though she looked at him, she did not see him. And he sank his head.

'This is another Moest,' she said, presenting the stranger. 'He knows Richard, too.'

The young man, a German of about thirty, with a clean-shaven æsthetic face, long black hair brushed back a little wearily or bewildered from his brow, and inclined to fall in an odd loose strand again, so that he nervously put it back with his fine hand, looked at Moest and bowed. He had a finely-cut face, but his dark-blue eyes were strained, as if he did not quite know where he was. He sat down again, and his pleasant figure took a self-conscious attitude, of a man whose business it was to say things that should be listened to. He was not conceited or affected—naturally sensitive and rather naïve; but he could only move in an atmosphere of literature and literary ideas; yet he seemed to know there was something else, vaguely, and he felt rather at a loss. He waited for the conversation to move his way, as, inert, an insect waits for the sun to set it flying.

'Another Moest,' Paula was pronouncing emphatically. 'Actually another Moest, of whom we have never heard, and under the same roof with us.'

The stranger laughed, his lips moving nervously over his teeth.

'You are in this house?' Peter asked, surprised.

The young man shifted in his chair, dropped his head, looked up again.

'Yes,' he said, meeting Moest's eyes as if he were somewhat dazzled. 'I am staying with the Lauriers, on the second floor.'

He spoke English slowly, with a quaint, musical quality in his voice, and a certain rhythmic enunciation.

'I see; and the telegram was for you?' said the host.

'Yes,' replied the stranger, with a nervous little laugh.

'My husband,' broke in Paula, evidently repeating to the German what she had said before, for Peter's benefit this time, 'was quite convinced I had an *affaire*'—she pronounced it in the French fashion 'with this terrible Richard.'

The German gave his little laugh, and moved, painfully self-conscious, in his chair.

'Yes,' he said, glancing at Moest.

'Did you spend a night of virtuous indignation?' Paula laughed to her husband, 'imagining my perfidy?'

'I did not,' said her husband. 'Were you at Madge's?'

'No,' she said. Then, turning to her guest: 'Who is Richard, Mr Moest?'

'Richard,' began the German, word by word, 'is my cousin.' He glanced quickly at Paula, to see if he were understood. She rustled her skirts, and arranged herself comfortably, lying, or almost squatting, on the sofa by the fire. 'He lives in Hampstead.'

'And what is he like?' she asked, with eager interest.

The German gave his little laugh. Then he moved his fingers across his brow, in his dazed fashion. Then he looked, with his beautiful blue eyes, at his beautiful hostess.

'I—' He laughed again nervously. 'He is a man whose

parts—are not very much—very well known to me. You see,' he broke forth, and it was evident he was now conversing to an imaginary audience—'I cannot easily express myself in English. I–I never have talked it. I shall speak, because I know nothing of modern England, a kind of Renaissance English.'

'How lovely!' cried Paula. 'But if you would rather, speak German. We shall understand sufficiently.'

'I would rather hear some Renaissance English,' said Moest.

Paula was quite happy with the new stranger. She listened to descriptions of Richard, shifting animatedly on her sofa. She wore a new dress, of a rich red-tile colour, glossy and long and soft, and she had threaded daisies, like buttons, in the braided plait of her hair. Her husband hated her for these familiarities. But she was beautiful too, and warm-hearted. Only, through all her warmth and kindliness, lay, he said, at the bottom, an almost feline selfishness, a coldness.

She was playing to the stranger—nay, she was not playing, she was really occupied by him. The young man was the favourite disciple of the most famous present-day German poet and *Meister*. He himself was occupied in translating Shakespeare. Having been always a poetic disciple, he had never come into touch with life save through literature, and for him, since he was a rather fine-hearted young man, with a human need to live, this was a tragedy. Paula was not long in discovering what ailed him, and she was eager to come to his rescue.

It pleased her, nevertheless, to have her husband sitting by, watching her. She forgot to give tea to anyone. Moest and the German both helped themselves, and the former attended also to his wife's cup. He sat rather in the background, listening, and waiting. She had made a fool of him with her talk to this stranger of 'Richard'; lightly and flippantly she had made a fool of him. He minded, but was used to it. Now she had absorbed herself in this dazed, starved, literature-bewildered young German, who was, moreover, really lovable, evidently a gentleman. And she was seeing in him her mission—'just as', said Moest bitterly to himself, 'she saw her mission in me, a year ago. She is no woman. She's got a big heart for everybody, but it must be like a common-room; she's got no private, sacred heart, except perhaps for herself, where there's no room for a man in it.'

At length the stranger rose to go, promising to come again.

'Isn't he adorable?' cried Paula, as her husband returned to the drawing-room. 'I think he is simply adorable.'

'Yes!' said Moest.

'He called this morning to ask about the telegram. But, poor devil, isn't it a shame what they've done to him?'

'What who have done to him?' her husband asked coldly, jealous.

'Those literary creatures. They take a young fellow like that, and stick him up among the literary gods, like a mantelpiece ornament, and there he has to sit being a minor ornament, while all his youth is gone. It is criminal.'

'He should get off the mantelpiece, then,' said Moest.

But inside him his heart was black with rage against her. What had she, after all, to do with this young man, when he himself was being smashed up by her? He loathed her pity and her kindliness, which was like a charitable institution. There was no core to the woman. She was full of generosity and bigness and kindness, but there was no heart in her, no security, no place for one single man. He began to understand now sirens and sphinxes and the other Greek fabulous female things. They had not been created by fancy, but out of bitter necessity of the man's human heart to express itself.

'Ha!' she laughed, half contemptuous. 'Did *you* get off your miserable, starved isolation by yourself?—you didn't. You had to be fetched down, and I had to do it.'

'Out of your usual charity,' he said.

'But you can sneer at another man's difficulties,' she said.

'Your name ought to be Panacea, not Paula,' he replied.

He felt furious and dead against her. He could even look at her without the tenderness coming. And he was glad. He hated her. She seemed unaware. Very well; let her be so.

'Oh, but he makes me so miserable, to see him!' she cried. 'Self-conscious, can't get into contact with anybody, living a false literary life like a man who takes poetry as a drug.—One *ought* to help him.'

She was really earnest and distressed.

'Out of the frying-pan into the fire,' he said.

'I'd rather be in the fire any day, than in a frying-pan,' she said, abstractedly, with a little shudder. She never troubled to see the meaning of her husband's sarcasms.

They remained silent. The maid came in for the tray, and to ask him if he would be in to dinner. He waited for his wife to answer. She sat with her chin in her hands, brooding over the young German, and did not hear. The rage flashed up in his heart. He would have liked to smash her out of this false absorption.

'No,' he said to the maid. 'I think not. Are you at home

for dinner, Paula?'

'Yes,' she said.

And he knew by her tone, easy and abstracted, that she intended him to stay, too. But she did not trouble to say anything.

At last, after some time, she asked:

'What did you do?'

'Nothing—went to bed early,' he replied.

'Did you sleep well?'

'Yes, thank you.'

And he recognised the ludicrous civilities of married people, and he wanted to go. She was silent for a time. Then she asked, and her voice had gone still and grave:

'Why don't you ask me what I did?'

'Because I don't care—you just went to somebody's for dinner.'

'Why don't you care what I do? Isn't it your place to care?'

'About the things you do to spite me?—no!'

'Ha!' she mocked. 'I did nothing to spite you. I was in deadly earnest.'

'Even with your Richard?'

'Yes,' she cried. 'There *might* have been a Richard. What did you care!'

'In that case you'd have been a liar and worse, so why should I care about you then?'

'You *don't* care about me,' she said, sullenly.

'You say what you please,' he answered.

She was silent for some time.

'And did you do absolutely nothing last night?' she asked.

'I had a bath and went to bed.'

Then she pondered.

'No,' she said, 'you don't care for me.'

He did not trouble to answer. Softly, a little china clock rang six.

'I shall go to Italy in the morning,' he said.

'Yes.'

'And,' he said, slowly, forcing the words out, 'I shall stay at the Aquila Nera at Milan—you know my address.'

'Yes,' she answered.

'I shall be away about a month. Meanwhile, you can rest.'

'Yes,' she said, in her throat, with a little contempt of him and his stiffness. He, in spite of himself, was breathing heavily. He knew that this parting was the real separation of their souls, marked the point beyond which they could go no farther, but accepted the marriage as a comparative failure. And he had built all his life on his marriage. She accused him of not loving her. He gripped the arms of his chair. Was there something in it? Did he only want the attributes which went along with her, the peace of heart which a man has in living to one woman, even if the love between them be not complete; the singleness and unity in his life that made it easy; the fixed establishment of himself as a married man with a home; the feeling that he belonged somewhere, that one woman existed—not was paid but *existed*—really to take care of him; was it these things he wanted, and not her? But he wanted her for these purposes—her, and nobody else. But was that not enough for her? Perhaps he wronged her—it was possible. What she said against him was in earnest. And what she said in earnest he had to believe, in the long run, since it was the utterance of her being. He felt miserable and tired.

When he looked at her, across the gathering twilight of the room, she was staring into the fire and biting her finger-nail, restlessly, restlessly, without knowing. And all his limbs went suddenly weak, as he realised that she suffered too, that something was gnawing at her. Something in the look of her, the crouching, dogged, wondering look made him faint with tenderness for her.

'Don't bite your finger-nails,' he said quietly, and, obediently, she took her hand from her mouth. His heart was beating quickly. He could feel the atmosphere of the room changing. It had stood aloof, the room, like something placed round him, like a great box. Now everything got softer, as if it partook of the atmosphere, of which he partook himself, and they were all one.

His mind reverted to her accusations, and his heart beat like a caged thing against what he could not understand. She said he did not love her. But he knew that in his way, he did. In his way—but was his way wrong? His way was himself, he thought, struggling. Was there something wrong, something missing in his nature, that he could not love? He struggled, as if he were in a mesh, and could not get out. He did not want to believe that he was deficient in his nature. Wherein was he deficient? It was nothing physical. She said he would not come out of himself, that he was no good to her, because he coud not get outside himself. What did she mean? Not outside himself! It seemed like some acrobatic fear, some slippery, contortionist trick. No, he could not understand. His heart flashed hot with resentment. She did nothing but find fault with him. What did she care about him, really, when she could taunt him with not being able to take a light woman when he was in Paris? Though his heart, forced to do her justice, knew that for this she loved him, really.

But it was too complicated and difficult, and already,

as they sat thinking, it had gone wrong between them and things felt twisted, horribly twisted, so that he could not breathe. He must go. He could dine at the hotel and go to the theatre.

'Well,' he said casually, 'I must go. I think I shall go and see "The Black Sheep." '

She did not answer. Then she turned and looked at him with a queer, half-bewildered, half-perverse smile that seemed conscious of pain. Her eyes, shining rather dilated and triumphant, and yet with something heavily yearning behind them, looked at him. He could not understand, and, between her appeal and her defiant triumph, he felt as if his chest was crushed so that he could not breathe.

'My love,' she said, in a little singing, abstract fashion, her lips somehow sipping towards him, her eyes shining dilated; and yet he felt as if he were not in it, himself.

His heart was a flame that prevented his breathing. He gripped the chair like a man who is going to be put under torture.

'What?' he said, staring back at her.

'Oh, my love!' she said softly, with a little, intense laugh on her face, that made him pant. And she slipped from her sofa and came across to him quickly, and put her hand hesitating on his hair. The blood struck like flame across his consciousness, and the hurt was keen like joy, like the releasing of something that hurts as the pressure is relaxed and the movement comes, before the peace. Afraid, his fingers touched her hand, and she sank swiftly between his knees, and put her face on his breast. He held her head hard against his chest, and again and again the flame went down his blood, as he felt her round, small, nut of a head between his hands pressing into his chest where the hurt had been bruised in so deep. His wrists quivered as he pressed her head to him, as he felt the deadness going out of him; the real life released, flowing into his body again. How hard he had shut it off, against her, when she hated him. He was breathing heavily with relief, blindly pressing her head against him. He believed in her again.

She looked up, laughing, childish, inviting him with her lips. He bent to kiss her, and as his eyes closed, he saw hers shut. The feeling of restoration was almost unbearable.

'Do you love me?' she whispered, in a little ecstasy.

He did not answer, except with the quick tightening of his arms, clutching her a little closer against him. And he loved the silkiness of her hair, and its natural scent. And it hurt him that the daisies she had threaded in should begin to wither. He resented their hurting her by their dying.

He had not understood. But the trouble had gone off. He was quiet, and he watched her from out of his sensitive stillness, a little bit dimly, unable to recover. She was loving to him, protective, and bright, laughing like a glad child too.

'We must tell Maud I shall be in to dinner,' he said.

That was like him—always aware of the practical side of the case, and the appearances. She laughed a little bit ironically. Why should she have to take her arm from round him, just to tell Maud he would be in to dinner?

'I'll go,' she said.

He drew the curtains and turned on the light in the big lamp that stood in a corner. The room was dim, and palely warm. He loved it dearly.

His wife, when she came back, as soon as she had closed the door, lifted her arms to him in a little ecstasy, coming to him. They clasped each other closer, body to body. And the intensity of his feeling was so fierce, he felt himself going dim, fusing into something soft and plastic between her hands. And this connection with her was bigger than life or death. And at the bottom of his heart was a sob.

She was gay and winsome at the dinner. Like lovers, they were just deliciously waiting for the night to come up. But there remained in him always the slightly broken feeling which the night before had left.

'And you won't go to Italy,' she said, as if it were an understood thing.

She gave him the best things to eat, and was solicitous of his welfare—which was not usual with her. It gave him deep, shy pleasure. He remembered a verse she was often quoting as one she loved. He did not know it for himself:

> 'On my breasts I warm thy foot-soles;
> Wine I pour, and dress thy meats;
> Humbly, when my lord disposes,
> Lie with him on perfumed sheets.'

She said it to him sometimes, looking up at him from the pillow. But it never seemed real to him. She might, in her sudden passion, put his feet between her breasts. But he never felt like a lord, never more pained and insignificant than at those times. As a little girl, she must have subjected herself before her dolls. And he was something like her lordliest plaything. He liked that too. If only . . .

Then, seeing some frightened little way of looking at him which she had, the pure pain came back. He loved her, and it would never be peace between them; she would never belong to him, as a wife. She would take him and reject him, like a mistress. And perhaps for that reason he would love her all the more; it might be so.

But then, he forgot. Whatever was or was not, now she loved him. And whatever came after, this evening he was the lord. What matter if he were deposed to-morrow, and she hated him!

Her eyes, wide and candid, were staring at him a little bit wondering, a little bit forlorn. She knew he had not quite come back. He held her close to him.

'My love,' she murmured consolingly. 'My love.'

And she put her fingers through his hair, arranging it in little, loose curves, playing with it and forgetting everything else. He loved that dearly, to feel the light lift and touch—touch of her finger-tips making his hair, as she said, like an Apollo's. She lifted his face to see how he looked, and, with a little laugh of love, kissed him. And he loved to be made much of by her. But he had the dim, hurting sense that she would not love him to-morrow, that it was only her great need to love that exalted him to-night. He *knew* he was no king; he did not feel a king, even when she was crowning and kissing him.

'Do you love me?' she asked, playfully whispering.

He held her fast and kissed her, while the blood hurt in his heart-chambers.

'You know,' he answered, with a struggle.

Later, when he lay holding her with a passion intense like pain, the words blurted from him:

'Flesh of my flesh. Paula!—Will you—?'

'Yes, my love,' she answered consolingly.

He bit his mouth with pain. For him it was almost an agony of appeal.

'But, Paula—I mean it—flesh of my flesh—a wife?'

She tightened her arms round him without answering. And he knew and she knew, that she put him off like that.

IV

Two months later, she was writing to him in Italy: 'Your idea of your woman is that she is an expansion, no, a *rib* of yourself, without any existence of her own. That I am a being by myself is more than you can grasp. I wish I could absolutely submerge myself in a man—and *so I do*. I *always* loved you . . .

'You will say "I was patient." Do you call that patient, hanging on for your needs, as you have done? The innermost life you have *always* had of me, and you held yourself aloof because you were afraid.

'The unpardonable thing was you told me you loved me.—Your *feelings* have hated me these three months, which did not prevent you from taking my love and every breath from me.—Underneath you undermined me, in some subtle, corrupt way that I did not see because I believed you, when you told me you loved me. . .

'The insult of the way took me these last three months I shall never forgive you. I honestly *did* give myself, and always in vain and rebuffed. The strain of it all has driven me quite mad.

'You say I am a tragédienne, but I don't do any of your perverse undermining tricks. You are always luring one into the open like a clever enemy, but you keep safely under cover all the time.

'This practically means, for me, that life is over, my belief in life—I hope it will recover, but it never could do so with you . . .'

To which he answered: 'If I kept under cover it is funny, for there isn't any cover now. —And you can hope, pretty easily, for your own recovery apart from me. For my side, without you, I am done . . . But you lie to yourself. You *wouldn't* love *me*, and you won't be able to love anybody else—except yourself.'

THE PRUSSIAN OFFICER

I

THEY had marched more than thirty kilometres since dawn, along the white, hot road where occasional thickets of trees threw a moment of shade, then out into the glare again. On either hand, the valley, wide and shallow, glittered with heat; dark-green patches of rye, pale young corn, fallow and meadow and black pine woods spread in a dull, hot diagram under a glistening sky. But right in front the mountains ranged across, pale blue and very still, snow gleaming gently out of the deep atmosphere. And towards the mountains, on and on, the regiment marched between the rye-fields and the meadows, between the scraggy fruit trees set regularly on either side of the high road. The burnished, dark-green rye threw off a suffocating heat, the mountains drew gradually nearer and more distinct. While the feet of the soldiers grew hotter, sweat ran through their hair under their helmets, and their knapsacks could burn no more in contact with their shoulders, but seemed instead to give off a cold, prickly sensation.

He walked on and on in silence, staring at the mountains ahead, that rose sheer out of the land, and stood fold behind fold, half earth, half heaven, the heaven, the barrier with slits of soft snow, in the pale, bluish peaks.

He could now walk almost without pain. At the start, he had determined not to limp. It had made him sick to take the first steps, and during the first mile or so, he had compressed his breath, and the cold drops of sweat had stood on his forehead. But he had walked it off. What were they after all but bruises! He had looked at them, as he was getting up: deep bruises on the backs of his thighs. And since he had made his first step in the morning, he had been conscious of them. Till now he had a tight, hot place in his chest, with suppressing the pain, and holding himself in. There seemed no air when he breathed. But he walked almost lightly.

The Captain's hand had trembled at taking his coffee at dawn: his orderly saw it again. And he saw the fine figure of the Captain wheeling on horseback at the farmhouse ahead, a handsome figure in pale-blue uniform with facings of scarlet, and the metal gleaming on the black helmet and the sword-scabbard, and dark streaks of sweat coming on the silky bay horse. The orderly felt he was connected with that figure moving so suddenly on horseback: he followed it like a shadow, mute and inevitable and damned by it. And the officer was always aware of the tramp of the company behind, the march of his orderly among the men.

The Captain was a tall man of about forty, grey at the temples. He had a handsome, finely-knit figure, and was one of the best horsemen in the West. His orderly, having to rub him down, admired the amazing riding-muscles of his loins.

For the rest, the orderly scarcely noticed the officer any more than he noticed himself. It was rarely he saw his master's face: he did not look at it. The Captain had reddish-brown, stiff hair, that he wore short upon his skull. His moustache was also cut short and bristly over a full, brutal mouth. His face was rather rugged, the cheeks thin. Perhaps the man was the more handsome for the deep lines in his face, the irritable tension of his brow, which gave him the look of a man who fights with life. His fair eyebrows stood bushy over light-blue eyes that were always flashing with cold fire.

He was a Prussian aristocrat, haughty and overbearing. But his mother had been a Polish countess. Having made too many gambling debts when he was young, he had ruined his prospects in the Army, and remained an infantry captain. He had never married: his position did not allow of it, and no woman had ever moved him to it. His time he spent riding—occasionally he rode one of his own horses at the races and at the officers' club. Now and then he took himself a mistress. But after such an event, he returned to duty with his brow still more tense, his eyes still more hostile and irritable. With the men, however, he was merely impersonal, though a devil when roused; so that, on the whole, they feared him, but had no great aversion from him. They accepted him as the inevitable.

To his orderly he was at first cold and just and indifferent: he did not fuss over trifles. So that his servant knew practically nothing about him, except just what orders he would give, and how he wanted them obeyed. That was quite simple. Then the change gradually came.

The orderly was a youth of about twenty-two, of medium height, and well built. He had strong, heavy limbs, was swarthy, with a soft, black, young moustache. There was something altogether warm and young about him. He had firmly marked eyebrows over dark, expressionless eyes, that seemed never to have thought, only to have received life direct through his senses, and acted straight from instinct.

Gradually the officer had become aware of his servant's young, vigorous, unconscious presence about him. He could not get away from the sense of the youth's person, while he was in attendance. It was like a warm flame upon the older man's tense, rigid body, that had become almost unliving, fixed. There was something so free and self-contained about him, and something in the young fellow's movement, that made the officer aware of him. And this irritated the Prussian. He did not choose to be touched into life by his servant. He might easily have changed his man, but he did not. He now very rarely looked direct at his orderly, but kept his face averted, as if to avoid seeing him. And yet as the young soldier moved unthinking about the apartment, the elder watched him, and would notice the movement of his strong young shoulders under the blue cloth, the bend of his neck. And it irritated him. To see the soldier's young, brown, shapely peasant's hand grasp the loaf or the wine-bottle sent a flash of hate or of anger through the elder man's blood. It was not that the youth was clumsy: it was rather the blind, instinctive sureness of movement of an unhampered young animal that irritated the officer to such a degree.

Once, when a bottle of wine had gone over, and the red gushed out on to the tablecloth, the officer had started up with an oath, and his eyes, bluey like fire, had held those of the confused youth for a moment. It was a shock for the young soldier. He felt something sink deeper, deeper into his soul, where nothing had ever gone before. It left him rather blank and wondering. Some of his natural completeness in himself was gone, a little uneasiness took its place. And from that time an undiscovered feeling had held between the two men.

Henceforward the orderly was afraid of really meeting his master. His subconsciousness remembered those steely blue eyes and the harsh brows, and did not intend to meet them again. So he always stared past his master, and avoided him. Also, in a little anxiety, he waited for the three months to have gone, when his time would be up. He began to feel a constraint in the Captain's presence, and the soldier even more than the officer wanted to be left alone, in his neutrality as servant.

He had served the Captain for more than a year, and knew his duty. This he performed easily, as if it were natural to him. The officer and his commands he took for granted, as he took the sun and the rain, and he served as a matter of course. It did not implicate him personally.

But now if he were going to be forced into a personal interchange with his master he would be like a wild thing caught; he felt he must get away.

But the influence of the young soldier's being had penetrated through the officer's stiffened discipline, and perturbed the man in him. He, however, was a gentleman, with long, fine hands and cultivated movements, and was not going to allow such a thing as the stirring of his innate self. He was a man of passionate temper, who had always kept himself suppressed. Occasionally there had been a duel, an outburst before the soldiers. He knew himself to be always on the point of breaking out. But he kept himself hard to the idea of the Service. Whereas the young soldier seemed to live out his warm, full nature, to give it off in his very movements, which had a certain zest, such as wild animals have in free movement. And this irritated the officer more and more.

In spite of himself, the Captain could not regain his neutrality of feeling towards his orderly. Nor could he leave the man alone. In spite of himself, he watched him, gave him sharp orders, tried to take up as much of his time as possible. Sometimes he flew into a rage with the young soldier, and bullied him. Then the orderly shut himself off, as it were out of earshot, and waited, with sullen, flushed face, for the end of the noise. The words never pierced to his intelligence, he made himself, protectively, impervious to the feelings of his master.

He had a scar on his left thumb, a deep seam going across the knuckle. The officer had long suffered from it, and wanted to do something to it. Still it was there, ugly and brutal on the young, brown hand. At last the Captain's reserve gave way. One day, as the orderly was smoothing out the tablecloth, the officer pinned down his thumb with a pencil, asking:

'How did you come by that?'

The young man winced and drew back at attention.

'A wood axe, Herr Hauptmann,' he answered.

The officer waited for further explanation. None came. The orderly went about his duties. The elder man was sullenly angry. His servant avoided him. And the next day he had to use all his will-power to avoid seeing the scarred thumb. He wanted to get hold of it and—a hot flame ran in his blood.

He knew his servant would soon be free, and would be glad. As yet, the soldier had held himself off from the elder man. The Captain grew madly irritable. He could not rest when the soldier was away, and when he was present, he glared at him with tormented eyes. He hated those fine, black brows over the unmeaning, dark eyes; he was infuriated by the free movement of the handsome limbs, which no military discipline could make stiff. And he became harsh and cruelly bullying, using contempt and satire. The young soldier only grew more mute and expressionless.

'What cattle were you bred by, that you can't keep

straight eyes? Look me in the eyes when I speak to you.'

And the soldier turned his dark eyes to the other's face, but there was no sight in them: he stared with the slightest possible cast, holding back his sight, perceiving the blue of his master's eyes, but receiving no look from them. And the elder man went pale, and his reddish eyebrows twitched. He gave his order, barrenly.

Once he flung a heavy military glove into the young soldier's face. Then he had the satisfaction of seeing the black eyes flare up into his own, like a blaze when straw is thrown on a fire. And he had laughed with a little tremor and a sneer.

But there were only two months more. The youth instinctively tried to keep himself intact: he tried to serve the officer as if the latter were an abstract authority and not a man. All his instinct was to avoid personal contact, even definite hate. But in spite of himself the hate grew, responsive to the officer's passion. However, he put it in the back-ground. When he had left the Army he could dare acknowledge it. By nature he was active, and had many friends. He thought what amazing good fellows they were. But, without knowing it, he was alone. Now this solitariness was intensified. It would carry him through his term. But the officer seemed to be going irritably insane, and the youth was deeply frightened.

The soldier had a sweetheart, a girl from the mountains, independent and primitive. The two walked together, rather silently. He went with her, not to talk, but to have his arm round her, and for the physical contact. This eased him, made it easier for him to ignore the Captain; for he could rest with her head fast against his chest. And she, in some unspoken fashion, was there for him. They loved each other.

The Captain perceived it, and was mad with irritation. He kept the young man engaged all the evenings long, and took pleasure in the dark look that came on his face. Occasionally, the eyes of the two men met, those of the younger sullen and dark, doggedly unalterable, those of the elder sneering with restless contempt.

The officer tried hard not to admit the passion that had got hold of him. He would not know that his feeling for his orderly was anything but that of a man incensed by his stupid, perverse servant. So, keeping quite justified, and conventional in his consciousness, he let the other thing run on. His nerves, however, were suffering. At last he slung the end of a belt in his servant's face. When he saw the youth start back, the pain-tears in his eyes and the blood on his mouth, he had felt at once a thrill of deep pleasure and of shame.

But this, he acknowledged to himself, was a thing he had never done before. The fellow was too exasperating. His own nerves must be going to pieces. He went away for some days with a woman.

It was a mockery of pleasure. He simply did not want the woman. But he stayed on for his time. At the end of it, he came back in an agony of irritation, torment, and misery. He rode all the evening, then came straight in to supper. His orderly was out. The officer sat with his long, fine hands lying on the table, perfectly still, and all his blood seemed to be corroding.

At last his servant entered. He watched the strong, easy young figure, the fine eyebrows, the thick black hair. In a week's time the youth had got back his old well-being. The hands of the officer twitched and seemed to be full of mad flame. The young man stood at attention, unmoving, shut off.

The meal went in silence. But the orderly seemed eager. He made a clatter with the dishes.

'Are you in a hurry?' asked the officer, watching the intent, warm face of his servant. The other did not reply.

'Will you answer my question?' said the Captain.

'Yes, sir,' replied the orderly, standing with his pile of deep Army plates. The Captain waited, looked at him, then asked again:

'Are you in a hurry?'

'Yes, sir,' came the answer, that sent a flash through the listener.

'For what?'

'I was going out, sir.'

'I want you this evening.'

There was a moment's hesitation. The officer had a curious stiffness of countenance.

'Yes, sir,' replied the servant, in his throat.

'I want you to-morrow evening also—in fact you may consider your evenings occupied, unless I give you leave.'

The mouth with the young moustache set close.

'Yes, sir,' answered the orderly, loosening his lips for a moment.

He again turned to the door.

'And why have you a piece of pencil in your ear?'

The orderly hesitated, then continued on his way without answering. He set the plates in a pile outside the door, took the stump of pencil from his ear, and put it in his pocket. He had been copying a verse for his sweetheart's birthday card. He returned to finish clearing the table. The officer's eyes were dancing, he had a little, eager smile.

'Why have you a piece of pencil in your ear?' he asked.

The orderly took his hands full of dishes. His master was standing near the great green stove, a little smile on his face, his chin thrust forward. When the young soldier saw him his heart suddenly ran hot. He felt blind. Instead of answering, he turned dazedly to the door. As he was crouching to set down the dishes, he was pitched forward by a kick from behind. The pots went in a stream down the stairs, he clung to the pillar of the banisters. And as he was rising he was kicked heavily again and again, so that he clung sickly to the post for some moments. His master had gone swiftly into the room and closed the door. The maid-servant downstairs looked up the staircase and made a mocking face at the crockery disaster.

The officer's heart was plunging. He poured himself a glass of wine, part of which he spilled on the floor, and gulped the remainder, leaning against the cool, green stove. He heard his man collecting the dishes from the stairs. Pale, as if intoxicated, he waited. The servant entered again. The Captain's heart gave a pang, as of pleasure, seeing the young fellow bewildered and uncertain on his feet with pain.

'Schöner!' he said.

The soldier was a little slower in coming to attention.

'Yes, sir!'

The youth stood before him, with pathetic young moustache, and fine eyebrows very distinct on his forehead of dark marble.

'I asked you a question.'

'Yes, sir.'

The officer's tone bit like acid.

'Why had you a pencil in your ear?'

Again the servant's heart ran hot, and he could not breathe. With dark, strained eyes, he looked at the officer, as if fascinated. And he stood there sturdily planted, unconscious. The withering smile came into the Captain's eyes, and he lifted his foot.

'I forgot it—sir,' panted the soldier, his dark eyes fixed on the other man's dancing blue ones.

'What was it doing there?'

He saw the young man's breast heaving as he made an effort for words.

'I had been writing.'

'Writing what?'

Again the soldier looked him up and down. The officer could hear him panting. The smile came into the blue eyes. The soldier worked his dry throat, but could not speak. Suddenly the smile lit like a flame on the officer's face, and a kick came heavily against the orderly's thigh. The youth moved sideways. His face went dead, with two black, staring eyes.

'Well?' said the officer.

The orderly's mouth had gone dry, and his tongue rubbed in it as on dry brown-paper. He worked his throat. The officer raised his foot. The servant went stiff.

'Some poetry, sir,' came the crackling, unrecognisable sound of his voice.

'Poetry, what poetry?' asked the Captain, with a sickly smile.

Again there was the working in the throat. The Captain's heart had suddenly gone down heavily, and he stood sick and tired.

'For my girl, sir,' he heard the dry, inhuman sound.

'Oh!' he said, turning away. 'Clear the table.'

'Click!' went the soldier's throat; then again, 'Click!' and then the half-articulate:

'Yes, sir.'

The young soldier was gone, looking old, and walking heavily.

The officer, left alone, held himself rigid, to prevent himself from thinking. His instinct warned him that he must not think. Deep inside him was the intense gratification of his passion, still working powerfully. Then there was a counteraction, a horrible breaking down of something inside him, a whole agony of reaction. He stood there for an hour motionless, a chaos of sensations, but rigid with a will to keep blank his consciousness, to prevent his mind grasping. And he held himself so until the worst of the stress had passed, when he began to drink, drank himself to an intoxication, till he slept obliterated. When he woke in the morning he was shaken to the base of his nature. But he had fought off the realisation of what he had done. He had prevented his mind from taking it in, had suppressed it along with his instincts, and the conscious man had nothing to do with it. He felt only as after a bout of intoxication, weak, but the affair itself all dim and not to be recovered. Of the drunkenness of his passion he scuccessfully refused remembrance. And when his orderly appeared with coffee, the officer assumed the same self he had had the morning before. He refused the event of the past night—denied it had ever been—and was successful in his denial. He had not done any such thing—not he himself. Whatever there might be lay at the door of a stupid insubordinate servant.

The orderly had gone about in a stupor all the evening. He drank some beer because he was parched, but not much, the alcohol made his feeling come back, and he could not bear it. He was dulled, as if nine-tenths of the ordinary man in him were inert. He crawled about disfigured. Still, when he thought of the kicks, he went sick, and when he thought of the threat of more kicking, in the room afterwards, his heart went hot and faint, and he panted, remembering the one that had come. He had been forced to say: 'For my girl.' He was much too done even to want to cry. His mouth hung slightly open, like an idiot's. He felt vacant, and wasted. So, he wandered at his work, painfully, and very slowly and clumsily, fumbling blindly with the brushes, and finding it difficult, when he sat down, to summon the energy to move again. His limbs, his jaw, were slack and nerveless. But he was very tired. He got to bed at last, and slept inert, relaxed, in a sleep that was rather stupor than slumber, a dead night of stupefaction shot through with gleams of anguish.

In the morning were the manoeuvres. But he woke even before the bugle sounded. The painful ache in his chest, the dryness of his throat, the awful steady feeling of misery made his eyes come awake and dreary at once. He knew, without thinking, what had happened. And he knew that the day had come again, when he must go on with his round. The last bit of darkness was being pushed out of the room. He would have to move his inert body and go on. He was so young, and had known so little trouble, that he was bewildered. He only wished it would stay night, so that he could lie still, covered up by the darkness. And yet nothing would prevent the day from coming, nothing would save him from having to get up and saddle the Captain's horse, and make the Captain's coffee. It was there, inevitable. And then, he thought, it was impossible. Yet they would not leave him free. He must go and take the coffee to the Captain. He was too stunned to understand it. He only knew it was inevitable—inevitable, however long he lay inert.

At last, after heaving at himself, for he seemed to be a mass of inertia, he got up. But he had to force every one of his movements from behind, with his will. He felt lost, and dazed, and helpless. Then he clutched hold of the bed, the pain was so keen. And looking at his things he saw the darker bruises on his swarthy flesh, and he knew that if he pressed one of his fingers on one of the bruises, he should faint. But he did not want to faint—he did not want anybody to know. No one should ever know. It was between him and the Captain. There were only the two people in the world now—himself and the Captain.

Slowly, economically, he got dressed and forced himself to walk. Everything was obscure, except just what he had his hands on. But he managed to get through his work. The very pain revived his dull senses. The worst remained yet. He took the tray and went up to the Captain's room. The officer, pale and heavy, sat at the table. The orderly, as he saluted, felt himself put out of existence. He stood still for a moment submitting to his own nullification—then he gathered himself, seemed to regain himself, and then the Captain began to grow vague, unreal, and the younger soldier's heart beat up. He clung to this situation—that the Captain did not exist—so that he himself might live. But when he saw his officer's hand tremble as he took the coffee, he felt everything falling shattered. And he went away, feeling as if he himself were coming to pieces, disintegrated. And when the Captain was there on horseback, giving orders, while he himself stood, with rifle and knapsack, sick with pain, he felt as if he must shut his eyes—as if he must shut his eyes on everything. It was only the long agony of marching with a parched throat that filled him with one single, sleep-heavy intention: to save himself.

II

He was getting used even to his parched throat. That the snowy peaks were radiant among the sky, that the whity-green glacier-river twisted through its pale shoals, in the valley below, seemed almost supernatural. But he was going mad with fever and thirst. He plodded on uncomplaining. He did not want to speak, not to anybody. There were two gulls, like flakes of water and snow, over the river. The scent of green rye soaked in sunshine came like a sickness. And the march continued, monotonously, almost like a bad sleep.

At the next farmhouse, which stood low and broad near the high road, tubs of water had been put out. The soldiers clustered round to drink. They took off their helmets, and the steam mounted from their wet hair. The Captain sat on horseback, watching. He needed to see his orderly. His helmet threw a dark shadow over his light, fierce eyes, but his moustache and mouth and chin were distinct in the sunshine. The orderly must move under the presence of the figure of the horseman. It was not that he was afraid, or cowed. It was as if he was disembowelled, made empty, like an empty shell. He felt himself as nothing, a shadow creeping under the sunshine. And, thirsty as he was, he could scarcely drink, feeling the Captain near him. He would not take off his helmet to wipe his wet hair. He wanted to stay in shadow, not to be forced into consciousness. Starting, he saw the light heel of the officer prick the belly of the horse; the Captain cantered away, and he himself could relapse into vacancy.

Nothing, however, could give him back his living place in the hot, bright morning. He felt like a gap among it all. Whereas the Captain was prouder, overriding. A hot flash went through the young servant's body. The Captain was firmer and prouder with life, he himself was empty as a shadow. Again the flash went through him, dazing him out. But his heart ran a little firmer.

The company turned up the hill, to make a loop for the return. Below, from among the trees, the farm-bell clanged. He saw the labourers, mowing bare-foot at the thick grass, leave off their work and go downhill, their scythes hanging over their shoulders, like long, bright claws curving down behind them. They seemed like dream-people, as if they had no relation to himself. He felt as in a blackish dream: as if all the other things were there and had form, but he himself was only a consciousness, a gap that could think and perceive.

The soldiers were tramping silently up the glaring hillside. Gradually his head began to revolve, slowly, rhythmically. Sometimes it was dark before his eyes, as if he saw this world through a smoked glass, frail shadows and unreal. It gave him a pain in his head to walk.

The air was too scented, it gave no breath. All the lush green-stuff seemed to be issuing its sap, till the air was deathly, sickly with the smell of greenness. There was the perfume of clover, like pure honey and bees. Then there grew a faint acrid tang—they were near the beeches; and then a queer clattering noise, and a suffocating, hideous smell; they were passing a flock of sheep, a shepherd in a black smock, holding his crook. Why should the sheep huddle together under this fierce sun? He felt that the shepherd would not see him, though he could see the shepherd.

At last there was the halt. They stacked rifles in conical stack, put down their kit in a scattered circle around it, and dispersed a little, sitting on a small knoll high on the hill-side. The chatter began. The soldiers were steaming with heat, but were lively. He sat still, seeing the blue mountains rising upon the land, twenty kilometres away. There was a blue fold in the ranges, then out of that, at the foot, the broad, pale bed of the river, stretches of whity-green water between pinkish grey shoals among the dark pine woods. There it was, spread out a long way off. And it seemed to come downhill, the river. There was a raft being steered, a mile away. It was a strange country. Nearer, a redroofed, broad farm with white base and square dots of windows crouched beside the wall of beech foliage on the wood's edge. There were long strips of rye and clover and pale green corn. And just at his feet, below the knoll, was a darkish bog, where globe flowers stood breathless still on their slim stalks. And some of the pale gold bubbles were burst, and a broken fragment hung in the air. He thought he was going to sleep.

Suddenly something moved into this coloured mirage before his eyes. The Captain, a small, light-blue and scarlet figure, was trotting evenly between the strips of corn, along the level brow of the hill. And the man making flag-signals was coming on. Proud and sure moved the horseman's figure, the quick, bright thing, in which was concentrated all the light of this morning, which for the rest lay fragile, shining shadow. Submissive, apathetic, the young soldier, sat and stared. But as the horse slowed to a walk, coming up the last steep path, the great flash flared over the body and soul of the orderly. He sat waiting. The back of his head felt as if it were weighted with a heavy piece of fire. He did not want to eat. His hands trembled slightly as he moved them. Meanwhile the officer on horseback was approaching slowly and proudly. The tension grew in the orderly's soul. Then again, seeing the

Captain ease himself on the saddle, the flash blazed through him.

The Captain looked at the path of light blue and scarlet, and dark head, scattered closely on the hill-side. It pleased him. The command pleased him. And he was feeling proud. His orderly was among them in common subjection. The officer rose a little on his stirrups to look. The young soldier sat with averted, dumb face. The Captain relaxed on his seat. His slim-legged, beautiful horse, brown as a beech nut, walked proudly uphill. The Captain passed into the zone of the company's atmosphere: a hot smell of men, of sweat, of leather. He knew it very well. After a word with the lieutenant, he went a few paces higher, and sat there, a dominant figure, his sweat-marked horse swishing its tail, while he looked down on his men, on his orderly, a non-entity among the crowd.

The young soldier's heart was like fire in his chest, and he breathed with difficulty. The officer, looking downhill, saw three of the young soldiers, two pails of water between them, staggering across a sunny green field. A table had been set up under a tree, and there the slim lieutenant stood, importantly busy. Then the Captain summoned himself to an act of courage. He called his orderly.

The flame leapt into the young soldier's throat as he heard the command, and he rose blindly, stifled. He saluted, standing below the officer. He did not look up. But there was the flicker in the Captain's voice.

'Go to the inn and fetch me . . .' the officer gave his commands. 'Quick!' he added.

At the last word, the heart of the servant leapt with a flash, and he felt the strength come over his body. But he turned in mechanical obedience, and set off at a heavy run downhill, looking almost like a bear, his trousers bagging over his military boots. And the officer watched this blind, plunging run all the way.

But it was only the outside of the orderly's body that was obeying so humbly and mechanically. Inside had gradually accumulated a core into which all the energy of that young life was compact and concentrated. He executed his commission, and plodded quickly back uphill. There was a pain in his head as he walked that made him twist his features unknowingly. But hard there in the centre of his chest was himself, himself, firm, and not to be plucked to pieces.

The Captain had gone up into the wood. The orderly plodded through the hot, powerfully smelling zone of the company's atmosphere. He had a curious mass of energy inside him now. The Captain was less real than himself. He approached the green entrance to the wood. There, in the half-shade, he saw the horse standing, the sunshine and the flickering shadow of leaves dancing over his brown body. There was a clearing where timber had lately been felled. Here, in the gold-green shade beside the brilliant cup of sunshine, stood two figures, blue and pink, the bits of pink showing out plainly. The Captain was talking to his lieutenant.

The orderly stood on the edge of the bright clearing, where great trunks of trees, stripped and glistening, lay stretched like naked, brownskinned bodies. Chips of wood littered the trampled floor, like splashed light, and the bases of the felled trees stood here and there, with their raw, level tops. Beyond was the brilliant, sunlit green of a beech.

'Then I will ride forward,' the orderly heard his

Captain say. The lieutenant saluted and strode away. He himself went forward. A hot flash passed through his belly, as he tramped towards his officer.

The Captain watched the rather heavy figure of the young soldier stumble forward, and his veins, too, ran hot. This was to be man to man between them. He yielded before the solid, stumbling figure with bent head. The orderly stooped and put the food on a level-sawn tree-base. The Captain watched the glistening, sun-inflamed, naked hands. He wanted to speak to the young soldier, but could not. The servant propped a bottle against his thigh, pressed open the cork, and poured out the beer into the mug. He kept his head bent. The Captain accepted the mug.

'Hot!' he said, as if amiably.

The flame sprang out of the orderly's heart, nearly suffocating him.

'Yes, sir,' he replied, between shut teeth.

And he heard the sound of the Captain's drinking, and he clenched his fists, such a strong torment came into his wrists. Then came the faint clang of the closing of the pot-lid. He looked up. The Captain was watching him. He glanced swiftly away. Then he saw the officer stoop and take a piece of bread from the tree-base. Again the flash of flame went through the young soldier, seeing the stiff body stoop beneath him, and his hands jerked. He looked away. He could feel the officer was nervous. The bread fell as it was being broken. The officer ate the other piece. The two men stood tense and still, the master laboriously chewing his bread, the servant staring with averted face, his fist clenched.

Then the young soldier started. The officer had pressed open the lid of the mug again. The orderly watched the lid of the mug, and the white hand that clenched the handle, as if he were fascinated. It was raised. The youth followed it with his eyes. And then he saw the thin, strong throat of the elder man moving up and down as he drank, the strong jaw working. And the instinct which had been jerking at the young man's wrists suddenly jerked free. He jumped, feeling as if it were rent in two by a strong flame.

The spur of the officer caught in a tree root, he went down backwards with a crash, the middle of his back thudding sickeningly against a sharp-edged tree-base, the pot flying away. And in a second the orderly, with serious, earnest young face, and underlip between his teeth, had got his knee in the officer's chest and was pressing the chin backward over the farther edge of the tree-stump, pressing, with all his heart behind in a passion of relief, the tension of his wrists exquisite with relief. And with the base of his palms he shoved at the chin, with all his might. And it was pleasant, too, to have that chin, that hard jaw already slightly rough with beard, in his hands. He did not relax one hair's breadth, but, all the force of all his blood exulting in his thrust, he shoved back the head of the other man, till there was a little 'cluck' and a crunching sensation. Then he felt as if his head went to vapour. Heavy convulsions shook the body of the officer, frightening and horrifying the young soldier. Yet it pleased him, too, to repress them. It pleased him to keep his hands pressing back the chin, to feel the chest of the other man yield in expiration to the weight of his strong, young knees, to feel the hard twitchings of the prostrate body jerking his own whole frame, which was pressed down on it.

But it went still. He could look into the nostrils of the

other man, the eyes he could scarcely see. How curiously the mouth was pushed out, exaggerating the full lips, and the moustache bristling up from them. Then, with a start, he noticed the nostrils gradually filled with blood. The red brimmed, hesitated, ran over, and went in a thin trickle down the face to the eyes.

It shocked and distressed him. Slowly, he got up. The body twitched and sprawled there, inert. He stood and looked at it in silence. It was a pity *it* was broken. It represented more than the thing which had kicked and bullied him. He was afraid to look at the eyes. They were hideous now, only the whites showing, and the blood running to them. The face of the orderly was drawn with horror at the sight. Well, it was so. In his heart he was satisfied. He had hated the face of the Captain. It was extinguished now. There was a heavy relief in the orderly's soul. That was as it should be. But he could not bear to see the long, military body lying broken over the tree-base, the fine fingers crisped. He wanted to hide it away.

Quickly, busily, he gathered it up and pushed it under the felled tree trunks, which rested their beautiful, smooth length either end on the logs. The face was horrible with blood. He covered it with the helmet. Then he pushed the limbs straight and decent, and brushed the dead leaves off the fine cloth of the uniform. So, it lay quite still in the shadow under there. A little strip of sunshine ran along the breast, from a chink between the logs. The orderly sat by it for a few moments. Here his own life also ended.

Then, through his daze, he heard the lieutenant, in a loud voice, explaining to the men outside the wood, that they were to suppose the bridge on the river below was held by the enemy. Now they were to march to the attack in such and such a manner. The lieutenant had no gift of expression. The orderly, listening from habit, got muddled. And when the lieutenant began it all again he ceased to hear.

He knew he must go. He stood up. It surprised him that the leaves were glittering in the sun, and the chips of wood reflecting white from the ground. For him a change had come over the world. But for the rest it had not—all seemed the same. Only he had left it. And he could not go back. It was his duty to return with the beer-pot and the bottle. He could not. He had left all that. The lieutenant was still hoarsely explaining. He must go, or they would overtake him. And he could not bear contact with anyone now.

He drew his fingers over his eyes, trying to find out where he was. Then he turned away. He saw the horse standing in the path. He went up to it and mounted. It hurt him to sit in the saddle. The pain of keeping his seat occupied him as they cantered through the wood. He would not have minded anything, but he could not get away from the sense of being divided from the others. The path led out of the trees. On the edge of the wood he pulled up and stood watching. There in the spacious sunshine of the valley soldiers were moving in a little swarm. Every now and then, a man harrowing on a strip of fallow shouted to his oxen, at the turn. The village and the white-towered church was small in the sunshine. And he no longer belonged to it—he sat there, beyond, like a man outside in the dark. He had gone out from everyday life into the unknown and he could not, he even did not want to go back.

Turning from the sun-blazing valley, he rode deep into the wood. Tree trunks, like people standing grey and still, took no notice as he went. A doe, herself a moving bit of sunshine and shadow, went running through the flecked shade. There were bright green rents in the foliage. Then it was all pine wood, dark and cool. And he was sick with pain, and had an intolerable, great pulse in his head, and he was sick. He had never been ill in his life. He felt lost, quite dazed with all this.

Trying to get down from the horse, he fell, astonished at the pain and his lack of balance. The horse shifted uneasily. He jerked its bridle and sent it cantering jerkily away. It was his last connection with the rest of things.

But he only wanted to lie down and not be disturbed. Stumbling through the trees, he came on a quiet place where beeches and pine trees grew on a slope. Immediately he had lain down and closed his eyes, his consciousness went racing on without him. A big pulse of sickness beat in him as if it throbbed through the whole earth. He was burning with dry heat. But he was too busy, too tearingly active in the incoherent race of delirium to observe.

III

He came to with a start. His mouth was dry and hard, his heart beat heavily, but he had not the energy to get up. His heart beat heavily. Where was he?–The barracks–at home? There was something knocking. And, making an effort, he looked round–trees, and litter of greenery, and reddish, bright, still pieces of sunshine on the floor. He did not believe he was himself, he did not believe what he saw. Something was knocking. He made a struggle towards consciousness, but relapsed. Then he struggled again. And gradually his surroundings fell into relationship with himself. He knew, and a great pang of fear went through his heart. Somebody was knocking. He could see the heavy, black rags of a fir tree overhead. Then everything went black. Yet he did not believe he had closed his eyes. He had not. Out of the blackness sight slowly emerged again. And someone was knocking. Quickly, he saw the blood-disfigured face of his Captain, which he hated. And he held himself still with horror. Yet, deep inside him, he knew that it was so, the Captain should be dead. But the physical delirium got hold of him. Someone was knocking. He lay perfectly still, as if dead, with fear. And he went unconscious.

When he opened his eyes again he started, seeing something creeping swiftly up a tree trunk. It was a little bird. And the bird was whistling overhead. Tap-tap-tap— it was the small, quick bird rapping the tree trunk with its beak, as if its head were a little round hammer. He watched it curiously. It shifted sharply, in its creeping fashion. Then, like a mouse, it slid down the bare trunk. Its swift creeping sent a flash of revulsion through him. He raised his head. It felt a great weight. Then, the little bird ran out of the shadow across a still patch of sunshine, its little head bobbing, swiftly, its white legs twinkling brightly for a moment. How neat it was in its build, so compact, with piece of white on its wings. There were several of them. They were so pretty—but they crept like swift, erratic mice, running here and there among the beech-mast.

He lay down again exhausted, and his consciousness lapsed. He had a horror of the little creeping birds. All his blood seemed to be darting and creeping in his head. And yet he could not move.

He came to with a further ache of exhaustion. There was the pain in his head, and the horrible sickness, and his inability to move. He had never been ill in his life. He did not know where he was or what he was. Probably he had got sunstroke. Or what else?—He had silenced the Captain for ever—some time ago—oh, a long time ago. There had been blood on his face, and his eyes had turned upwards. It was all right, somehow. It was peace. But now he had got beyond himself. He had never been here before. Was it life, or not life? He was by himself. They were in a big, bright place, those others, and he was outside. The town, all the country, a big bright place of light: and he was outside, here, in the darkened open beyond, where each thing existed alone. But they would all have to come out there sometime, those others. Little, and left behind him, they all were. There had been father and mother and sweetheart. What did they all matter? This was the open land.

He sat up. Something scuffled. It was a little brown squirrel running in lovely undulating bounds over the floor, its red tail completing the undulation of its body—and then, as it sat up, furling and unfurling. He watched it, pleased. It ran on again, friskily, enjoying itself. It flew wildly at another squirrel, and they were chasing each other, and making little scolding, chattering noises. The soldier wanted to speak to them. But only a hoarse sound came out of his throat. The squirrels burst away—they flew up the trees. And then he saw the one peeping round at him, half-way up a tree trunk. A start of fear went through him, though in so far as he was conscious, he was amused. It still stayed, its little keen face staring at him half-way up the tree trunk, its little ears pricked up, its clawey little hands clinging to the bark, its white breast reared. He started from it in panic.

Struggling to his feet, he lurched away. He went on

walking, walking, looking for something—for a drink. His brain felt hot and inflamed for want of water. He stumbled on. Then he did not know anything. He went unconscious as he walked. Yet he stumbled on, his mouth open.

When, to his dumb wonder, he opened his eyes on the world again, he no longer tried to remember what it was. There was thick, golden light behind golden-green glitterings, and tall, grey-purple shafts, and darknesses farther off, surrounding him, growing deeper. He was conscious of a sense of arrival. He was amid the reality, on the real, dark bottom. But there was the thirst burning in his brain. He felt lighter, not so heavy. He supposed it was, newness. The air was muttering with thunder. He thought he was walking wonderfully swiftly and was coming straight to relief—or was it to water?

Suddenly he stood still with fear. There was a tremendous flare of gold, immense—just a few dark trunks like bars between him and it. All the young level wheat was burnished gold glaring on its silky green. A woman, full-skirted, a black cloth on her head for head-dress, was passing like a block of shadow through the glistening, green corn, into the full glare. There was a farm, too, pale blue in shadow, and the timber black. And there was a church spire, nearly fused away in the gold. The woman moved on, away from him. He had no language with which to speak to her. She was the bright, solid unreality. She would make a noise of words that would confuse him, and her eyes would look at him without seeing him. She was crossing there to the other side. He stood against a tree.

When at last he turned, looking down the long, bare grove whose flat bed was already filling dark, he saw the mountains in a wonder-light, not far away, and radiant.

Behind the soft, grey ridge of the nearest range the farther mountains stood golden and pale grey, the snow all radiant like pure, soft gold. So still, gleaming in the sky, fashioned pure out of the ore of the sky, they shone in their silence. He stood and looked at them, his face illuminated. And like the golden, lustrous gleaming of the snow he felt his own thirst bright in him. He stood and gazed, leaning against a tree. And then everything slid away into space.

During the night the lightning fluttered perpetually, making the whole sky white. He must have walked again. The world hung livid round him for moments, fields a level sheen of grey-green light, trees in dark bulk, and the range of clouds black across a white sky. Then the darkness fell like a shutter, and the night was whole. A faint flutter of a half-revealed world, that could not quite leap out of the darkness!—Then there again stood a sweep of pallor for the land, dark shapes looming, a range of clouds hanging overhead. The world was a ghostly shadow, thrown for a moment upon the pure darkness, which returned ever whole and complete.

And the mere delirium of sickness and fever went on inside him—his brain opening and shutting like the night—then sometimes convulsions of terror from something with great eyes that stared round a tree—then the long agony of the march, and the sun decomposing his blood—then the pang of hate for the Captain, following by a pang of tenderness and ease. But everything was distorted, born of an ache and resolving into an ache.

In the morning he came definitely awake. Then his brain flamed with the sole horror or thirstiness! The sun was on his face, the dew was steaming from his wet clothes. Like one possessed, he got up. There, straight in front of him, blue and cool and tender, the mountains ranged across the pale edge of the morning sky. He wanted them—he wanted them alone—he wanted to leave himself and be identified with them. They did not move, they were still and soft, with white, gentle markings of snow. He stood still, mad with suffering, his hands crisping and clutching. Then he was twisting in a paroxysm on the grass.

He lay still, in a kind of dream of anguish. His thirst seemed to have separated itself from him, and to stand apart, a single demand. Then the pain he felt was another single self. Then there was the clog of his body, another separate thing. He was divided among all kinds of separate things. There was some strange, agonised connection between them, but they were drawing farther apart. Then they would all split. The sun, drilling down on him, was drilling through the bond. Then they would all fall, fall through the everlasting lapse of space. Then again, his consciousness reasserted itself. He roused on to his elbow and stared at the gleaming mountains. There they ranked, all still and wonderful between earth and heaven. He stared till his eyes went black, and the mountains, as they stood in their beauty, so clean and cool, seemed to have it, that which was lost in him.

IV

When the soldiers found him, three hours later, he was lying with his face over his arm, his black hair giving off heat under the sun. But he was still alive. Seeing the open, black mouth the young soldiers dropped him in horror.

He died in the hospital at night, without having seen again.

The doctors saw the bruises on his legs, behind, and were silent.

The bodies of the two men lay together, side by side, in the mortuary, the one white and slender, but laid rigidly at rest, the other looking as if every moment it must rouse into life again, so young and unused, from a slumber.

THE HORSE DEALER'S DAUGHTER

'WELL, Mabel, and what are you going to do with yourself?' asked Joe, with foolish flippancy. He felt quite safe himself. Without listening for an answer, he turned aside, worked a grain of tobacco to the tip of his tongue, and spat it out. He did not care about anything, since he felt safe himself.

The three brothers and the sister sat round the desolate breakfast-table, attempting some sort of desultory consultation. The morning's post had given the final tap to the family fortunes, and all was over. The dreary dining-room itself, with its heavy mahogany furniture, looked as if it were waiting to be done away with.

But the consultation amounted to nothing. There was a strange air of ineffectuality about the three men, as they sprawled at table, smoking and reflecting vaguely on their own condition. The girl was alone, a rather short, sullen-looking young woman of twenty-seven. She did not share the same life as her brothers. She would have been good-looking, save for the impressive fixity of her face, 'bull-dog', as her brothers called it.

There was a confused tramping of horses' feet outside. The three men all sprawled round in their chairs to watch. Beyond the dark holly bushes that separated the strip of lawn from the high-road, they could see a cavalcade of shire horses swinging out of their own yard, being taken for exercise. This was the last time. These were the last horses that would go through their hands. The young men watched with critical, callous look. They were all frightened at the collapse of their lives, and the sense of disaster in which they were involved felt them no inner freedom.

Yet they were three fine, well-set fellows enough. Joe, the eldest, was a man of thirty-three, broad and handsome in a hot, flushed way. His face was red, he twisted his black moustache over a thick finger, his eyes were shallow and restless. He had a sensual way of uncovering his teeth when he laughed, and his bearing was stupid. Now he watched the horses with a glazed look of helplessness in his eyes, a certain stupor of downfall.

The great draught-horses swung past. They were tied head to tail, four of them, and they heaved along to where a lane branched off from the high-road, planting their great hoofs floutingly in the fine black mud, swinging their great rounded haunches sumptuously, and trotting a few sudden steps as they were led into the lane, round the corner. Every movement showed a massive, slumbrous strength, and a stupidity which held them in subjection. The groom at the head looked back, jerking the leading rope. And the cavalcade moved out of sight up the lane, the tail of the last horse, bobbed up tight and stiff, held out taut from the swinging great haunches as they rocked behind the hedges in a motion-like sleep.

Joe watched with glazed hopeless eyes. The horses were almost like his own body to him. He felt he was done for now. Luckily he was engaged to a woman who was old as himself, and therefore her father, who was steward of a neighbouring estate, would provide him with a job. He would marry and go into harness. His life was over, he would be a subject animal now.

He turned uneasily aside, the retreating steps of the horses echoing in his ears. Then, with foolish restlessness, he reached for the scraps of bacon-rind from the plates, and making a faint whistling sound, flung them to the terrier that lay against the fender. He watched the dog swallow them, and waited till the creature looked into his eyes. Then a faint grin came on his face, and in a high, foolish voice he said:

'You won't get much more bacon shall you, you little b——?'

The dog faintly and dismally wagged its tail, then lowered its haunches, circled round, and lay down again.

There was another helpless silence at the table. Joe sprawled uneasily in his seat, not willing to go till the family conclave was dissolved. Fred Henry, the second brother, was erect, clean-limbed, alert. He had watched the passing of the horses with more sang-froid. If he was an animal, like Joe, he was an animal which controls, not one which is controlled. He was master of any horse, and he carried himself with a well-tempered air of mastery. But he was not master of the situations of life. He pushed his coarse brown moustache upwards, off his lip, and glanced irritably at his sister, who sat impassive and inscrutable.

'You'll go and stop with Lucy for a bit, shan't you?' he asked. The girl did not answer.

'I don't see what else you can do,' persisted Fred Henry.

'Go as skivvy,' Joe interpolated laconically.

The girl did not move a muscle.

'If I was her, I should go in for training for a nurse,' said Malcolm, the youngest of them all. He was the baby of the family, a young man of twenty-two, with a fresh, jaunty *museau*.

But Mabel did not take any notice of him. They had talked at her and round her for so many years, that she hardly heard them at all.

The marble clock on the mantelpiece softly chimed the half-hour, the dog rose uneasily from the hearth-rug and looked at the party at the breakfast-table. But still they sat on in ineffectual conclave.

'Oh, all right,' said Joe suddenly, apropos of nothing. 'I'll get a move on.'

He pushed back his chair, straddled his knees with a downward jerk, to get them free, in horsey fashion, and went to the fire. Still, he did not go out of the room; he was curious to know what the others would do or say. He began to change his pipe, looking down at the dog and saying in a high, affected voice:

'Going wi' me? Going wi' me are ter? Tha'rt goin' further than tha counts on just now, dost hear?'

The dog faintly wagged its tail, the man stuck out his jaw and covered his pipe with his hands, and puffed intently, losing himself in the tobacco, looking down all the while at the dog with an absent brown eye. The dog looked up at him in mournful distrust. Joe stood with his knees stuck out, in real horsey fashion.

'Have you had a letter from Lucy?' Fred Henry asked of his sister.

'Last week,' came the neutral reply.

'And what does she say?'

There was no answer.

'Does she *ask* you to go and stop there?' persisted Fred Henry.

'She says I can if I like.'

'Well, then, you'd better. Tell her you'll come on Monday.'

This was received in silence.

'That's what you'll do then, is it?' said Fred Henry, in

some exasperation.

But she made no answer. There was a silence of futility and irritation in the room. Malcolm grinned fatuously.

'You'll have to make up your mind between now and next Wednesday,' said Joe loudly, 'or else find yourself lodgings on the kerbstone.'

The face of the young woman darkened, but she sat on immutable.

'Here's Jack Fergusson!' exclaimed Malcolm, who was looking aimlessly out of the window.

'Where?' exclaimed Joe loudly.

'Just gone past.'

'Coming in?'

Malcolm craned his neck to see the gate.

'Yes,' he said.

There was a silence. Mabel sat on like one condemned, at the head of the table. Then a whistle was heard from the kitchen. The dog got up and barked sharply. Joe opened the door and shouted:

'Come on'.

After a moment a young man entered. He was muffled up in overcoat and a purple woollen scarf, and his tweed cap which he did not remove, was pulled down on his head. He was of medium height, his face was rather long and pale, his eyes looked tired.

'Hello, Jack! Well, Jack!' exclaimed Malcolm and Joe. Fred Henry merely said: 'Jack.'

'What's doing?' asked the newcomer, evidently addressing Fred Henry.

'Same. We've got to be out by Wednesday. Got a cold?'

'I have—got it bad, too.'

'Why don't you stop in?'

'*Me* stop in? When I can't stand on my legs, perhaps I

shall have a chance.' The young man spoke huskily. He had a slight Scotch accent.

'It's a knock-out, isn't it,' said Joe, boisterously, 'if a doctor goes round croaking with a cold. Looks bad for the patients, doesn't it?'

The young doctor looked at him slowly.

'Anything the matter with *you,* then?' he asked sarcastically.

'Not as I know of. Damn your eyes, I hope not. Why?'

'I thought you were very concerned about the patients, wondered if you might be one yourself.'

'Damn it, no, I've never been patient to no flaming doctor, and hope I never shall be,' returned Joe.

At this point Mabel rose from the table, and they all seemed to become aware of her existence. She began putting the dishes together. The young doctor looked at her, but did not address her. He had not greeted her. She went out of the room with the tray, her face impassive and unchanged.

'When are you off then, all of you?' asked the doctor.

'I'm catching the eleven-forty,' replied Malcolm. 'Are you goin' down wi' th' trap, Joe?'

'Yes, I've told you I'm going down wi' th' trap, haven't I?'

'We'd better be getting her in then. So long, Jack, if I don't see you before I go,' said Malcolm, shaking hands.

He went out, followed by Joe, who seemed to have his tail between his legs.

'Well, this is the devil's own,' exclaimed the doctor, when he was left alone with Fred Henry. 'Going before Wednesday, are you?'

'That's the orders,' replied the other.

'Where, no Northampton?'

'That's it.'

'The devil!' exclaimed Fergusson, with quiet chagrin. And there was silence between the two.

'All settled up, are you?' asked Fergusson.

'About.'

There was another pause.

'Well, I shall miss yer, Freddy, boy,' said the young doctor.

'And I shall miss thee, Jack,' returned the other.

'Miss you like hell,' mused the doctor.

Fred Henry turned aside. There was nothing to say. Mabel came in again, to finish clearing the table.

'What are *you* going to do, then, Miss Pervin?' asked Fergusson. 'Going to your sister's, are you?'

Mabel looked at him with her steady, dangerous eyes, that always made him uncomfortable, unsettling his superficial ease.

'No,' she said.

'Well, what in the name of fortune *are* you going to do? Say what you mean to do,' cried Fred Henry, with futile intensity.

But she only averted her head, and continued her work. She folded the white table-cloth, and put on the chenille cloth.

'The sulkiest bitch that ever trod!' muttered her brother.

But she finished her task with perfectly impassive face, the young doctor watching her interestedly all the while. Then she went out.

Fred Henry stared after her, clenching his lips, his blue eyes fixing in sharp antagonism, as he made a grimace of sour exasperation.

'You could bray her into bits, and that's all you'd get out of her,' he said, in a small, narrowed tone.

The doctor smiled faintly.

'What's she *going* to do, then?' he asked.

'Strike me if *I* know!' returned the other.

There was a pause. Then the doctor stirred.

'I'll be seeing you to-night, shall I?' he said to his friend.

'Ay—where's it to be? Are we going over to Jessdale?'

'I don't know. I've got such a cold on me. I'll come round to the "Moon and Stars", anyway.'

'Let Lizzie and May miss their night for once, eh?'

'That's it—if I feel as I do now.'

'All's one—'

The two young men went through the passage and down to the back door together. The house was large, but it was servantless now, and desolate. At the back was a small bricked house-yard and beyond that a big square, gravelled fine and red, and having stables on two sides. Sloping, dank, winter-dark fields stretched away on the open sides.

But the stables were empty. Joseph Pervin, the father of the family, had been a man of no education, who had become a fairly large horse dealer. The stables had been full of horses, there was a great turmoil and come-and-go of horses and of dealers and grooms. Then the kitchen was full of servants. But of late things had declined. The old man had married a second time, to retrieve his fortunes. Now he was dead and everything was gone to the dogs, there was nothing but debt and threatening.

For months, Mabel had been servantless in the big house, keeping the home together in penury for her ineffectual brothers. She had kept house for ten years. But previously it was with unstinted means. Then, however brutal and coarse everything was, the sense of money had kept her proud, confident. The men might be foul-mouthed, the women in the kitchen might have bad reputations, her brothers might have illegitimate children. But so long as there was money, the girl felt herself established, and brutally proud, reserved.

No company came to the house, save dealers and coarse men. Mabel had no associates of her own sex, after her sister went away. But she did not mind. She went regularly to church, she attended to her father. And she lived in the memory of her mother, who had died when she was fourteen, and whom she had loved. She had loved her father, too, in a different way, depending upon him, and feeling secure in him, until at the age of fifty-four he married again. And then she had set hard against him. Now he had died and left them all hopelessly in debt.

She had suffered badly during the period of poverty. Nothing, however, could shake the curious, sullen, animal pride that dominated each member of the family. Now, for Mabel, the end had come. Still she would not cast about her. She would follow her own way just the same. She would always hold the keys of her own situation. Mindless and persistent she endured from day to day. Why should she think? Why should she answer anybody? It was enough that this was the end, and there was no way out. She need not pass any more darkly along the main street of the small town, avoiding every eye. She need not demean herself any more, going into the shops and buying the cheapest food. This was at an end. She thought of nobody, not even of herself. Mindless and persistent, she seemed in a sort of ecstasy to be coming nearer to her fulfilment, her own glorification, approaching her dead mother, who was glorified.

In the afternoon she took a little bag, with shears and

sponge and a small scrubbing-brush, and went out. It was a grey wintry day, with saddened, dark green fields and an atmosphere blackened by the smoke of foundries not far off. She went quickly, darkly along the causeway, heeding nobody, through the town to the churchyard.

There she always felt secure, as if no one could see her, although as a matter of fact she was exposed to the stare of everyone who passed along under the churchyard wall. Nevertheless, once under the shadow of the great looming church, among the graves, she felt immune from the world, reserved within the thick churchyard wall as in another country.

Carefully she clipped the grass from the grave, and arranged the pinky white, small chrysanthemums in the tin cross. When this was done, she took an empty jar from a neighbouring grave, brought water, and carefully, most scrupulously sponged the marble headstone and the coping-stone.

It gave her sincere satisfaction to do this. She felt in immediate contact with the world of her mother. She took minute pains, went through the park in a state bordering on pure happiness, as if in performing this task she came into a subtle, intimate connection with her mother. For the life she followed here in the world was far less real than the world of death she inherited from her mother.

The doctor's house was just by the church. Fergusson, being a mere hired assistant, was slave to the countryside. As he hurried now to attend to the out-patients in the surgery, glancing across the graveyard with his quick eye, he saw the girl at her task at the grave. She seemed so intent and remote, it was like looking into another world. Some mystical element was touched in him. He slowed down as he walked, watching her as if spellbound.

She lifted her eyes, feeling him looking. Their eyes met. And each looked again at once, each feeling, in some way, found out by the other. He lifted his cap and passed on down the road. There remained distinct in his consciousness, like a vision, the memory of her face, lifted from the tombstone in the churchyard, and looking at him with slow, large, portentous eyes. It *was* portentous, her face. It seemed to mesmerise him. There was a heavy power in her eyes which laid hold of his whole being, as if he had drunk some powerful drug. He had been feeling weak and done before. Now the life came back into him, he felt delivered from his own fretted, daily self.

He finished his duties at the surgery as quickly as might be, hastily filling up the bottles of the waiting people with cheap drugs. Then, in perpetual haste, he set of again to visit several cases in another part of his round, before tea-time. At all times he preferred to walk if he could, but particularly when he was not well. He fancied the motion restored him.

The afternoon was falling. It was grey, deadened, and wintry, with a slow, moist, heavy coldness sinking in and deadening all the faculties. But why should he think or notice? He hastily climbed the hill and turned across the dark green fields, following the black cinder-track. In the distance, across a shallow dip in the country, the small town was clustered like smouldering ash, a tower, a spire, a heap of low, raw, extinct houses. And on the nearest fringe of the town, sloping into the dip, was Oldmeadow, the Pervins' house. He could see the stables and the outbuildings distinctly, as they lay towards him on the slope. Well, he would not go there many more times! Another resource would be lost to him, another place gone: the only company he cared for in the alien, ugly little town he was losing. Nothing but work, drudgery, constant hastening from dwelling to dwelling among the colliers and the iron-workers. It wore him out, but at the same time he had a craving for it. It was a stimulant to him to be in the homes of the working people, moving, as it were, through the innermost body of their life. His nerves were excited and gratified. He could come so near, into the very lives of the rough, inarticulate, powerfully emotional men and women. He grumbled, he said he hated the hellish hole. But as a matter of fact it excited him, the contact with the rough, strongly-feeling people was a stimulant applied direct to his nerves.

Below Oldmeadow, in the green, shallow, soddened hollow of fields, lay a square, deep pond. Roving across the landscape, the doctor's quick eye detected a figure in black passing through the gate of the field, down towards the pond. He looked again. It would be Mabel Pervin. His mind suddenly became alive and attentive.

Why was she going down there? He pulled up on the path on the slope above, and stood staring. He could just make sure of the small black figure moving in the hollow of the failing day. He seemed to see her in the midst of such obscurity, that he was like a clairvoyant, seeing rather with the mind's eye than with ordinary sight. Yet he could see her positively enough, whilst he kept his eye attentive. He felt, if he looked away from her, in the thick, ugly falling dusk, he would lose her altogether.

He followed her minutely as she moved, direct and intent, like something transmitted rather than stirring in voluntary activity, straight down the field towards the pond. There she stood on the bank for a moment. She never raised her head. Then she waded slowly into the water.

He stood motionless as the small black figure walked slowly and deliberately towards the centre of the pond, very slowly, gradually moving deeper into the motionless water, and still moving forward as the water got up to her breast. Then he could see her no more in the dusk of the dead afternoon.

'There!' he exclaimed. 'Would you believe it?'

And he hastened straight down, running over the wet, soddened fields, pushing through the hedges, down into the depression of callous wintry obscurity. It took him several minutes to come to the pond. He stood on the bank, breathing heavily. He could see nothing. His eyes seemed to penetrate the dead water. Yes, perhaps that was the dark shadow of her black clothing beneath the surface of the water.

He slowly ventured into the pond. The bottom was deep, soft clay, he sank in, and the water clasped dead cold round his legs. As he stirred he could smell the cold, rotten clay that foulded up into the water. It was objectionable in his lungs. Still, repelled and yet not heeding, he moved deeper into the pond. The cold water rose over his thighs, over his loins, upon his abdomen. The lower part of his body was all sunk in the hideous cold element. And the bottom was so deeply soft and uncertain, he was afraid of pitching with his mouth underneath. He could not swim, and was afraid.

He crouched a little, spreading his hands under the water and moving them round, trying to feel for her. The dead cold pond swayed upon his chest. He moved again, a little deeper, and again, with his hands underneath, felt all around under, and again, with his hands underneath, he felt all around under the water. And he touched her clothing. But it evaded his fingers. He made a desperat effort to grasp it.

And so doing he lost his balance and went under, horribly, suffocating in the foul earthy water, struggling madly for a few moments. At last, after what seemed an eternity, he got his footing, rose again into the air and looked around. He gasped, and knew he was in the world. Then he looked at the water. She had risen near him. He grasped her clothing, and drawing her nearer, turned to take his way to land again.

He went very slowly, carefully, absorbed in the slow process. He rose higher, climbing out of the pond. The water was now only about his legs; he was thankful, full of relief to be out of the clutches of the pond. He lifted her and staggered on to the bank, out of the horror of wet, grey clay.

He laid her down on the bank. She was quite unconscious and running with water. He made the water come from her mouth, he worked to restore her. He did not have to work very long before he could feel the breathing begin again in her; she was breathing naturally. He worked a little longer. He could feel her live beneath his hands; she was coming back. He wiped her face, wrapped her in his overcoat, looked round into the dim, dark grey world, then lifted her and staggered down the bank and across the fields.

It seemed an unthinkably long way, and his burden so heavy he felt he would never get to the house. But at last he was in the stable-yard, and then in the house-yard. He opened the door and went into the house. In the kitchen he laid her down on the hearth-rug and called. The house was empty. But the fire was burning in the grate.

Then again he kneeled to attend to her. She was ...ng regularly, her eyes were wide open and as if conscious, but there seemed something missing in her look. She was conscious in herself, but unconscious of her surroundings.

He ran upstairs, took blankets from a bed, and put them before the fire to warm. Then he removed her saturated, earthy-smelling clothing, rubbed her dry with a towel, and wrapped her naked in the blankets. Then he went into the dining-room, to look for spirits. There was a little whisky. He drank a gulp himself, and put some into her mouth.

The effect was instantaneous. She looked full into his face, as if she had been seeing him for some time, and yet had only just become conscious of him.

'Dr. Fergusson?' she said.

'What?' he answered.

He was divesting himself of his coat, intending to find some dry clothing upstairs. He could not bear the smell of the dead, clayed water, and he was mortally afraid for his own health.

'What did I do?' she asked.

'Walked into the pond,' he replied. He had begun to shudder like one sick, and could hardly attend to her. Her eyes remained full on him, he seemed to be going dark in his mind, looking back at her helplessly. The shuddering became quieter in him, his life came back to him, dark and unknowing, but strong again.

'Was I out of my mind?' she asked, while her eyes were fixed on him all the time.

'Maybe, for the moment,' he replied. He felt quiet, because his strength had come back. The strange fretful strain had left him.

'Am I out of my mind now?' she asked.

'Are you?' he reflected a moment. 'No,' he answered truthfully, 'I don't see that you are.' He turned his face aside. He was afraid now, because he felt dazed, and felt dimly that her power was stronger than his, in this issue. And she continued to look at him fixedly all the time.

'Can you tell me where I shall find some dry things to put on?' he asked.

'Did you dive into the pond for me?' she asked.

'No,' he answered. 'I walked in. But I went in overhead as well.'

There was silence for a moment. He hesitated. He very much wanted to go upstairs to get into dry clothing. But there was another desire in him. And she seemed to hold him. His will seemed to have gone to sleep, and left him, standing there slack before her. But he felt warm inside himself. He did not shudder at all, though his clothes were sodden on him.

'Why did you?' she asked.

'Because I didn't want you to do such a foolish thing,' he said.

'It wasn't foolish,' she said, still gazing at him as she lay on the floor, with a sofa cushion under her head. 'It was the right thing to do. *I* knew best, then.'

'I'll go and shift these wet things,' he said. But still he had not the power to move out of her presence, until she sent him. It was as if she had the life of his body in her hands, and he could not extricate himself. Or perhaps he did not want to.

Suddenly she sat up. Then she became aware of her own immediate condition. She felt the blankets about her, she knew her own limbs. For a moment it seemed as if her reason were going. She looked round, with wild eye, as if seeking something. He stood still with fear. She saw her clothing lying scattered.

'Who undressed me?' she asked, her eyes resting full

and inevitable on his face.

'I did,' he replied, 'to bring you round.'

For some moments she sat and gazed at him awfully, her lips parted.

'Do you love me, then?' she asked.

He only stood and stared at her, fascinated. His soul seemed to melt.

She shuffled forward on her knees, and put her arms round him, round his legs, as he stood there, pressing her breasts against his knees and thighs, clutching him with strange, convulsive certainty, pressing his thighs against her, drawing him to her face, her throat, as she looked up at him with flaring, humble eyes and transfiguration, triumphant in first possession.

'You love me,' she murmured, in strange transport, yearning and triumphant and confident. 'You love me. I know you love me, I know.'

And she was passionately kissing his knees, through the wet clothing, passionately and indiscriminately kissing his knees, his legs, as if unaware of everything.

He looked down at the tangled wet hair, the wild, bare, animal shoulders. He was amazed, bewildered, and afraid. He had never thought of loving her. He had never wanted to love her. When he rescued her and restored her, he was a doctor, and she was a patient. He had had no single personal thought of her. Nay, this introduction of the personal element was very distasteful to him, a violation of his professional honour. It was horrible to have her there embracing his knees. It was horrible. He revolted from it, violently. And yet—and yet—he had not the power to break away.

She looked at him again, with the same supplication of powerful love, and that same transcendent, frightening light of triumph. In view of the delicate flame which seemed to come from her face like a light, he was powerless. And yet he had never intended to love her. He had never intended. And something stubborn in him could not give way.

'You love me,' she repeated, in a murmur of deep, rhapsodic assurance. 'You love me.'

Her hands were drawing him, drawing him down to her. He was afraid, even a little horrified. For he had, really, no intention of loving her. Yet her hands were drawing him towards her. He put out his hand quickly to steady himself, and grasped her bare shoulder. A flame seemed to burn the hand that grasped her soft shoulder. He had no intention of loving her: his whole will was against his yielding. It was horrible. And yet wonderful was the touch of her shoulders, beautiful the shining of her face. Was she perhaps mad? He had a horror of yielding to her. Yet something in him ached also.

He had been staring away at the door, away from her. But his hand remained on her shoulder. She had gone suddenly very still. He looked down at her. Her eyes were now wide with fear, with doubt, the light was dying from her face, a shadow of terrible greyness was returning. He could not bear the touch of her eyes' question upon him, and the look of death behind the question.

With an inward groan he gave way, and let his heart yield towards her. A sudden gentle smile came on his face. And her eyes, which never left his face, slowly, slowly filled with tears. He watched the strange water rise in her eyes, like some slow fountain coming up. And his heart seemed to burn and melt away in his breast.

He could not bear to look at her any more. He dropped on his knees and caught her head with his arms and pressed her face against his throat. She was very still. His heart, which seemed to have broken, was burning with a kind of agony in his breast. And he felt her slow, hot tears wetting his throat. But he could not move.

He felt the hot tears wet his neck and the hollows of his neck, and he remained motionless, suspended through one of man's eternities. Only now it had become indispensable to him to have her face pressed close to him; he could never let her go again. He could never let her head go away from the close clutch of his arm. He wanted to remain like that for ever, with his heart hurting him in a pain that was also life to him. Without knowing, he was looking down on her damp, soft brown hair.

Then, as it were suddenly, he smelt the horrid stagnant smell of that water. And at the same moment she drew away from him and looked at him. Her eyes were wistful and unfathomable. He was afraid of them, and he fell to kissing her, not knowing what he was doing. He wanted her eyes not to have that terrible, wistful, unfathomable look.

When she turned her face to him again, a faint delicate flush was glowing, and there was again dawning that terrible shining of joy in her eyes, which really terrified him, and yet which he now wanted to see, because he feared the look of doubt still more.

'You love me?' she said, rather faltering.

'Yes.' The word cost him a painful effort. Not because it wasn't true. But because it was too newly true, the *saying* seemed to tear open again his newly-torn heart. And he hardly wanted it to be true, even now.

She lifted her face to him, and he bent forward and kissed her on the mouth, gently, with the one kiss that is an eternal pledge. And as he kissed her his heart strained again in his breast. He never intended to love her. But now it was over. He had crossed over the gulf to her, and all that he had left behind had shrivelled and become void.

After the kiss, her eyes again slowly filled with tears. She sat still, away from him, with her face drooped aside, and her hands folded in her lap. The tears fell very slowly. There was complete silence. He too sat there motionless and silent on the hearth-rug. The strange pain of his heart that was broken seemed to consume him. That he should love her? That this was love! That he should be ripped open in this way! Him, a doctor! How they would all jeer if they knew! It was agony to him to think they might know.

In the curious naked pain of the thought he looked again to her. She was sitting there drooped into a muse. He saw a tear fall, and his heart flared hot. He saw for the first time that one of her shoulders was quite uncovered, one arm bare, he could see one of her small breasts; dimly, because it had become almost dark in the room.

'Why are you crying?' he asked, in an altered voice.

She looked up at him, and behind her tears the consciousness of her situation for the first time brought a dark look of shame to her eyes.

'I'm not crying, really,' she said, watching him, half frightened.

He reached his hand, and softly closed it on her bare arm.

'I love you! I love you!' he said in a soft, low vibrating voice, unlike himself.

She shrank, and dropped her head. The soft, penetrating grip of his hand on her arm distressed her. She looked up at him.

'I want to go,' she said. 'I want to go and get you some dry things.'

'Why?' he said. 'I'm all right.'

'But I want to go,' she said. 'And I want you to change your things.'

He released her arm, and she wrapped herself in the blanket, looking at him rather frightened. And still she did not rise.

'Kiss me,' she said wistfully.

He kissed her, but briefly, half in anger.

Then, after a second, she rose nervously, all mixed up in the blanket. He watched her in her confusion as she tried to extricate herself and wrap herself up so that she could walk. He watched her relentlessly, as she knew. And as she went, the blanket trailing, and as he saw a glimpse of her feet and her white leg, he tried to remember her as she was when he had wrapped her in the blanket. But then he didn't want to remember, because she had been nothing to him then, and his nature revolted from remembering her as she was when she was nothing to him.

A tumbling, muffled noise from within the dark house startled him. Then he heard her voice: 'There are clothes.' He rose and went to the foot of the stairs, and gathered up the garments she had thrown down. Then he came back to the fire, to rub himself down and dress. He grinned at his own appearance when he had finished.

The fire was sinking, so he put on coal. The house was now quite dark, save for the light of a street-lamp that shone in faintly from beyond the holly trees. He lit the gas with matches he found on the mantelpiece. Then he emptied the pockets of his own clothes, and threw all his wet things in a heap into the scullery. After which he gathered up her sodden clothes, gently, and put them in a separate heap on the copper-top in the scullery.

It was six o'clock on the clock. His own watch had

stopped. He ought to go back to the surgery. He waited, and still she did not come down. So he went to the foot of the stairs and called:

'I shall have to go.'

Almost immediately he heard her coming down. She had on her best dress of black voile, and her hair was tidy, but still damp. She looked at him—and in spite of herself, smiled.

'I don't like you in those clothes,' she said.

'Do I look a sight?' he answered.

They were shy of one another.

'I'll make you some tea,' she said.

'No, I must go.'

'Must you?' And she looked at him again with the wide, strained, doubtful eyes. And again, from the pain of his breast, he knew how he loved her. He went and bent to kiss her, gently, passionately, with his heart's painful kiss.

'And my hair smells so horrible,' she murmured in distraction. 'And I'm so awful, I'm so awful! Oh, no, I'm too awful.' And she broke into bitter, heart-broken sobbing. 'You can't want to love me, I'm horrible.'

'Don't be silly, don't be silly,' he said, trying to comfort her, kissing her, holding her in his arms. 'I want you, I want to marry you, we're going to be married, quickly, quickly—to-morrow if I can.'

But she only sobbed terribly, and cried:

'I feel awful. I feel awful. I feel I'm horrible to you.'

'No, I want you, I want you,' was all he answered, blindly, with that terrible intonation which frightened her almost more than her horror lest he should *not* want her.

FANNY AND ANNIE

FLAME-LURID his face as he turned among the throng of flame-lit and dark faces upon the platform. In the light of the furnace she caught sight of his drifting countenance, like a piece of floating fire. And the nostalgia, the doom of home-coming went through her veins like a drug. His eternal face, flame-lit now! The pulse and darkness of red fire from the furnace towers in the sky, lighting the desultory, industrial crowd on the wayside station, lit him and went out.

Of course he did not see her. Flame-lit and unseeing! Always the same, with his meeting eyebrows, his common cap, and his red-and-black scarf knotted round his throat. Not even a collar to meet her! The flames had sunk, there was shadow.

She opened the door of her grimy, branch-line carriage, and began to get down her bags. The porter was nowhere, of course, but there was Harry, obscure, on the outer edge of the little crowd, missing her, of course.

'Here! Harry!' she called, waving her umbrella in the twilight. He hurried forward.

'Tha's come, has ter?' he said, in a sort of cheerful welcome. She got down, rather flustered, and gave him a peck of a kiss.

'Two suit-cases!' she said.

Her soul groaned within her, as he clambered into the carriage after her bags. Up shot the fire in the twilight sky, from the great furnace behind the station. She felt the red flame go across her face. she had come back, she had come back for good. And her spirit groaned dismally. She doubted if she could bear it.

There, on the sordid little station under the furnaces, she stood, tall and distinguished, in her well-made coat and skirt and her broad grey velour hat. She held her umbrella, her bead chatelaine, and a little leather case in her grey-gloved hands, while Harry staggered out of the ugly little train with her bags.

'There's a trunk at the back,' she said in her bright voice. But she was not feeling bright. The twin black cones of the iron foundry blasted their sky-high fires into the night. The whole scene was lurid. The train waited cheerfully. It would wait another ten minutes. She knew it. It was all so deadly familiar.

Let us confess it at once. She was a lady's maid, thirty years old, come back to marry her first-love, a foundry worker, after having kept him dangling off and on, for a dozen years. Why had she come back? Did she love him? No. She didn't pretend to. She had loved her brilliant and ambitious cousin, who had jilted her, and who had died. She had had other affairs which had come to nothing. So here she was, come back suddenly to marry her first-love, who had waited—or remained single—all these years.

'Won't a porter carry these?' she said, as Harry strode with his workman's stride down the platform towards the guard's van.

'I can manage,' he said.

And with her umbrella, her chatelaine, and her little leather case, she followed him.

The trunk was there.

'We'll get Heather's greengrocer's cart to fetch it up,' he said.

'Isn't there a cab?' said Fanny, knowing dismally

enough that there wasn't.

'I'll just put it aside o' the penny-in-the-slot, and Heather's greengrocess'll fetch it about half-past eight,' he said.

He seized the box by its two handles and staggered with it across the level-crossing, bumping his legs against it as he waddled. Then he dropped it by the red sweetmeats machine.

'Will it be safe there?' she said.

'Ay—safe as houses,' he answered. He returned for the two bags. Thus, laden, they started to plod up the hill, under the great long black building of the foundry. She walked beside him—workman of workmen he was, trudging with that luggage. The red light flared over the deepening darkness. From the foundry came the horrible, slow clang clang, clang of iron, a great noise, with an interval just long enough to make it unendurable.

Compare this with the arrival at Gloucester: the carriage for her mistress, the dog-cart for herself with the luggage! The drive out past the river, the pleasant trees of the carriage-approach; and herself sitting beside Arthur, everybody so polite to her.

She had come home—for good! Her heart nearly stopped beating as she trudged up that hideous and interminable hill, beside the laden figure. What a come-down! What a come-down! She could not take it with her usual bright cheerfulness. She knew it all too well. It is easy to bear up against the unusual, but the deadly familiarity of an old stale past!

He dumped the bags down under a lamp-post, for a rest. There they stood, the two of them, in the lamp-light. Passers-by stared at her, and gave good-night to Harry. Her they hardly knew, she had become a stranger.

'They're too heavy for you, let me carry one,' she said.

'They begin to weigh a bit by the time you've gone a mile,' he answered.

'Let me carry the little one,' she insisted.

'Tha can ha'e it for a minute, if ter's a mind,' he said, handing over the valise.

And thus they arrived in the streets of shops of the little ugly town on top of the hill. How everybody stared at her; my word, how they stared! And the cinema was just going in, and the queues were tailing down the road to the corner. And everybody took full stock of her.

'Night, Harry!' shouted the fellows, in an interested voice.

However, they arrived at her aunt's—a little sweet-shop in a side street. They 'pinged' the door-bell, and her aunt came running forward out of the kitchen.

'There you are, child! Dying for a cup of tea, I'm sure. How are you?'

Fanny's aunt kissed her, and it was all Fanny could do to refrain from bursting into tears, she felt so low. Perhaps it was her tea she wanted.

'You've had a drag with that luggage,' said Fanny's aunt to Harry.

'Ay—I'm not sorry to put it down,' he said, looking at his hand which was crushed and cramped by the bag handle.

Then he departed to see about Heather's greengrocery cart.

When Fanny sat at tea, her aunt, a grey-haired, fair-faced little woman, looked at her with an admiring heart, feeling bitterly sore for her. For Fanny was beautiful: tall, erect, finely coloured, with her delicately arched nose, her rich brown hair, her large lustrous-grey eyes. A passionate woman—a woman to be afraid of. So proud, so inwardly violent! She came of a violent race.

It needed a woman to sympathise with her. Men had not the courage. Poor Fanny! She was such a lady, and so straight and magnificent. And yet everything seemed to do her down. Every time she seemed to be doomed to humiliation and disappointment, this handsome, brilliantly sensitive woman, with her nervous, over-wrought laugh.

'So you've really come back, child?' said her aunt.

'I really have, Aunt,' said Fanny.

'Poor Harry! I'm not sure, you know, Fanny, that you're not taking a bit of an advantage of him.'

'Oh, Aunt, he's waited so long, he may as well have what he's waited for.' Fanny laughed grimly.

'Yes, child, he's waited so long, that I'm not sure it isn't a bit hard on him. You know, I *like* him, Fanny—though as you know quite well, I don't think he's good enough for you. And I think he thinks so himself, poor fellow.'

'Don't you be so sure of that, Aunt. Harry is common, but he's not humble. He wouldn't think the Queen was any too good for him, if he's a mind to her.'

'Well—it's as well if he has a proper opinion of himself.'

'It depends what you call proper,' said Fanny. 'But he's got his good points—'

'Oh, he's a nice fellow, and I like him, I do like him. Only, as I tell you he's not good enough for you.'

'I've made up my mind, Aunt,' said Fanny, grimly.

'Yes,' mused the aunt. 'They say all things come to him who waits—'

'More than he's bargained, for, eh, Aunt?' laughed Fanny rather bitterly.

The poor aunt, this bitterness grieved her for her niece.

They were interrupted by the ping of the shop-bell, and Harry's call of 'Right!' But as he did not come in at once, Fanny, feeing solicitous for him presumably at the moment, rose and went into the shop. She saw a cart outside, and went to the door.

And the moment she stood in the doorway, she heard a woman's common vituperative voice crying from the darkness of the opposite side of the road:

'Tha'rt theer, are ter? I'll shame thee, Mester, I'll shame there, see if I dunna.'

Startled, Fanny started across the darkness, and saw a woman in a black bonnet go under one of the lamps up the side street.

Harry and Bill Heather had dragged the trunk off the little dray, and she retreated before them as they came up the shop step with it.

'Wheer shal ha'e it?' asked Harry.

'Best take it upstairs,' said Fanny.

She went up first to light the gas.

When Heather had gone, and Harry was sitting down having tea and pork-pie, Fanny asked:

'Who was that woman shouting?'

'Nay, I canna tell thee. To somebody, I s'd think,' replied Harry. Fanny looked at him, but asked no more.

He was a fair-haired fellow of thirty-two, with a fair moustache. He was broad in his speech, and looked like a foundry-hand, which he was. But women always liked him. There was something of a mother's lad about him—something warm and playful and really sensitive.

He had his attractions even for Fanny. What she rebelled against so bitterly was that he had no sort of ambition. He was a moulder, but of very commonplace skill. He was thirty-two years old, and hadn't saved twenty pounds. She would have to provide the money for the home. He didn't care. He just didn't care. He had no initiative at all. He had no vices—no obvious ones. But he was just indifferent, spending as he went, and not caring. Yet he did not look happy. She remembered his face in the fire-glow: something haunted, abstracted about it. As he sat there eating his pork-pie, bulging his cheek out, she felt he was like a doom to her. And she raged against the doom of him. It wasn't that he was gross. His *way* was common, almost on purpose. But he himself wasn't really common. For instance, his food was not particularly important to him, he was not greedy. He had a charm, too, particularly for women, with his blondness and his sensitiveness and his way of making a woman feel that she was a higher being. But Fanny knew him, knew the peculiar obstinate limitedness of him, that would nearly send her mad.

He stayed till about half-past nine. She went to the door with him.

'When are you coming up?' he said, jerking his head in the direction, presumably, of his own home.

'I'll come to-morrow afternoon,' she said brightly. Between Fanny and Mrs. Goodall, his mother, there was naturally no love lost.

Again she gave him an awkward little kiss, and said good-night.

'You can't wonder, you know, child, if he doesn't seem so very keen,' said her aunt, 'It's your own fault.'

'Oh, Aunt, I couldn't stand him when he was keen. I can do with him a lot better as he is.'

The two women sat and talked far into the night. They understood each other. The aunt, too, had married as Fanny was marrying: a man who was no companion to her, a violent man, brother of Fanny's father. He was dead, Fanny's father was dead.

Poor Aunt Lizzie, she cried woefully over her bright niece, when she had gone to bed.

Fanny paid the promised visit to his people the next afternoon. Mrs. Goodall was a large woman with smooth-parted hair, a common, obstinate woman, who had spoiled her four lads and her one vixen of a married daughter. She was one of those old-fashioned powerful natures that couldn't do with looks or education or any form of showing-off. She fairly hated the sound of correct English. She *thee'd* and *tha'd* her prospective daughter-in-law, and said:

'I'm none as ormin' as I look, seest ta.'

Fanny did not think her prospective mother-in-law looked at all orming, so the speech was unnecessary.

'I towd him mysen,' said Mrs. Goodall, ' 'Er's held back all this long, let 'er stop as 'er is. 'E'd none ha' had thee for *my* tellin'–tha hears. No, 'e's a fool, an' I know it. I says to him: "Tha looks a man, doesn't ter, at thy age, goin' an' openin' to her when ter hears her scart' at th' gate, after she's done gallivantin' round wherever she's a mind. That looks rare an' soft." But it's no use o' any talking: he answered that letter o' thine and made his own bad bargain.

But in spite of the old woman's anger, she was also flattered at Fanny's coming back to Harry. For Mrs. Goodall was impressed by Fanny–a woman of her own match. And more than this, everybody knew that Fanny's Aunt Kate had left her two hundred pounds, this apart from the girl's savings.

So there was high tea in Princess Street when Harry came home back from work, and a rather acrid odour of cordiality, the vixen Jinny darting in to say vulgar things. Of course Jinny lived in a house whose garden end joined the paternal garden. They were a clan who stuck together, these Goodalls.

It was arranged that Fanny should come to tea again on the Sunday, and the wedding was discussed. It should take place in a fortnight's time at Morley Chapel. Morley was a hamlet on the edge of the real country, and in its little Congregational Chapel Fanny and Harry had first met.

What a creature of habit he was! He was still in the choir of Morley Chapel-not very regular. He belonged just because he had a tenor voice, and enjoyed singing. Indeed, his solos were only spoilt to local fame because when he sang he handled his aitches so hopelessly.

*'And I saw 'eaven hopened
And be'old, a wite 'orse—'*

This was one of Harry's classics, only surpassed by the fine outburst of his heaving:

'Hangels—hever bright an' fair—'

It was a pity, but it was unalterable. He had a good voice, and he sang with a certain lacerating fire, but his pronunciation made it all funny. And *nothing* could alter him.

So he was never heard save at cheap concerts and in the little, poorer chapels. The other scoffed.

Now the month was September, and Sunday was Harvest Festival at Morley Chapel, and Harry was singing solos. So that Fanny was to go to service, and come home to a grand spread of Sunday tea with him. Poor Fanny! One of the most wonderful afternoons had been a Sunday afternoon service, with her cousin Luther at her side, Harvest Festival in Morley Chapel. Harry had sung solos then—ten years ago. She remembered his pale-blue tie, and the purple asters and the great vegetable marrows in which he was famed, and her cousin Luther at her side, young, clever, come down from London, where he was getting on well, learning his Latin and his French and German so brilliantly.

However, once again it was Harvest Festival at Morley Chapel, and once again, as ten years before, a soft, exquisite September day, with the last roses pink in the cottage gardens, the last dahlias crimson, the last sunflowers yellow. And again the little old chapel was a bower, with its famous sheaves of corn and corn-plaited pillars, its great bunches of grapes dangling like tassels from the pulpit corners, its marrows and potatoes and pears and apples and damsons, its purple asters and yellow Japanese sunflowers. Just as before, the red dahlias round the pillars were dropping, weak-headed among the oats. The place was crowded and hot, the plates of tomatoes seemed balanced perilous on the gallery front, the Rev. Enderby was weirder than ever to look at, so long and emaciated and hairless.

The Rev. Enderby, probably forewarned, came and shook hands with her and welcomed her, in his broad northern, melancholy sing-song before he mounted the pulpit. Fanny was handsome in a gauzy dress and a beautiful lace hat. Being a little late, she sat in a chair in the side-aisle wedged in, right in front of the chapel. Harry was in the gallery above, and she could only see him from the eyes upwards. She noticed again how his eyebrows met, blond and not very marked, over his nose. He was attractive, too: physically lovable, very. If only—if only her *pride* had not suffered! She felt he dragged her down.

> '*Come, ye thankful people, come,*
> *Raise the song of harvest-home.*
> *All is safely gathered in*
> *Ere the winter storms begin—*'

Even the hymn was a falsehood, as the season had been wet, and half the crops were still out, and in a poor way.

Poor Fanny! She sang little, and looked beautiful through that inappropriate hymn. Above her stood Harry— mercifully in a dark suit and a dark tie, looking almost handsome. And his lacerating, pure tenor sounded well, when the words were drowned in the general commotion. Brilliant she looked, and brilliant she felt, for she was hot and angrily miserable and inflamed with a sort of fatal despair. Because there was about him a physical attraction which she really hated, but which she could not escape from. He was the first man who had ever kissed her. And his kisses, even while she rebelled from them, had lived in her blood and sent roots down into her soul. After all this time she had come back to them. And her soul groaned, for she felt dragged down, dragged down to earth, as a bird which some dog has got down in the dust. She knew her life would be unhappy. She knew that what she was doing was fatal. Yet it was her doom. She had to come back to him.

He had to sing two solos this afternoon: one before the 'address' from the pulpit and one after. Fanny looked in him, and wondered he was not too shy to stand up there in front of all the people. But no, he was not shy. He had even a kind of assurance on his face as he looked down from the choir gallery at her: the assurance of a common man deliberately entrenched in his commonness. Oh, such a rage went through her veins as she saw the air of triumph, laconic, indifferent triumph which sat so obstinately and recklessly on his eyelids as he looked down at her. Ah, she despised him! But there he stood up in that choir gallery like Balaam's ass in front of her, and she could not get beyond him. A certain winsomeness also about him. A certain physical winsomeness, and as if his flesh were new and lovely to touch. The thorn of desire rankled bitterly in her heart.

He, it goes without saying, sang like a canary, this particular afternoon, with a certain defiant passion which pleasantly crisped the blood of the congregation. Fanny felt the crisp flames go through her veins as she listened. Even the curious loud-mouthed vernacular had a certain fascination. But, oh, also, it was so repugnant. He would triumph over her, obstinately he would drag her right back into the common people: a doom, a vulgar doom.

The second performance was an anthem, in which Harry sang the solo parts. It was clumsy, but beautiful, with lovely words.

'They that sow in tears shall reap in joy,
He that goeth forth and weepeth, bearing precious seed
Shall doubtless come again rejoicing, bring his
sheaves with him—'

'*Shall doubtless come, Shall doubtless come—*' softly intoned the altos–'*Bringing his she-e-eaves with him,*' the trebles flourished brightly, and then again began the half-wistful solo:

'They that sow in tears shall reap in joy—'

Yes, it was effective and moving.

But at the moment when Harry's voice sank carelessly down to his close, and the choir, standing behind him, were opening their mouths for the final triumphant outburst, a shouting female voice rose up from the body of the congregation. The organ gave one startled trump, and went silent; the choir stood transfixed.

'You look well standing there, singing in God's holy house,' came the loud, angry female shout. Everybody turned electrified. A stoutish, red-faced woman in a black bonnet was standing up denouncing the soloist. Almost fainting with shock, the congregation realised it. 'You look well, don't you, standing there singing solos in God's holy house, you, Goodall. But I said I'd shame on you. You look well, bringing your young woman here with you, don't you? I'll let her know who she's dealing with. A scamp as won't take the consequences of what he's done.' The hard-faced, frenzied woman turned in the direction of Fanny. '*That's* what Harry Goodall is, if you want to know.'

And she sat down again in her seat. Fanny, startled like all the rest, had turned to look. She had gone white, and then a burning red, under the attack. She knew the woman: a Mrs. Nixon, a devil of a woman, who beat her pathetic, drunken, red-nosed second husband, Bob, and her two lanky daughters, grown-up as they were. A notorious character. Fanny turned round again, and sat motionless as eternity in her seat.

There was a minute of perfect silence and suspense. The audience was open-mouthed and dumb; the choir stood like Lot's wife; and Harry, with his music-sheet, stood there uplifted, looking down with a dumb sort of indifference on Mrs. Nixon, his face naive and faintly mocking. Mrs. Nixon sat defiant in her seat, braving them all.

Then a rustle, like a wood when the wind suddenly catches the leaves. And then the tall, weird minister got to his feet, and in his strong, bell-like, beautiful voice—the only beautiful thing about him—he said with infinite mournful pathos:

'Let us unite in singing the last hymn on the hymn-sheet; the last hymn on the hymn-sheet, number eleven.

> *"Fair waved the golden corn*
> *In Canaan's pleasant land."*

The organ tuned up promptly. During the hymn the offertory was taken. And after the hymn, the prayer.

Mr. Enderby came from Northumberland. Like Harry, he had never been able to conquer his accent, which was very broad. He was a little simple, one of God's fools, perhaps, an odd bachelor soul, emotional, ugly, but very gentle.

'And if, O our dear Lord, beloved Jesus, there should fall a shadow of sin upon our harvest, we leave it to Thee to judge, for Thou art judge. We lift our spirits and our sorrow, Jesus, to Thee, and our mouths are dumb. O Lord, keep us from forward speech, restrain us from foolish words and thoughts, we pray Thee, Lord Jesus, who knowest all and judgest all.'

Thus the minister said in his sad, resonant voice, washed his hands before the Lord. Fanny bent forward open-eyed during the prayer. She could see the roundish head of Harry, also bent forward. His face was inscrutable and expressionless. The shock left her bewildered. Anger perhaps was her dominating emotion.

The audience began to rustle to its feet, to ooze slowly and excitedly out of the chapel, looking with wildly interested eyes at Fanny, at Mrs. Nixon, and at Harry. Mrs.

Nixon, shortish, stood defiant in her pew, facing the aisle, as if announcing that, without rolling her sleeves up, she was ready for anybody. Fanny sat quite still. Luckily the people did not have to pass her. And Harry, with red ears, was making his way sheepishly out of the gallery. The loud noise of the organ covered all the downstairs commotion of exit.

The minister sat silent and inscrutable in his pulpit, rather like a death's-head, while the congregation filed out. When the last lingerers had unwillingly departed, craning their necks to stare at the still seated Fanny, he rose, stalked in his hooked fashion down the little country chapel and fastened the door. Then he returned and sat down by the silent young woman.

'This is most unfortunate, most unfortunate!' he moaned. 'I am so sorry, I am so sorry, indeed, indeed, ah, indeed!' he sighed himself to a close.

'It's a sudden surprise, that's one thing,' said Fanny brightly.

'Yes—yes—indeed. Yes, a surprise, yes. I don't know the woman, I don't know her.'

'I know her,' said Fanny. 'She's a bad one.'

'Well! Well!' said the minister. 'I don't know her. I don't understand. I don't understand at all. But it is to be regretted, it is very much to be regretted. I am very sorry.'

Fanny was watching the vestry door. The gallery stairs communicated with the vestry, not with the body of the chapel. She knew the choir members had been peeping for information.

At last Harry came—rather sheepishly—with his hat in his hand.

'Well!' said Fanny, rising to her feet.

'We've had a bit of an extra,' said Harry.

'I should think so,' said Fanny.

'A most unfortunate circumstance— a most *unfortunate* circumstance. Do you understand it, Harry? I don't understand it at all.'

'Ay, I understand it. The daughter's goin' to have a childt, an' 'er lays it to me.'

'And has she no occasion to?' asked Fanny, rather censorious.

'It's no more mine than it is some other chap's,' said Harry, looking aside.

There was a moment of pause.

'Which girl is it?' asked Fanny.

'Annie—the young one—'

There followed another silence.

'I don't think I know them, do I?' asked the minister.

'I shouldn't think so. Their name's Nixon—mother married old Bob for her second husband. She's a tanger, she's driven the gel to what she is. They live in Manners Road.'

'Why, what's amiss with the girl?' asked Fanny sharply. 'She was all right when I knew her.'

'Ay—she's all right. But she's always in an' out o' th' pubs, wi' th' fellows,' said Harry.

'A nice thing!' said Fanny.

Harry glanced towards the door. He wanted to get out.

'Most distressing, indeed!' the minister slowly shook his head.

'What about to-night, Mr. Enderby?' asked Harry, in rather a small voice. 'Shall you want me?'

Mr. Enderby looked up painedly, and put his hand to his brow. He studied Harry for some time, vacantly. There was the faintest sort of a resemblance between the two men.

'Yes,' he said. 'Yes, I think. I think we must take no notice and cause as little remark as possible.'

Fanny hesitated. Then she said to Harry:

'But *will* you come?'

He looked at her.

'Ay, I s'll come,' he said.

Then he turned to Mr. Enderby.

'Well, good afternoon, Mr. Enderby,' he said.

'Good afternoon, Harry, good afternoon,' replied the mournful minister. Fanny followed Harry to the door, and for some time they walked in silence through the late afternoon.

'And it's yours as much as anybody else's?' she said.

'Ay,' he answered shortly.

And they went without another word, for the long mile or so, till they came to the corner of the street where Harry lived. Fanny hesitated. Should she go on to her aunt's? Should she? It would mean leaving all this, for ever. Harry stood silent.

Some obstinacy made her turn with him along the road to his own home. When they entered the house-place, the whole family was there mother and father and Jinny, with Jinny's husband and children and Harry's two brothers.

'You've been having your ears warmed, they tell me,' said Mrs. Goodall grimly.

'Who telled thee?' asked Harry shortly.

'Maggie and Luke's both been in.'

'You look well, don't you!' said interfering Jinny.

Harry went and hung his hat up, without replying.

'Come upstairs and take your hat off,' said Mrs. Goodall to Fanny almost kindly. It would have annoyed her very much if Fanny had dropped her son at this moment.

'What's' 'er say, then? asked the father secretly of Harry, jerking his head in the direction of the stairs whence Fanny had disappeared.

'Nowt yet,' said Harry.

'Serve you right if she chucks you now,' said Jinny. 'I'll bet it's right about Annie Nixon an' you.'

'Tha bets so much, ' said Harry.

'Yi—but you con't deny it,' said Jinny.

'I can if I've a mind.'

His father looked at him inquiringly.

'It's no more mine than it is Bill Bower's, or Ted Slaney's, or six or seven on 'em,' said Harry to his father.

And the father nodded silently.

'That'll not get you out of it, in court,' said Jinny.

Upstairs Fanny evaded all the thrusts made by his mother, and did not declare her hand. She tidied her hair, washed her hands, and put the tiniest bit of powder on her face, for coolness, there in front of Mrs. Goodall's indignant gaze. It was like a declaration of independence. But the old woman said nothing.

They came down to Sunday tea, with sardines and tinned salmon and tinned peaches, besides tarts and cakes. The chatter was general. It concerned the Nixon family and the scandal.

'Oh, she's a foul-mouthed woman,' said Jinny of Mrs. Nixon. 'She may well talk about God's holy house, *she* had. It's first time she's set foot in it, ever since she dropped off from being converted. She's a devil and she always was one. Can't you remember how she treated Bob's children, mother, when we lived down in the Buildings? I can remember when I was a little girl she used to bathe them in the yard, in the cold, so that they shouldn't splash the house. She'd half kill them if they made a mark on the floor, and the language she'd use! And one Saturday I can remember Garry, that was Bob's own girl, she ran off when her stepmother was going to bathe her—ran off without a rag of clothes on—can you remember, mother? And she hid in Smedley's closes—it was the time of mowing-grass—and nobody could find her. She hid out there all night, didn't she, mother? Nobody could find her. My word, there was a talk. They found her on Sunday morning—'

'Fred Coutts threatened to break every bone in the woman's body, if she touched the children again,' put in the father.

'Anyhow, they frightened her,' said Jinny. 'But she was nearly as bad with her own two. And anybody can see that she'd driven old Bob till he's gone soft.'

'Ah, soft as mush,' said Jack Goodall. ' 'E'd never addle a week's wages, nor yet a day's, if th' chaps didn't make it up to him.'

'My word, if he didn't bring her a week's wage, she'd pull his head off,' said Jinny.

'But a clean woman, and respectable, except for her foul mouth,' said Mr. Goodall. 'Keeps to herself like a bulldog. Never lets anybody come near the house, and neighbours with nobody.'

'Wanted it thrashed out of her,' said Mr. Goodall, a silent, evasive sort of man.

'Where Bob gets the money for his drink from is a mystery,' said Jinny.

'Chaps treats him,' said Harry.

'Well, he's got the pair of frightenedest rabbit-eyes you'd wish to see,' said Jinny.

'Ay, with a drunken man's murder in them, *I* think,' said Mrs. Goodall.

So the talk went on after tea, till it was practically time to start off to the chapel again.

'You'll have to be getting ready, Fanny,' said Mrs. Goodall.

'I'm not going to-night,' said Fanny abruptly. And there was a sudden halt in the family. 'I'll stop with *you* to-night, mother,' she added.

'Best you had, my gel,' said Mrs. Goodall, flattered and assured.

THE WOMAN WHO RODE AWAY

I

She had thought that this marriage, of all marriages, would be an adventure. Not that the man himself was exactly magical to her. A little, wiry, twisted fellow, twenty years older than herself, with brown eyes and greying hair, who had come to America a scrap of a wastrel, from Holland, years ago, as a tiny boy, and from the gold-mines of the west had been kicked south into Mexico, and now as more or less rich, owning silver-mines in the wilds of the Sierra Madre: it was obvious that the adventure lay in his circumstances, rather than his person. But he was still a little dynamo of energy, in spite of accidents survived, and what he had accomplished he had accomplished alone. One of those human oddments there is no accounting for.

When she actually *saw* what he had accomplished, her heart quailed. Great green-covered, unbroken mountain-hills, and in the midst of the lifeless isolation, the sharp pinkish mounds of the dried mud from the silver-works. Under the nakedness of the works, the walled-in, one-storey adobe house, with its garden inside, and its deep inner veranda with tropical climbers on the sides. And when you looked up from this shut-in flowered patio, you saw the huge pink cone of the silver refuse, and the machinery of the extracting plant against heaven above. No more.

To be sure, the great wooden doors were often open. And then she could stand outside, in the vast open world. And see great, void, tree-clad hills piling behind one another, from nowhere into nowhere. They were green in autumn-time. For the rest, pinkish, stark, dry, and abstract.

And in his battered Ford car her husband would take her into the dead, thrice-dead little Spanish town forgotten among the mountains. The great, sun-dried dead church, the dead portales, the hopeless covered market-place, where, the first time she went, she saw a dead dog lying between the meat-stalls and the vegetable array, stretched out as if for ever, nobody troubling to throw it away. Deadness within dead-ness.

Everybody feebly talking silver, and showing bits of ore. But silver was at a standstill. The great war came and went. Silver was a dead market. Her husband's mines were closed down. But she and he lived on in the abode house under the works, among the flowers that were never very flowery to her.

She had two children, a boy and a girl. And her eldest, the boy, was nearly ten years old before she aroused from her stupor of subjected amazement. She was now thirty-three, a large, blue-eyed, dazed woman, beginning to grow stout. Her little, wiry, tough, twisted, brown-eyed husband was fifty-three, a man as tough as wire, tenacious as wire, still full of energy, but dimmed by the lapse of silver from the market, and by some curious inaccessibility on his wife's part.

He was a man of principles, and a good husband. In a way, he doted on her. He never quite got over his dazzled admiration of her. But essentially, he was still a bachelor. He had been thrown out on the world, a little bachelor, at the age of ten. When he married he was over forty, and had enough money to marry on. But his capital was all a bachelor's. He was boss of his own works, and marriage was the last and most intimate bit of his own works.

He admired his wife to extinction, he admired her body, all her points. And she was to him always the rather dazzling Californian girl from Berkeley, whom he had first known. Like any sheikh, he kept her guarded among those mountains of Chihuahua. He was jealous of her as he was of his silver-mine: and that is saying a lot.

At thirty-three she really was still the girl from Berkeley, in all but physique. Her conscious development had stopped mysteriously with her marriage, completely arrested. Her husband had never become real to her, neither mentally nor physically. In spite of his late sort of passion for her, he never meant anything to her, physically. Only morally he swayed her, downed her, kept her in an invincible slavery.

So the years went by, in the adobe house strung round the sunny patio, with the silver-works overhead. Her husband was never still. When the silver went dead, he ran a ranch lower down, some twenty miles away, and raised pure-bred hogs, splendid creatures. At the same time, he hated pigs. He was a squeamish waif of an idealist, and really hated the physical side of life. He loved work, work, work, and making things. His marriage, his children, were something he was making, part of his business, but with a sentimental income this time.

Gradually her nerves began to go wrong. She must get out. So he took her to El Paso for three months. And at least it was the United States.

But he kept his spell over her. The three months ended: back she was, just the same, in her adobe house among those eternal green or pinky-brown hills, void as only the undiscovered is void. She taught her children, she supervised the Mexican boys who were her servants. And sometimes her husband brought visitors, Spaniards or Mexicans or occasionally white men.

He really loved to have white men staying on the place. Yet he had not a moment's peace when they were there. It was as if his wife were some peculiar secret vein of ore in his mines, which no one must be aware of except himself. And she was fascinated by the young gentlemen, mining engineers, who were his guests at times. He, too, was fascinated by a real gentleman. But he was an old-timer miner with a wife, and if a gentleman looked at his wife, he felt as if his mind were being looted, the secrets of it pried out.

It was one of these young gentlemen who put the idea into her mind. They were all standing outside the great wooden doors of the patio, looking at the outer world. The eternal, motionless hills were all green, it was September, after the rains. There was no sign of anything, save the deserted mine, the deserted works, and a bunch of half-deserted mines' dwellings.

'I wonder,' said the young man, 'what there is behind those great blank hills.'

'More hills,' said Lederman. 'If you go that way, Sonora and the coast. This way is the desert—you came from there—and the other way, hills and mountains.'

'Yes, but what *lives* in the hills and the mountains? *Surely* there is something wonderful? It looks *so* like nowhere on earth: like being on the moon.'

'There's plenty of game, if you want to shoot. And Indians, if you call *them* wonderful.'

'Wild ones?'

'Wild enough.'

'But friendly?'

'It depends. Some of them are quite wild, and they don't let anybody near. They kill a missionary at sight. And where a missionary can't get, nobody can.'

'But what does the government say?'

'They're so far from everywhere , the government leaves 'em alone.'

And they're wily; if they think there'll be trouble, they send a delegation to Chihuahua and make a formal submission. The government is glad to leave it at that.

'And do they live quite wild, with their own savage customs and religion?'

'Oh, yes. They use nothing but bows and arrows. I've seen them in town, in the Plaza, with funny sort of hats with flowers round them, and a bow in one hand, quite naked except for a sort of shirt, even in cold weather–striding round with their savage's bare legs.'

'But don't you suppose it's wonderful, up there in their secret villages?'

'No. What would there be wonderful about it? Savages are savages, and all savages behave more or less alike: rather low-down and dirty, unsanitary, with a few cunning tricks, and struggling to get enough to eat.'

'But surely they have old, old religions and mysteries–it *must* be wonderful, surely it must.'

'I don't know about mysteries–howling and heathen practices more or less indecent. No, I see nothing wonderful in that kind of stuff. And I wonder that you should, when you have lived in London or Paris or New York–'

'Ah, *everybody* lives in London or Paris or New York'–said the young man, as if this were an argument.

And this particular vague enthusiasm for unknown

Indians found a full echo in the woman's heart. She was overcome by a foolish romanticism more unreal than a girl's. She felt it was her destiny to wander into the secret haunts of these timeless, mysterious, marvellous Indians of the mountains.

She kept her secret. The young man was departing, her husband was going with him down to Torreon, on business: would be away for some days. But before the departure, she made her husband talk about the Indians, about the wandering tribes, resembling the Navajo, who were still wandering free; and the Yaquis of Sonora; and the different groups in the different valleys of Chihuahua State.

There was supposed to be one tribe, the Chilchuis, living in a high valley to the south, who were the sacred tribe of all the Indians. The descendants of Montezuma and the old Aztec or Totonac kings still lived among them, and the old priests still kept up the ancient religion, and offered human sacrifices—so it was said. Some scientists had been to the Chilchui country, and had come back gaunt and exhausted with hunger and bitter privation, bringing various curious, barbaric objects of worship, but having seen nothing extaordinary in the hungry, stark village of savages.

Though Lederman talked in this off-hand way, it was obvious he felt some of the vulgar excitement at the idea of ancient and mysterious savages.

'How far away are they?' she asked.

'Oh—three days on horseback—past Cuchitee and a little lake there is up there.'

Her husband and the young man departed. The woman made her crazy plans. Of late, to break the monotony of her life, she had harassed her husband into letting her go riding with him, occasionally, on horseback. She was never allowed to go out alone. The country truly was not safe, lawless and crude.

But she had her own horse, and she dreamed of being free as she had been as a girl, among the hills of California.

Her daughter, nine years old, was now in a tiny convent in the little half-deserted Spanish mining-town five miles away.

'Manuel,' said the woman to her house-servant, 'I'am going to ride to the convent to see Margarita, and take her a few things. Perhaps I shall stay the night in the convent. You look after Freddy and see everything is all right till I come back.'

'Shall I ride with you on the master's horse, or shall Juan?' asked the servant.

'Neither of you. I shall go alone.'

The young man looked her in the eyes, in protest. Absolutely impossible that the woman should ride alone!

'I shall go alone,' repeated the large, placid-seeming, fair-complexioned woman, with peculiar overbearing emphasis. And the man silently, unhappily yielded.

'Why are you going alone, mother?' asked her son, as she made up parcels of food.

'Am I *never* to be let alone? Not one moment of my life?' she cried, with sudden explosion of energy. And the child, like the servant, shrank into silence.

She set off without a qualm, riding astride on her strong roan horse, and wearing a riding-suit of coarse linen, a riding-skirt over her linen breeches, a scarlet neck-tie over her white blouse, and a black felt hat on her head. She had food in her saddle-bags, an army canteen with water, and a large, native blanket tied on behind the saddle. Peering into the distance, she set off from her home.

Manuel and the little boy stood in the gateway to watch her go. She did not even turn to wave them farewell.

But when she had ridden about a mile, she left the wild road and took a small trail to the right, that led into another valley, over steep places and past great trees, and through another deserted mining settlement. It was September, the water was running freely in the little stream that had fed the now-abandoned mine. She got down to drink, and let the horse drink too.

She saw natives coming through the trees, away up the slope. They had seen her, and were watching her closely. She watched in turn. The three people, two women and a youth, were making a wide detour, so as not to come too close to her. She did not care. Mounting, she trotted ahead up the silent valley, beyond the silver-works, beyond any trace of mining. There was still a rough trail that led over rocks and loose stones into the valley beyond. This trail she had already ridden, with her husband. Beyond that she knew she must go south.

Curiously she was not afraid, although it was a frightening country, the silent, fatal-seeming mountain slopes, the occasional distant, suspicious, elusive natives among the trees, the great carrion birds occasionally hovering, like great flies, in the distance, over some carrion of some ranch-house or some group of huts.

As she climbed, the trees shrank and the trail ran through a thorny scrub, that was trailed over with blue convolvulus and an occasional pink creeper. Then these flowers lapsed. She was nearing the pine trees.

She was over the crest, and before her another silent, void, greenclad valley. It was past midday. Her horse turned to a little runlet of water, so she got down to eat her midday meal. She sat in silence looking at the motionless, unliving valley, and at the sharp-peaked hills, rising higher to rock and pine trees, southwards. She rested two hours in the heat of the day, while the horse cropped around her.

Curious that she was neither afraid nor lonely. Indeed, the loneliness was like a drink of cold water to one who is very thirsty. And a strange elation sustained her from within.

She travelled on, and camped at night in a valley beside a stream, deep among the bushes. She had seen cattle and had crossed several trails. There must be a ranch not far off. She heard the strange wailing shriek of a mountain-lion, and the answer of dogs. But she sat by her small camp-fire in a secret hollow place and was not really afraid. She was buoyed up always by the curious, bubbling elation within her.

It was very cold before dawn. She lay wrapped in her blanket looking at the stars, listening to her horse shivering, and feeling like a woman who has died and passed beyond. She was not sure that she had not heard, during the night, a great crash at the centre of herself, which was the crash of her own death. Or else it was a crash at the centre of the earth, and meant something big and mysterious.

With the first peep of light she got up, numb with cold, and made a fire. She ate hastily, gave her horse some pieces of oil-seed cake, and set off again. She avoided any meeting—and since she met nobody, it was evident that she in turn was avoided. She came at last in sight of the village of Cuchitee, with its black houses with their reddish roofs, a sombre, dreary little cluster below another silent, long-abandoned mine. And beyond, a long, great mountain-side, rising up green and light to the darker, shaggier green of pine trees. And beyond the pine trees stretches of naked rock against the sky, rock slashed already and brindled with white stripes of snow. High up, the new snow had already begun to fall.

And now, as she neared, more or less, her destination, she began to go vague and disheartened. She had passed the little lake among yellowing aspen trees whose white trunks were round and suave like the white round arms of some woman. What a lovely place! In California she would have raved about it. But here she looked and saw that it was lovely, but she didn't care. She was weary and spent with her two nights in the open, afraid of the coming night. She didn't know where she was going, or what she was going for. Her horse plodded dejectedly on, towards that immense and forbidding mountain-slope, following a stony little trail. And if she had had any will of her own left, she would have turned back, to the village, to be protected and sent home to her husband.

But she had no will of her own. Her horse splashed through a brook, and turned up a valley, under immense yellowing cottonwood trees. She must have been near nine thousand feet above sea-level, and her head was light with the altitude and with weariness. Beyond the cottonwood trees she could see, on each side, the steep sides of mountain-slopes hemming her in, sharp-plumaged with overlapping aspen, and, higher up, with sprouting, pointed spruce and pine tree. Her horse went on automatically. In this tight valley, on this slight trail, there was nowhere to go but ahead, climbing.

Suddenly her horse jumped, and three men in dark blankets were on the trail before her.

'*Adios!*' came the greeting, in the full, restrained Indian voice.

'*Adios!*' she replied, in her assured, American woman's voice.

'Where are you going?' came the quiet question, in Spanish.

The men in the dark sarapes had come closer, and were looking up at her.

'On ahead,' she replied coolly, in her hard, Saxon Spanish.

These were just natives to her: dark-faced, strongly-built men in dark sarapes and straw hats. They would have been the same as the men who worked for her husband, except, strangely, for the long black hair that fell over their shoulders. She noted this long black hair with a certain distaste. These must be the wild Indians she had come to see.

'Where do you come from?' the same man asked. It was always the one man who spoke. He was young, with quick, large, bright black eyes that glanced sideways at her. He had a soft black moustache on his dark face, and a sparse tuft of beard, loose hairs on his chin. His long black hair, full of life, hung unrestrained on his shoulders. Dark as he was, he did not look as if he had washed lately.

His two companions were the same, but older men, powerful and silent. One had a thin black line of moustache, but was beardless. The other had the smooth cheeks and the sparse dark hairs marking the lines of his chin with the beard characteristic of the Indians.

'I come from far away,' she replied, with half-jocular evasion.

This was received in silence.

'But where do you live?' asked the young man, with that same quiet insistence.

'In the north,' she replied airily.

Again there was a moment's silence. The young man conversed quietly, in Indian, with his two companions.

'Where do you want to go, up this way?' he asked suddenly, with challenge and authority, pointing briefly up the trail.

'To the Chilchui Indians,' answered the woman laconically.

The young man looked at her. His eyes were quick and black, and inhuman. He saw, in the full evening light, the faint sub-smile of assurance on her rather large, calm, fresh-complexioned face; the weary, bluish lines under her large blue eyes; and in her eyes, as she looked down at him, a half-childish, half-arrogant confidence in her own female power. But in her eyes also, a curious look of trance.

'*Usted es Señora?* You are a lady?' the Indian asked her.

'Yes, I am a lady,' she replied complacently.

'With a family?'

'With a husband and two children, boy and girl,' she said.

The Indian turned to his companion and translated, in the low, gurgling speech, like hidden water running. They were evidently at a loss.

'Where is your husband?' asked the young man.

'Who knows?' she replied airily. 'He has gone away on business for a week.'

The black eyes watched her shrewdly. She, for all her weariness, smiled faintly in the pride of her own adventure and the assurance of her own womanhood, and the spell of the madness that was on her.

'And who do *you* want to do?' the Indian asked her.

'I want to visit the Chilchui Indians—to see their houses

and to know their gods,' she replied.

The young man turned and translated quickly, and there was a silence almost of consternation. The grave elder men were glancing at her sideways, with strange looks, from under their decorated hats. And they said something to the young man, in deep chest voices.

The latter still hesitated. Then he turned to the woman.

'Good!' he said. 'Let us go. But we cannot arrive until to-morrow. We shall have to make a camp to-night.'

'Good!' she said. 'I can make a camp.'

Without more ado, they set off at a good speed up the stony trail. The young Indian ran alongside her horse's head, the other two ran behind. One of them had taken a thick stick, and occasionally he struck her horse a resounding blow on the haunch, to urge him forward. This made the horse jump, and threw her back in the saddle, which, tired as she was, made her angry.

'Don't do that!' she cried, looking round angrily at the fellow. She met his black, large, bright eyes, and for the first time her spirit really quailed. The man's eyes were not human to her, and they did not see her as a beautiful white woman. He looked at her with a black, bright inhuman look, and saw no woman in her at all. As if she were some strange, unaccountable *thing*, incomprehensible to him, but inimical. She sat in her saddle in wonder, feeling once more as if she had died. And again he struck her horse, and jerked her badly in the saddle.

All the passionate anger of the spoilt white woman rose in her. She pulled her horse to a standstill, and turned with blazing eyes to the man at her bridle.

'Tell that fellow not to touch my horse again,' she cried.

She met the eyes of the young man, and in their bright black inscrutability she saw a fine spark, as in a snake's eye, of derision. He spoke to his companion in the rear, in the low tones of the Indian. The man with the stick listened without looking. Then, giving a strange low cry to the horse, he struck it again on the rear, so that it leaped forward spasmodically up the stony trail, scattering the stones, pitching the weary woman in her seat.

The anger flew like a madness into her eyes, she went white at the gills. Fiercely she reined in her horse. But before she could turn, the young Indian had caught the reins under the horse's throat, jerked them forward, and was trotting ahead rapidly, leading the horse.

The woman was powerless. And along with her supreme anger there came a slight thrill of exultation. She knew she was dead.

The sun was setting, a great yellow light flooded the last of the aspens, flared on the trunks of the pine trees, the pine needles bristled and stood out with dark lustre, the rocks glowed with unearthly glamour. And through the effulgence the Indian at her horse's head trotted unweariedly on, his dark blanket swinging, his bare legs glowing with a strange transfigured ruddiness in the powerful light, and his straw hat with its half-absurd decorations of flowers and feathers shining showily above his river of long black hair. At times he would utter a low call to the horse, and then the other Indian, behind, would fetch the beast a whack with the stick.

The wonder-light faded off the mountains, the world began to grow dark, a cold air breathed down. In the sky, half a moon was struggling against the glow in the west. Huge shadows came down from steep rocky slopes. Water was rushing. The woman was conscious only of her fatigue, her unspeakable fatigue, and the old wind from the heights. She was not aware how moonlight replaced daylight. It happened while she travelled unconscious with weariness.

For some hours they travelled by moonlight. Then suddenly they came to a standstill. The men conversed in low tones for a moment.

'We camp here,' said the young man.

She waited for him to help her down. He merely stood holding the horse's bridle. She almost fell from the saddle, so fatigued.

They had chosen a place at the foot of rocks that still gave off a little warmth of the sun. One man cut pine boughs, another erected little screens of pine boughs against the rock for shelter, and put boughs of balsam pine for beds. The third made a small fire, to heat tortillas. They worked in silence.

The woman drank water. She did not want to eat—only to lie down.

'Where do I sleep?' she asked.

The young man pointed to one of the shelters. She crept in and lay inert. She did not care what hapened to her, she was so weary, and so beyond everything. Through the twigs of spruce she could see the three men squatting round the fire on their hams, chewing the tortillas they picked from the ashes with their dark fingers, and drinking water from a gourd. They talked in low, muttering tones, with long intervals of silence. Her saddle and saddle-bags lay not far from the fire, unopened, untouched. The men were not interested in her nor her belongings. There they squatted with their hats on their heads, eating, eating mechanically, like animals, the dark sarape with its fringe falling to the ground before and behind, the powerful dark legs naked and squatting like an animal's showing the dirty white shirt and the sort of loin-cloth which was the only other garment, underneath. And they showed no more sign of interest in her than if she had been a piece of venison they were bringing home from the hunt, and had hung inside a shelter.

After a while they carefully extinguished the fire, and went inside their own shelter. Watching through the screen boughs, she had a moment's thrill of fear and anxiety, seeing the dark forms cross and pass silently in the moonlight. Would they attack her now?

But no! They were as if oblivious to her. Her horse was hobbled; she could hear it hopping wearily. All was silent, mountain-silent, cold, deathly. She slept and woke and slept in a semi-conscious numbness of cold and fatigue. A long, long night, icy and eternal, and she aware that she had died.

II

Yet when there was a stirring, and a clink of flint and steel, and the form of a man crouching like a dog over a bone, at a red splutter of fire, and she knew it was morning coming, it seemed to her the night had passed too soon.

When the fire was going, she came out of her shelter with one real desire left: for coffee. The men were warming more tortillas.

'Can we make coffee?' she asked.

The young man looked at her, and she imagined the same faint spark of derision in his eyes. He shook his head.

'We don't take it,' he said. 'There is no time.'

And the elder men, squatting on their haunches, look up at her in the terrible paling dawn, and there was not even derision in their eyes. Only that intense, yet remote, inhuman glitter which was terrible to her. They were inaccessible. They could not see her as a woman at all. As if she *were* not a woman. As if, perhaps, her whiteness took away all her womanhood, and left her as some giant, female white ant. That was all they could see in her.

Before the sun was up, she was in the saddle again, and they were climbing steeply, in the icy air. The sun came, and soon she was very hot, exposed to the glare in the bare places. It seemed to her they were climbing to the roof of the world. Beyond against heaven were slashes of snow.

During the course of the morning, they came to a place where the horse could not go farther. They rested for a time with a great slant of living rock in front of them, like the glossy breast of some earth-beast. Across this rock, along a wavering crack, they had to go. It seemed to her that for hours she went in torment, on her hands and knees, from crack to crevice, along the slanting face of this pure rock-mountain. An Indian in front and an Indian behind walked slowly erect, shod with sandals of braided leather. But she in her riding-boots dared not stand erect.

Yet what she wondered, all the time, was why she persisted in clinging and crawling along these mile-long sheets of rock. Why she did not hurl herself down, and have done! The world was below her.

When they emerged at last on a stony slope, she looked back, and saw the third Indian coming carrying her saddle and saddle-bags on his back, the whole hung from a band across his forehead. And he had his hat in his hand, as he stepped slowly, with the slow, soft, heavy tread of the

Indian, unwavering in the chinks of rock, as if along a scratch in the mountain's iron shield.

The stony slope led downwards. The Indians seemed to grow excited. One ran ahead at a slow trot, disappearing round the curve of stones. And the track curved round and down, till at last in the full blaze of the mid-morning sun, they could see a valley below them, between walls of rock, as in a great wide chasm let in the mountains. A green valley, with a river, and trees, and clusters of low flat sparkling houses. It was all tiny and perfect, three thousand feet below. Even the flat bridge over the stream, and the square with the houses around it, the bigger buildings piled up at opposite ends of the square, the tall cottonwood trees, the pastures and stretches of yellow-sere maize, the patches of brown sheep or goats in the distance, on the slopes, the railed enclosures by the stream-side. There it was, all small and perfect, looking magical, as any place will look magical seen from the mountains above. The unusual thing was that the low houses glittered white, white-washed, looking like crystals of salt, or silver. This frightened her.

They began the long, winding descent at the head of the barranca, following the stream that rushed and fell. At first it was all rocks; then the pine trees began, and soon the silver-limbed aspens. The flowers of autumn, big daisy-like flowers, and white ones, and many yellow flowers, were in profusion. But she had to sit down and rest, she was so weary. And she saw the bright flowers shadowily as pale shadows hovering, as one who is dead must see them.

At length came grass and pasture-slopes between mingled aspen and pine trees. A shepherd, naked in the sun save for his hat and his cotton loin-cloth, was driving his brown sheep away. In a grove of trees they sat and waited, she and the young Indian. The one with the saddle had also gone forward.

They heard a sound of someone coming. It was three men, in the fine sarapes of red and orange and yellow and black, and with brilliant feather head-dresses. The oldest had his grey hair braided with fur, and his red and orange-yellow sarape was covered with curious black markings, like a leopard-skin. The other two were not grey-haired, but they were elders too. Their blankets were in stripes, and their head-dresses not so elaborate.

The young Indian addressed the elders in a few quiet words. They listened without answering or looking at him or at the woman, keeping their faces averted and their eyes turned to the ground, only listening. And at length they turned and looked at the woman.

The old chief, or medicine-man, whatever he was, had a deeply wrinkled and lined face of dark bronze, with a few sparse grey hairs round the mouth. Two long braids of grey hair, braided with fur and coloured feather, hung on his shoulders. And yet, it was only his eyes that mattered. They were black and of extraordinary piercing strength, without a qualm of misgiving in their demonish, dauntless power. He looked into the eyes of the white woman with a long piercing look, seeking she knew not what. She summoned all her strength to meet his eyes and keep up her guard. But it was no good. He was not looking at her as one human being looks at another. He never even perceived her resistance or her challenge, but looked past them both, into she knew not what.

She could see it was hopeless to expect a human communication with this old being.

He turned and said a few words to the young Indian.

'He asks what do you seek here?' said the young man in Spanish.

'I? Nothing! I only came to see what it was like.'

This was again translated, and the old man turned his eyes on her once more. Then he spoke again, in his low muttering tone, to the young Indian.

'He says, why does she leave her house with the white men? Does she want to bring the white man's God to the Chilchui?'

'No,' she replied, foolhardy. 'I came away from the white man's God myself. I came to look for the God of the Chilchui.'

Profound silence followed, when this was translated. Then the old man spoke again, in a small voice almost of weariness.

'Does the white woman seek the gods of the Chilchui because she is weary of her own God?' came the question.

'Yes, she does. She is tired of the white man's God,' she replied, thinking that was what they wanted her to say. She would like to serve the gods of the Chilchui.

She was aware of an extraordinary thrill of triumph and exultance passing through the Indians, in the tense silence that followed when this was translated. Then they all looked at her with piercing black eyes, in which a steely covetous intent glittered incomprehensible. She was the more puzzled, as there was nothing sensual or sexual in the look. It had a terrible glittering purity that was beyond her. She was afraid, she would have been paralysed with fear, had not something died within her, leaving her with a cold, watchful wonder only.

The elders talked a little while, then the two went away, leaving her with the young man and the oldest chief. The old man now looked at her with a certain solicitude.

'He says are you tired?' asked the young man.

'Very tired,' she said.

'The men will bring you a carriage,' said the young Indian.

The carriage, when it came, proved to be a litter consisting of a sort of hammock of dark woollen frieze, slung on to a pole which was borne on the shoulders of two long-haired Indians. The woolen hammock was spread on the ground, she sat down on it, and the two men raised the pole to their shoulders. Swinging rather as if she were in a sack, she was carried out of the grove of trees, following the old chief, whose leopard-spotted blanket moved curiously in the sunlight.

They had emerged in the valley-head. Just in front were the maize fields, with ripe ears of maize. The corn was not very tall, in this high altitude. The well-worn path went between it, and all she could see was the erect form of the old chief, in the flame and black sarape, stepping soft and heavy and swift, his head forward, looking neither to right nor left. Her bearers followed, stepping rhythmically, the long blue-black hair glistening like a river down the naked shoulders of the man in front.

They passed the maize, and came to a big wall or earthwork made of earth and adobe bricks. The wooden doors were open. Passing on, they were in a network of small gardens, full of flowers and herbs and fruit trees, each garden watered by a tiny ditch of running water. Among each cluster of trees and flowers was a small, glittering white house, windowless, and with closed door. The place was a network of little paths, small streams, and little bridges among square, flowering gardens.

Following the broadest path—a soft narrow track between leaves and grass, a path worn smooth by centuries of human feet, no hoof of horse nor any wheel to disfigure it—they came to the little river of swift bright water, and crossed on a log bridge. Everything was silent—there was not a human being anywhere. The road went on under magnificent cottonwood trees. It emerged suddenly outside the central plaza or square of the village.

This was a long oblong of low white houses with flat roofs, and two bigger buildings, having as it were little square huts piled on top of bigger long huts, stood at either end of the oblong, facing each other rather askew. Every little house was a dazzling white, save for the great round beam-ends which projected under the flat eaves, and for the flat roofs. Round each of the bigger buildings, on the outside of the square, was a stockyard fence, inside which was garden with trees and flowers, and various small houses.

Not a soul was in sight. They passed silently between the houses into the central square. This was quite bare and arid, the earth trodden smooth by endless generations of passing feet, passing across from door to door. All the doors of the windowless houses gave on to this blank square, but all doors were closed. The firewood lay near the threshold, a clay oven was still smoking, but there was no sign of moving life.

The old man walked straight across the square to the big house at the end, where the two upper storeys, as in a house of toy bricks, stood each one smaller than the lower one. A stone staircase, outside, led up to the roof of the first storey.

At the foot of this staircase the litter-bearers stood still, and lowered the woman to the ground.

'You will come up,' said the young Indian who spoke Spanish.

She mounted the stone stairs to the earthen roof of the first house, which formed a platform round the wall of the second storey. She followed around this platform to the back of the big house. There they descended again, into the garden at the rear.

So far they had seen no one. But now two men appeared, bareheaded, with long braided hair, and wearing a sort of white shirt gathered into a loin-cloth. These went along with the three newcomers, across the garden where red flowers and yellow flowers were blooming, to a long, low white house. There they entered without knocking.

It was dark inside. There was a low murmur of men's voices. Several men were present, their white shirts showing in the gloom, their dark face invisible. They were sitting on a great log of smooth old wood, that lay along the far wall. And save for this log, the room seemed empty. But no, in the dark at one end was a couch, a sort of bed, and someone lying there, covered with furs.

The old Indian in the spotted sarape, who had accompanied the woman, now took off his hat and his blanket and his sandals. Laying them aside, he approached the couch, and spoke in a low voice. For some moments there was no answer. Then an old man with the snow-white hair hanging round his darkly-visible face roused himself like a vision, and leaned on one elbow, looking vaguely at the company, in tense silence.

The grey-haired Indian spoke again, and then the young Indian, taking the woman's hand, led her forward. In her linen riding-habit, and black boots and hat, and her pathetic bit of a red tie, she stood there beside the fur-covered bed of the old, old man, who sat reared up, leaning on one elbow, remote as a ghost, his white hair streaming in disorder, his face almost black, yet with a far-off intentness, not of this world, leaning forward to look at her.

His face was so old, it was like dark glass, and the few curling hairs that sprang white from his lips and chin were quite incredible. The long white locks fell unbraided and disorderly on either side of the glassy dark face. And under a faint powder of white eyebrows, the black eyes of the old chief looked at her as if from the far, far dead, seeing something that was never to be seen.

At last he spoke a few deep, hollow words, as if to the dark air.

'He says, do you bring your heart to the god of the Chilchui?' translated the young Indian.

'Tell him yes,' she said, automatically.

There was a pause. The old Indian spoke again, as if to the air. One of the men present went out. There was a silence as if of eternity in the dim room that was lighted only through the open door.

The woman looked round. Four old men with grey hair sat on the log by the wall facing the door. Two other men, powerful and impassive, stood near the door. They all had long hair, and wore white shirts gathered into a loin-cloth. Their powerful legs were naked and dark. There was a silence like eternity.

At length the man returned, with white and dark clothing on his arm. The young Indian took them, and holding them in front of the woman, said:

'You must take off your clothes, and put these on.'

'If all you men will go out,' she said.

'No one will hurt you,' he said quietly.

'Not while you men are here,' she said.

He looked at the two men by the door. They came quickly forward, and suddenly gripped her arms as she stood, without hurting her, but with great power. Then two of the old men came, and with curious skill slit her boots down with keen knives, and drew them off, and slit her clothing so that it came away from her. In a few moments she stood there white and uncovered. The old man on the bed spoke, and they turned her round for him to see. He spoke again, and the young Indian deftly took the pins and comb from her fair hair, so that it fell over her shoulders in a bunchy tangle.

Then the old man spoke again. The Indian led her to the bedside. The white-haired, glassy-dark old man moistened his finger-tips at his mouth, and most delicately touched her on the breasts and on the body, men on the back. And she winced strangely each time, as the finger-tips drew along her skin, as if Death itself were touching her.

And she wondered, almost sadly, why she did not feel shamed in her nakedness. She only felt sad and lost. Because nobody felt ashamed. The elder men were all dark and tense with some other deep, gloomy, incomprehensible emotion, which suspended all her agitation, while the young Indian had a strange look of ecstasy on his face. And she, she was only utterly strange and beyond herself, as if her body were not her own.

They gave her the new clothing: a long white cotton shift, that came to her knees: then a tunic of thick blue woollen stuff, embroidered with scarlet and green flowers. It was fastened over one shoulder only, and belted with a braid sash of scarlet and black wool.

When she was thus dressed, they took her away, barefoot, to a little house in the stockaded garden. The young Indian told her she might have what she wanted. She asked for water to wash herself. He brought it in a jar, together with a long wooden bowl. Then he fastened the gatedoor of her house, and left her a prisoner. She could see through the bars of the gate-door of her house, the red flowers of the garden, and a humming-bird. Then from the roof of the big house she heard the long, heavy sound of a drum, unearthly to her in its summons, and an uplifted voice calling from the house-top in a strange language, with a far-away emotionless intonation, delivering some speech or message. And she listened as if from the dead.

But she was very tired. She lay down on a couch of skins, pulling over her the blanket of dark wool, and she slept, giving up everything.

When she woke it was late afternoon, and the young Indian was entering with a basket-tray containing food, tortillas, and corn-mush with bits of meat, probably mutton, and a drink made of honey, and some fresh plums. He brought her also a long garland of red and yellow flowers with knots of blue buds at the end. He sprinkled the garland with water from a jar, then offered it to her, with a smile. He seemed very gentle and thoughtful, and on his face and in his dark eyes was a curious look of triumph and ecstasy, that frightened her a little. The glitter had gone from the black eyes, with their curving dark lashes, and he would look at her with this strange soft glow of ecstasy that was not quite human, and terribly impersonal, and which made her uneasy.

'Is there anything you want?' he said, in his low, slow, melodious voice, that always seemed withheld, as if he were speaking aside to somebody else, or as if he did not want to let the sound come out to her.

'Am I going to be kept a prisoner here?' she asked.

'No, you can walk in the garden to-morrow,' he said

softly. Always this curious solicitude.

'Do you like that drink?' he said, offering her a little earthenware cup. 'It is very refreshing.'

She sipped the liquor curiously. It was made with herbs and sweetened with honey, and had a strange, lingering flavour. The young man watched her with gratification.

'It has a peculiar taste,' she said.

'It is very refreshing,' he replied, his black eyes resting on her always with that look of gratified ecstasy. Then he went away. And presently she began to be sick, and to vomit violently, as if she had no control over herself.

Afterwards she felt a great soothing languor, steal over her, her limbs felt strong and loose and full of languor, and she lay on her couch listening to the sounds of the village, watching the yellowing sky, smelling the scent of burning cedar wood, or pine wood. So distinctly she heard the yapping of tiny dogs, the shuffle of far-off feet, the murmur of voices, so keenly she detected the smell of smoke, and flowers, and evening falling, so vividly she saw the one bright star infinitely remote, stirring above the sunset, that she felt as if all her senses were diffused on the air, that she could distinguish the sound of evening flowers unfolding, and the actual crystal sound of the heavens, as the vast belts of the world-atmosphere slid past one another, and as if the moisture ascending and the moisture descending in the air resounded like some harp in the cosmos.

She was a prisoner in her house, and in the stockaded garden, but she scarcely minded. And it was days before she realised that she never was another woman. Only the men, the elderly men of the big house, that she imagined must be some sort of temple, and the men priests of some sort. For they always had the same colours, red, orange, yellow, and black, and the same grave, abstracted demeanour.

Sometimes an old man would come and sit in her room with her, in absolute silence. None spoke any language but Indian, save the one younger man. The older men would smile at her, and sit with her for an hour at a time, sometimes smiling at her when she spoke in Spanish, but never answering save with this slow, benevolent-seeming smile. And they gave off a feeling of almost fatherly solicitude. Yet their dark eyes, brooding over her, had something away in their depths that was awesomely ferocious and relentless. They would cover it with a smile, at once, if they felt her looking. But she had seen it.

Always they treated her with this curious impersonal solicitude, this utterly impersonal gentleness, as an old man treats a child. But underneath it she felt there was something else, something terrible. When her old visitor had gone away, in his silent, insidious, fatherly fashion, a shock of fear would come over her; though of what she knew not.

The young Indian would sit and talk with her freely, as if with great candour. But with him, too, she felt that everything real was unsaid. Perhaps it was unspeakable. His big dark eyes would rest on her almost cherishingly, touched with ecstasy, and his beautiful, slow, languorous voice would trail out its simple, ungrammatical Spanish. He told her he was the grandson of the old, old man, son of the man in the spotted sarape: and they were caciques, kings from the old, old days, before even the Spaniards came. But he himself had been in Mexico City, and also in the United States. He had worked as a labourer, building the roads in Los Angeles. He had travelled as far as Chicago.

'Don't you speak English, then?' she asked.

His eyes rested on her with a curious look of duplicity and conflict, and he mutely shook his head.

'What did you do with your long hair, when you were in the United States?' she asked. 'Did you cut it off?'

Again, with the look of torment in his eyes, he shook his head.

'No,' he said, in a low, subdued voice, 'I wore a hat, and a handkerchief tied round my head.'

And he relapsed into silence, as if of tormented memories.

'Are you the only man of your people who has been to the United States?' she asked him.

'Yes. I am the only one who has been away from here for a long time. The others come back soon, in one week. They don't stay away. The old men don't let them.'

'And why did you go?'

'The old men want me to go—because I shall be the cacique—'

He talked always with the same naïvete, and almost childish candour. But she felt that this was perhaps just the effect of his Spanish. Or perhaps speech altogether was unreal to him. Anyhow, she felt that all the real things were kept back.

He came and sat with her a good deal—sometimes more than she wished—as if he wanted to be near her. She asked him if he was married. He said he was—with two children.

'I should like to see your children,' she said.

But he answered only with that smile, a sweet, almost ecstatic smile, above which the dark eyes hardly change from their enigmatic abstraction.

It was curious, he would sit with her by the hour, without ever making her self-conscious, or sex-conscious.

He seemed to have no sex, as he sat there so still and gentle and apparently submissive with his head bent a little forward, and the river of glistening black hair streaming maidenly over his shoulders.

Yet when she looked again, she saw his shoulders broad and powerful, his eyebrows black and level, the short, curved, obstinate black lashes over his lowered eyes, the small, fur-like line or moustache above his blackish, heavy lips, and the strong chin, and she knew that in some other mysterious way he was darkly and powerfully male. And he, feeling her watching him, would glance up at her swiftly with a dark lurking look in his eyes, which immediately he veiled with that half-sad smile.

The days and the weeks went by, in a vague kind of contentment. She was uneasy sometimes, feeling she had lost the power over herself. She was not in her own power, she was under the spell of some other control. And at times she had moments of terror and horror. But then these Indians would come and sit with her, casting their insidious spell over her by their very silent presence, their silent, sexless, powerfull physical presence. As they sat they seemed to take her will away, and leaving her will-less and victim to her own indifference. And the young man would bring her sweetened drink, often the same emetic drink, but sometimes other kinds. And after drinking, the languor filled her heavy limbs, her senses seemed to float in the air, listening, hearing. They had brought her a little female dog, which she called Flora. And once, in the trace of her senses, she felt she *heard* the little dog conceive, in her tiny womb, and begin to be complex, with young. And another day she could hear the vast sound of the earth going round, like some immense arrow-string booming.

But as the days grew shorter and colder, when she was cold, she would get a sudden revival of her will, and a desire to go out, to go away. And she insisted to the young man, she wanted to go out.

So one day, they let her climb to the topmost roof of the big house where she was, and look down the square. It was the day of the big dance, but not everybody was dancing. Women with babies in their arms stood in their doorways, watching. Opposite, at the other end of the square, there was a throng before the other big house, and a small, brilliant group on the terrace roof of the first storey, in front of wide open doors of the upper storey. Through these wide open doors she could see fire glinting in darkness and priests in head-dresses of black and yellow and scarlet feathers, wearing robe-like blankets of black and red and yellow, with long green fringes, were moving about. A big drum was beating slowly and regularly, in the dense, Indian silence. The crowd below waited.

Then a drum started on a high beat, and there came the deep, powerful burst of men singing a heavy, savage music, like a wind roaring in some timeless forest, many mature men singing in one breath, like the wind; and long lines of dancers walked out from under the big house. Men with naked, golden-bronze bodies and streaming black hair, tufts of red and yellow feathers on their arms, and kilts of white frieze with a bar of heavy red and black and green embroidery round their waists, bending slightly forward and stamping the earth in their absorbed, monotonous stamp of the dance, a fox-fur, hung by the nose from their belt behind, swaying with the sumptuous swaying of a beautiful fox-fur, the tip of the tail writhing above the dancer's heels. And after each man, a woman with a strange elaborate head-dress of feathers and seashells, and wearing a short black tunic, moving erect, holding up tufts of feathers in each hand, swaying her wrists rhythmically and subtly beating the earth with her bare feet.

So, the long line of the dance unfurling from the big house opposite. And from the big house beneath her, strange scent of incense, strange tense silence, then the answering burst of inhuman male singing, and the long line of the dance unfurling.

It went on all day, the insistence of the drum, the cavernous, roaring, storm-like sound of male singing, the incessant swinging of the fox-skins behind the powerful, gold-bronze, stamping legs of the men, the autumn sun from a perfect blue heaven pouring on the rivers of black hair, men's and women's, the valley all still, the walls of rock beyond, the awful huge bulking of the mountain against the pure sky, its snow seething with sheer whiteness.

For hours and hours she watched, spellbound, and as if drugged. And in all the terrible persistence of the drumming and the primeval, rushing deep singing, and the endless stamping of the dance of fox-tailed men, the tread of heavy, bird-erect women in their black tunics, she seemed at last to feel her own death; her own obliteration. As if she were to be obliterated from the field of life again. In the strange towering symbols on the heads of the changeless, absorbed women she seemed to read once more the *Mene Mene Tekel Upharsin*. Her kind of womanhood, intensely personal and individual, was to be obliterated again, and the great primeval symbols were to tower once more over the fallen individual independence of woman. The sharpness and the quivering nervous consciousness of the highly-bred white woman was to be destroyed again, womanhood was to be cast once more into the great stream of impersonal sex and impersonal passion. Strangely, as if clairvoyant, she saw the immense sacrifice prepared. And she went back to her little house in a trance of agony.

After this, there was always a certain agony when she heard the drums at evening, and the strange uplifted savage sound of men singing round the drum, like wild creatures howling to the invisible gods of the moon and the vanished sun. Something of the chuckling, sobbing cry of the coyote, something of the exultant bark of the fox, the far-off wild melancholy exultance of the howling wolf, the torment of the puma's scream, and the insistence of the ancient fierce human male, with his lapses of tenderness and his abiding ferocity.

Sometimes she would climb the high roof after nightfall, and listen to the dim cluster of young men round the drum on the bridge just beyond the square, singing by the hour. Sometimes there would be a fire, and in the fire-glow, men in their white shirts or naked save for a loin-cloth, would be dancing and stamping like spectres, hour after hour in the dark cold air, within the fire-glow, forever dancing and stamping like turkeys, or dropping squatting by the fire to rest, throwing their blankets round them.

'Why do you all have the same colours?' she asked the young Indian.

'Why do you all have red and yellow and black, over your white shirts? And the women have black tunics?'

He looked into her eyes, curiously, and the faint, evasive smile came on to his face. Behind the smile lay a soft, strange malignancy.

'Because our men are the fire and the day-time, and our women are the spaces between the stars at night,' he said.

'Aren't the women even stars?' she said.

'No. We say they are the spaces between the stars, that keep the stars apart.'

He looked at her oddly, and again the touch of derision came into his eyes.

'White people,' he said, 'they know nothing. They are like children, always with toys. We know the sun, and we know the moon. And we say, when a white woman sacrifices herself to our gods, then our gods will begin to make the world again, and the white man's gods will fall to pieces.'

'How sacrifice herself?' she asked quickly.

And he, as quickly covered, covered himself with a subtle smile.

'She sacrifice her own gods and come to our gods, I mean that,' he said soothingly.

But she was not reassured. An icy pang of fear and certainty was at her heart.

'The sun he is alive at one end of the sky,' he continued, 'and the moon lives at the other end. And the man all the time have to keep the sun happy in his side of the sky, and the woman have to keep the moon quiet at her side of the sky. All the time she have to work at this. And the sun can't ever go into the house of the moon, and the moon can't ever go into the house of the sun, in the sky. So the woman, she asks the moon to come into her cave, inside her. And the man, he draws the sun down till he has the power of the sun. All the time he do this. Then when the man gets a woman, the sun goes into the cave of the moon, and that is how eveything in the world starts.'

She listened, watching him closely, as one enemy watches another who is speaking with double meaning.

'Then,' she said, 'why aren't you Indians masters of

the white men?'

'Because,' he said, 'the Indian got weak, and lost his power with the sun, so the white men stole the sun. But they can't keep him—they don't know how. They got him, but they don't know what to do with him, like a boy who catches a big grizzly bear, and can't kill him, and can't run away from him. The grizzly bear eats the boy that catch him, when he want to run away from him. White men don't know what they are doing with the sun, and white women don't know what they do with the moon. The moon she got angry with white women, like a puma when someone kills her little ones. The moon, she bites white women—here inside,' and he pressed his side. 'The moon, she is angry in a white woman's cave. The Indian can see it. And soon,' he added, 'the Indian women get the moon back and keep her quiet in their house. And the Indian men get the sun, and the power over all the world. White men don't know what the sun is. They never know.'

He subsided into a curious exultant silence.

'But,' she faltered, 'why do you hate us so? Why do you hate me?'

He looked up suddenly with a light on his face, and a startling flame of a smile.

'No, we don't hate,' he said softly, looking with a curious glitter into her face.

'You do,' she said, forlorn and hopeless.

And after a moment's silence, he rose and went away.

III

Winter had now come, in the high valley, with snow that melted in the day's sun, and nights that were bitter cold. She lived on, in a kind of daze, feeling her power ebbing more and more away from her, as if her will was leaving her. She felt always in the same relaxed, confused, victimised state, unless the sweetened herb drink would numb her mind altogether, and release her senses into a sort of heightened, mystic acuteness and a feeling as if she were diffusing out deliciously into the harmony of things. This at length became the only state of consciousness she really recognised: this exquisite sense of bleeding out into the higher beauty and harmony of things. Then she could actually hear the great stars in heaven, which she saw through her door, speaking from their motion and brightness, saying things perfectly to the cosmos, as they trod in perfect ripples, like bells on the floor of heaven, passing one another and grouping in the timeless dance, with the spaces of dark between. And she could hear the snow on a cold, cloudy day twittering and faintly whistling in the sky, like birds that flock and fly away in autumn, suddenly calling farewell to the invisible moon, and slipping out of the plains of the air, releasing peaceful warmth. She herself would call to the arrested snow to fall from the upper air. She would call to the unseen moon to cease to be angry, to make peace again with the unseen sun like a woman who ceases to be angry in her house. And she would smell the sweetness of the moon relaxing to the sun in the wintry heaven, when the snow fell in a faint, cold-perfumed relaxation, as the peace of the sun mingled again in a sort of unison with the peace of the moon.

She was aware too of the sort of shadow that was on the Indians of the valley, a deep stoical disconsolation, almost religious in its depth.

'We have lost our power over the sun, and we are trying

to get him back. But he is wild with us, and shy like a horse that has got away. We have to go through a lot.' So the young Indian said to her, looking into her eyes with a strained meaning. And she, as if bewitched, replied:

'I hope you will get him back.'

The smile of triumph flew over his face.

'Do you hope it?' he said.

'I do,' she answered fatally.

'Then all right,' he said. 'We shall get him.'

And he went away in exultance.

She felt she was drifting on some consummation, which she had no will to avoid, yet which seemed heavy and finally terrible to her.

It must have been almost December, for the days were short when she was taken again before the aged man, and stripped of her clothing, and touched with the old fingertips.

The aged cacique looked her in the eyes, with his eyes of lonely, far-off, black intentness, and murmured something to her.

'He wants you to make the sign of peace,' the young man translated, showing her the gesture. 'Peace and farewell to him.'

She was fascinated by the black, glass-like, intent eyes of the old cacique, that watched her without blinking, like a basilisk's, overpowering her. In their depths also she saw a certain fatherly compassion, and pleading. She put her hand before her face, in the required manner, making the sign of peace and farewell. He made the sign of peace back again to her, then sank among his furs. She thought he was going to die, and that he knew it.

There followed a day of ceremonial, when she was brought out before all the people, in a blue blanket with white fringe, and holding blue feathers in her hands. Before an altar of one house she was perfumed with incense and sprinkled with ash. Before the altar of the opposite house she was fumigated again with incense by the gorgeous, terrifying priests in yellow and scarlet and black, their faces painted with scarlet paint. And then they threw water on her. Meanwhile she was faintly aware of the fire on the altar, the heavy, heavy sound of a drum, the heavy sound of men beginning powerfully, deeply, savagely to sing, the swaying of the crowd of faces in the plaza below, and the formation for a sacred dance.

But at this time her commonplace ocnsciousness was numb, she was aware of her immediate surroundings as shadows, almost immaterial. With refined and heightened senses she could hear the sound of the earth winging on its journey, like a shot arrow, the ripple-rustling of the air, and the boom of the great arrow-string. And it seemed to her there were two great influences in the upper air, one golden towards the sun, and one invisible silver; the first travelling like rain ascending to the gold presence sunwards, the second like rain silverily descending the ladders of space towards the hovering, lurking clouds over the snowy mountain-top. There between them, another presence, waiting to shake himself free of moisture, of heavy white snow that had mysteriously collected about him. And in summer, like a scorched eagle, he would wait to shake himself clear of the weight of heavy sunbeams. And he was coloured like fire. And he was always shaking himself clear, of snow or of heavy heat, like an eagle rustling.

Then there was a still stranger presence, standing watching from the blue distance, always watching. Sometimes running in upon the wind, or shimmering in the heat-waves. The blue wind itself, rushing, as it were, out of the holes into the sky, rushing out of the sky down upon the earth. The blue wind, the go-between, the invisible ghost that belonged to two worlds, that played upon the ascending and the descending chords of the rains.

More and more her ordinary personal consciousness had left her, she had gone into that other state of passional cosmic consciousness, like one who is drugged. The Indians, with their heavy religious natures, had made her succumb to their vision.

Only one personal question she asked the young Indian:

'Why am I the only one that wears blue?'

'It is the colour of the wind. It is the colour of what goes away and is never coming back, but which is always here, waiting like death among us. It is the colour of the dead. And it is the colour that stands away off, looking at us from the distance, that cannot come near to us. When we go near, it goes farther. It can't be near. We are all brown and yellow and black hair, and white teeth and red blood. We are the ones that are here. You with blue eyes, you are the messengers from the far-away, you cannot stay, and now it is time for you to go back.'

'Where to?' she asked.

'To the way-off things like the sun and the blue mother of rain, and tell them that we are the people on the world again, and we can bring the sun to the moon again, like a red horse to a blue mare; we are the people. The white women have driven back the moon in the sky, won't let her come to the sun. So the sun is angry. And the Indian must give the moon to the sun.'

'How?' she said.

'The white woman got to die and go like a wind to the

sun, tell him the Indians will open the gate to him. And the Indian women will open the gate to the moon. The white women don't let the moon come down out of the blue coral. The moon used to come down among the Indian women, like a white goat among the flowers. And the sun want to come down to the Indian men, like an eagle to the pine trees. The sun, he is shut out behind the white man, and the moon she is shut out behind the white woman, and they can't get away. They are angry, everything in the world gets angrier. The Indian says he will give the white woman to the sun, so the sun will leap over the white man and come to the Indian again. And the moon will be surprised, she will see the gate open, and she will not know which way to go. But the Indian woman will call to the moon: *Come! Come! Come back into my grasslands. The wicked white woman can't harm you any more.* Then the sun will look over the heads of the white men, and see the moon in the pastures of our women, with the Red Men standing around like pine trees. Then he will leap over the heads of the white men, and come running past to the Indians through the spruce trees. And we, who are red and black and yellow, we who stay, we shall have the sun on our right hand and the moon on our left. So we can bring the rain down out of the blue meadows, and up out of the black; and we can call the wind that tells the corn to grow, when we ask him, and we shall make the clouds to break, and the sheep to have twin lambs. And we shall be full of power, like a spring day. But the white people will be a hard winter, without snow—'

'But,' said the white women, 'I don't shut out the moon—how can I?'

'Yes,' he said, 'you shut the gate, and then laugh, think you have it all your own way.'

She could never quite understand the way he looked at her. He was always so curiously gentle, and his smile was so soft. Yet there was such a glitter in his eyes, and an unrelenting sort of hate came out of his words, a strange, profound, impersonal hate. Personally he liked her, she was sure. He was gentle with her, attracted by her in some strange, soft, passionless way. But impersonally he hated her with a mystic hatred. He would smile at her, winningly. Yet if, the next moment, she glanced round at him unawares, she would catch that gleam of pure after-hate in his eyes.

'Have I got to die and be given to the sun?' she asked.

'Some time,' he said, laughing evasively 'Some time we all die.'

They were gentle with her, and very considerate with her. Strange men, the old priests and the young cacique alike, they watched over her and cared for her like women. In their soft, insidious understanding, there was something womanly. Yet their eyes, with that strange glitter, and their dark, shut mouths that would open to the broad jaw, the small, strong, white teeth, had something very primitively male and cruel.

One wintry day, when snow was falling, they took her to a great dark chamber in the big house. The fire was burning in a corner on a high raised dais under a sort of hood or canopy of adobe-work. She saw in the fire-glow the glowing bodies of the almost naked priests, and strange symbols on the roof and walls of the chamber. There was no door or window in the chamber, they had descended by a ladder, from the roof. And the fire of pinewood danced continually, showing walls painted with strange devices, which she could not understand, and a ceiling of poles making a curious pattern of black and red and yellow, and alcoves or niches in which were curious objects she could not discern.

The older priests were going through some ceremony near the fire, in silence, intense Indian silence. She was seated on a low projection of the wall, opposite the fire, two men seated beside her. Presently they gave her a drink from a cup, which she took gladly, because of the semitrance it would induce.

In the darkness and in the silence she was accurately aware of everything that happened to her: how they took off her clothes, and, standing her before a great, weird device on the wall, coloured blue and white and black, washed her all over with water and the amole infusion; washed even her hair, softly, carefully, and dried it on white clothes, till it was soft and glistening. Then they laid her on a couch under another great indecipherable image of red and black and yellow, and now rubbed all her body with sweet-scented oil, and massaged all her limbs, and her back, and her sides, with a long, strange, hypnotic massage. Their dark hands were incredibly powerful, yet soft with a watery softness she could not understand. And the dark faces, leaning near her white body, she saw were darkened with red pigment, with lines of yellow round the cheeks. And the dark eyes glittered absorbed, as the hands worked upon the soft white body of the woman.

They were so impersonal, absorbed in something that was beyond her. They never saw her as a personal woman: she could tell that. She was some mystic object to them, some vehicle of passions too remote for her to grasp Herself in a state of trance, she watched their faces bending over her, dark, strangely glistening with the transparent red paint, and lined with bars of yellow. And in this weird, luminous-dark mask of living face, the eyes were fixed with an unchanging steadfast gleam, and the purplish-pigmented lips were closed in a full, sinister, sad grimness. The immense fundamental sadness, the grimness of ultimate decision, the fixity of revenge, and the nascent exultance of those that are going to triumph—these things she could read in their faces, as she lay and was rubbed into a misty glow by their uncanny dark hands. Her limbs, her flesh, her very bones at last seemed to be diffusing into a roseate sort of mist, in which her consciousness hovered like some sungleam in a flushed cloud.

She knew the gleam would fade, the cloud would go grey. But at present she did not believe it. She knew she was a victim; that all this elaborate work upon her was the work of victimising her. But she did not mind. She wanted it.

Later, they put a short blue tunic on her and took her to the upper terrace, and presented her to the people. She saw the plaza below her full of dark faces and of glittering eyes. There was no pity: only the curious hard exultance. The people gave a subdued cry when they saw her, and she shuddered. But she hardly cared.

Next day was the last. She slept in a chamber of the big house. At dawn they put on her a big blue blanket with a fringe, and led her out into the plaza, among the throng of silent, dark-blanketed people. There was pure white snow on the ground, and the dark people in their dark-brown blankets looked like inhabitants of another world.

A large drum was slowly pounding, and an old priest was declaiming from a house-top. But it was not till noon that a litter came forth, and the people gave that low, animal cry which was so moving. In the sacklike litter sat

the old, old cacique, his white hair braided with black
briad and large turquoise stones. His face was like a piece
of obsidian. He lifted his hand in token, and the litter
stopped in front of her. Fixing her with his old eyes, he
spoke to her for a few moments, in his hollow voice. No
one translated.

Another litter came, and she was placed in it. Four
priests moved ahead, in their scarlet and yellow and black,
with plumed head-dresses. Then came the litter of the old
cacique. Then the light drums began, and two groups of
singers burst simultaneously into song, male and wild.
And the golden-red, almost naked men, adorned with
ceremonial feathers and kilts, the rivers of black hair down
their backs, formed into two files and began to tread the
dance. So they threaded out of the snowy plaza, in two
long, sumptuous lines of dark red-gold and black and fur,
swaying with a faint tinkle of bits of shell and flint,
winding over the snow between the two bee-clusters of
men who sang around the drums.

Slowly they moved out, and her litter, with its
attendance of feathered, lurid dancing priests, moved after.
Everybody danced the tread of the dance-step, even,
subtly, the litter-bearers. And out of the plaza they went,
past smoking ovens, on the trail to the great cottonwood
trees, that stood like grey-silver lace against the blue sky,
bare and exquisite above the snow. The river, diminished,
rushed among fangs of ice. The chequer-squares of
gardens within fences were all snowy, and the white
houses now looked yellowish.

The whole valley glitterd intolerably with pure snow,
away to the walls of the standing rock. And across the
flat cradle of snow-bed wound the long thread of the
dance, shaking slowly and sumptuously in its orange and

black motion. The high drums thudded quickly, and on the crystalline frozen air the swell and roar of the chant of savages was like an obsession.

She sat looking out of her litter with big, transfixed blue eyes, under which were the wan markings of her drugged weariness. She knew she was going to die, among the glisten of this snow, at the hands of this savage, sumptuous people. And as she stared at the blaze of the blue sky above the slashed and ponderous mountain, she thought: 'I am dead already. What difference does it make, the transition from the dead I am to the dead I shall be, very soon!' Yet her soul sickened and felt wan.

The strange procession trailed on, in perpetual dance, slowly across the plain of snow, and then entered the slopes between the pine tress. She saw the copper-dark men dancing the dance-tread, onwards, between the copper-pale tree trunks. And at last, she, too, in her swaying litter, entered the pine trees.

They were travelling on and on, upwards, across the snow under the trees, past superb shafts of pale, flaked copper, the rustle and shake and tread of the threading dance, penetrating into the forest, into the mountain. They were following a stream-bed: but the stream was dry, like summer, dried up by the frozenness of the head-waters. There were dark, red-bronze willow bushes with wattles like wild hair, and pallie aspen trees looking cold flesh against the snow. Then jutting dark rocks.

At last she could tell that the dancers were moving forward no more. Nearer and nearer she came upon the drums, as to a lair of mysterious animals. Then through the bushes she emerged into a strange amphitheatre. Facing was a great wall of hollow rock, down the front of which hung a great, dripping, fand-like spoke of ice. The ice came pouring over the rock from the precipice above, and then stood arrested, dripping out of high heaven, almost down to the hollow stones where the stream-pool should be below. But the pool was dry.

On either side the dry pool the lines of dancers had formed, and the dance was continuing without intermission, against a background of bushes.

But what she felt was that fanged inverted pinnacle of ice, hanging from the lip of the dark precipice above. And behind the great rope of ice she saw the leopard-like figures of priests climbing the hollow cliff face, to the cave that like a dark socket bored a cavity, an orifice, half-way up the crag.

Before she could realise, her litter-bearers were staggering in the footholds, climbing the rock. She, too, was behind the ice. There it hung, like a curtain that is not spread, but hangs like a great fang. And near above her was the orifice of the cave sinking dark into the rock. She watched it as she swayed upwards.

On the platform of the cave stood the priests, waiting in all their gorgeousness of feathers and fringed robes, watching her ascent. Two of them stooped to help her litter-bearer. And at length she was on the platform of the cave, far in behind the shaft of ice, above the hollow amphitheatre among the bushes below, where men were dancing, and the whole populace of the village was clustered in silence.

The sun was sloping down the afternoon sky, on the left. She knew that this was the shortest day of the year, and the last day of her life. They stood her facing the iridescent column of ice, which fell down marvellously arrested, away in front of her.

Some signal was given, and the dance below stopped.

There was now absolute silence. She was given a little to drink, then two priests took off her mantle and her tunic, and in her strange pallor she stood there, between the lurid robes of the priests, beyond the pillar of ice, beyond and above the dark-faced people. The throng below gave the low, wild cry. Then the priest turned her round, so she stood with her back to the open world, her long blonde hair to the people below. And they cried again.

She was facing the cave, inwards. A fire was burning and flickering in the depths. Four priests had taken off their robes, and were almost as naked as she was. They were powerful men in the prime of life, and they kept their dark, painted faces lowered.

From the fire came the old, old priest, with an incense-pan. He was naked and in a state of barbaric ecstasy. He fumigated his victim, reciting at the same time in a hollow voice. Behind him came another robeless priest, with two flint knives.

When she was fumigated, they laid her on a large flat stone, the four powerful men holding her by the outstretched arms and legs. Behind stood the aged man, like a skeleton covered with dark glass, holding knife and transfixedly watching the sun; and behind him again was another naked priest, with a knife.

She felt little sensation, though she knew all that was happening. Turning to the sky, she looked at the yellow sun. It was sinking. The shaft of ice was like a shadow between her and it. And she realised that the yellow rays were filling half the cave, though they had not reached the altar where the fire was, at the far end of the funnel-shaped cavity.

Yes, the rays were creeping round slowly. As they grew ruddier, they penetrated farther. When the red sun was about to sink, he would shine full through the shaft of ice deep into the hollow of the cave, to the innermost.

She understood now that this was what the men were waiting for. Even those that held her down were bent and twisted round, their black eyes watching the sun with a glittering eagerness, and awe, and craving. The black eyes of the aged cacique were fixed like black mirrors on the sun, as if sightless, yet containing some terrible answer to the reddening winter planet. And all the eyes of the priests were fixed and glittering on the sinking orb, in the reddening, icy silence of the winter afternoon.

They were anxious, terribly anxious, and fierce. Their ferocity wanted something, and they were waiting for the moment. And their ferocity was ready to leap out into mystic exultance, of triumph. But they were anxious.

Only the eyes of the oldest man were not anxious. Black, and fixed, and as if sightless, they watched the sun, seeing beyond the sun. And in their black, empty concentration there was power, power intensely abstract and remote, but deep, deep to the heart of the earth, and the heart of the sun. In absolute motionlessness he watched till the red sun should send his ray through the column of ice. Then the old man would strike, and strike home, accomplish the sacrifice and achieve the power.

The mastery that man must hold, and that passes from race to race.

THINGS

THEY were true idealists from New England. But that is some time ago: before the war. Several years before the war, they met and married; he a tall, keen-eyed young man from Connecticut, she a smallish, demure, Puritan-looking young woman from Massachusetts. They both had a little money. Not much, however. Even added together, it didn't make three thousand dollars a year. Still—they were free. Free!

Ah! Freedom! To be free to live one's own life! To be twenty-five and twenty-seven, a pair of true idealists with a mutual love of beauty, and an inclination towards 'Indian thought'—meaning, alas, Mrs. Besant—and an income a little under three thousand dollars a year! But what is money? All one wishes to do is to live a full and beautiful life. In Europe, of course, right at the fountain-head of tradition. It might possibly be done in America: in New England, for example. But at a forfeiture of a certain amount of 'beauty'. True beauty takes a long time to mature. The baroque is only half-beautiful, half-matured. No, the real silver bloom, the real golden-sweet bouquet of beauty had its roots in the Renaissance, not in any later or shallower period.

Therefore the two idealists, who were married in New Haven, sailed at once to Paris: Paris of the old days. They had a studio apartment on the Boulevard Montparnasse, and they became real Parisians, in the old, delightful sense, not in the modern, vulgar. It was the shimmer of the pure impressionists, Monet and his followers, the world seen in terms of pure light, light broken and unbroken. How lovely! How lovely the nights, the river, the mornings in the old streets and by the flower-stalls and the book-stalls, the afternoons up on Montmartre or in the Tuileries, the evenings on the boulevards!

They both painted, but not desperately. Art had not taken them by the throat, and they did not take Art by the throat. They painted: that's all. They knew people—nice people, if possible, though one had to take them mixed. And they were happy.

Yet it seems as if human beings must set their claws in *something*. To be 'free', to the 'living a full and beautiful life' you must, alas, be attached to something. A full and beautiful life means a tight attachment to *something*—at least, it is so for all idealists—or else a certain boredom supervenes; there is a certain waving of loose ends upon the air, like the waving, yearning nostrils of the vine that spread and rotate, seeking something to clutch, something up which to climb towards the necessary sun. Finding nothing, the vine can only trail, half-fulfilled, upon the ground. Such is freedom!—a clutching of the right pole. And human beings are all vines. But especially the idealist. He is a vine, and he needs to clutch and climb. And he despises the man who is a mere *potato*, or turnip, or lump of wood.

Our idealists were frightfully happy, but they were all the time reaching out for something to cotton on to. At first, Paris was enough. They explored Paris *thoroughly*. And they learned French till they almost felt like French people, they could speak it so glibly.

Still, you know, you never talk French with your *soul*. It can't be done. And though it's very thrilling, at first, talking in French to clever Frenchmen—they seem *so much* cleverer than oneself—still, in the long run, it is not satisfying. The endlessly clever *materialism* of the French leaves you cold, in the end, gives a sense of barenness and incompatibility with true New England depth. So our two idealists felt.

They turned away from France—but ever so gently. France had disappointed them. 'We've loved it, and we've got a great deal out of it. But after a while, after a considerable while, several years, in fact Paris leaves one feeling disappointed. It hasn't quite got what one wants.'

'But Paris isn't France.'

'No, perhaps not. France is quite different from Paris. And France is lovely—quite lovely. But *to us*, though we love it, it doesn't say a great deal.'

So, when the war came, the idealists moved to Italy. And they loved Italy. They found it beautiful, and more poignant than France. It seemed much nearer to the New England conception of beauty; something pure, and full of sympathy, without the *materialism* and the *cynicism* of the French. The two idealists seemed to breathe their own true air in Italy.

And in Italy, much more than in Paris, they felt they could thrill to the teachings of the Buddha. They entered the swelling stream of modern Buddhistic emotion, and they read the books, and they practised meditation, and they deliberately set themselves to eliminate from their own souls greed, pain, and sorrow. They did not realise—yet—that Buddha's very eagerness to free himself from pain and sorrow is in itself a sort of greed. No, they dreamed of a perfect world, from which all greed, and nearly all pain, and a great deal of sorrow, were eliminated.

But America entered the war, so the two idealists had to help. They did hospital work. And though their experience made them realise more than ever that greed, pain, and sorrow *should* be eliminated from the world, nevertheless the Buddhism, or the theosophy, didn't emerge very triumphant from the long crisis. Somehow, somewhere, in some part of themselves, they felt that greed, pain, and sorrow would never be eliminated, because most people don't care about eliminating them, and never will care. Our idealists were far too Western to think of abandoning all the world to damnation, while they saved their two selves. They were far too unselfish to sit tight under a bho tree and reach Nirvana in a mere couple.

It was more than that, though. They simply hadn't enough *Seitz-fleisch* to squat under a bho tree and get to Nirvana by contemplating anything, least of all their own navel. If the whole wide world was not going to be saved, they, personally, were not so very keen on being saved just by themselves. No, it would be so lonesome. They were New Englanders, so it must be all or nothing. Greed, pain, and sorrow must either be eliminated from *all the world,* or else, what was the use of eliminating them from oneself? No use at all! One was just a victim.

And so, although they still *loved* 'Indian thought', and felt very tender about it, well, to go back to our metaphor, the pole up which the green and anxious vines clambered so far now proved dry-rotten. It snapped, and the vines came slowly subsiding to earth again. There was no crack and crash. The vines held themselves up by their own foliage, for a while. But they subsided. The beanstalk of 'Indian thought' had given way before Jack and Jill had climbed off the tip of it to a further world.

They subsided with a slow rustle back to earth again. But they made no outcry. They were again 'disappointed'. But they never admitted it. 'Indian thought' had let them down. But they never complained. Even to one another, they never said a word. They were both disappointed, faintly but deeply disillusioned, and they both knew it. But the knowledge was tacit.

And they still had so much in their lives. They still had Italy—dear Italy. And they still had freedom, the priceless treasure. And they still had so much 'beauty' About the fullness of their lives they were not quite so sure. They had one little boy, whom they loved as parents should love their children, but whom they wisely refrained from fastening upon, to build their lives on him. No, no, they must live their own lives! They still had strength of mind to know that.

But they were now no longer very young. Twenty-five and twenty-seven had become thirty-five and thirty-seven. And though they had had a very wonderful time in Europe, and though they still loved Italy—dear Italy!—yet, they were disappointed. They had got a lot out of it: oh, a very great deal indeed! Still, it hadn't given them quite, not *quite*, what they had expected. Europe was lovely, but it was dead. Living in Europe, you were living on the past. And Europeans, with all their superficial charm were not *really* charming. They were materialistic, they had no *real* soul. They just did not understand the inner urge of the spirit, because the inner urge was dead in them, they were all survivals. There, that was the truth about Europeans: they were survivals, with no more getting ahead in them.

It was another bean-pole, another vine-support crumbled under the green life of the vine. And very bitter it was, this time. For up the old tree-trunk of Europe the green vine had been clambering silently for more than ten years, ten hugely important years, the years of real living. The two idealists had *lived* in Europe, lived on

Europe and on European life and European things as vines in an everlasting vineyard.

They had made their home here; a home such as you could never make in America. Their watchword had been 'beauty'. They had rented, the last four years, the second floor of an old palazzo on the Arno, and here they had all their 'things'. And they derived a profound, profound satisfaction from their apartment: the lofty, silent, ancient room with windows on the river, with glistening, dark-red floors, and the beautiful furniture that the idealists had 'picked up'.

Yes, unknown to themselves, the lives of the idealists had been running with a fierce swiftness horizontally, all the time. They had become tense, fierce, hunters of 'things' for their home. While their souls were climbing up to the sun of old European culture or old Indian thought, their passions were running horizontally, clutching at 'things'. Of course they did not buy the things for the things' sakes, but for the sake of 'beauty'. They looked upon their home as a place entirely furnished by loveliness, not by 'things' at all. Valerie had some very lovely curtains at the windows of the long *salotto*, looking on the river: curtains of queer ancient material that looked like finely-knitted silk, most beautifully faded down from vermilion and orange, and gold, and black, down to a sheer soft glow. Valerie hardly ever came into the *salotto* without mentally falling on her knees before the curtains. 'Chartres!' she said. 'To me they are Chartres!' And Melville never turned and looked at his sixteen-century Venetian bookcase, with its two or three dozen of choice books, without feeling his marrow stir in his bones. The holy of holies!

The child silently, almost sinisterly, avoided any rude

contact with these ancient monuments of furniture, as if they had been nests of sleeping cobras, or that 'thing' most perilous to the touch, the Ark of the Covenant. His childish awe was silent and cold, but final.

Still, a couple of New England idealists cannot live merely on the bygone glory of their furniture. At least, one couple could not. They got used to the marvellous Bologna Cupboard, they got used to the wonderful Venetian bookcase, and the books, and the Siena curtains and bronzes, and the lovely sofas and side-tables and chair they had 'picked up' in Paris. Oh, they had been picking things up since the first day they had landed in Europe. And they were still at it. It is the last interest Europe can offer to an outsider: or to an insider either.

When people came, and were thrilled by the Melville interion, then Valerie and Erasmus felt they had not lived in vain: that they still were living. But in the long mornings, when Erasmus was desultorily working at Renaissance Florentine literature, and Valerie was attending to the apartment: and in the long hours after lunch; and in the long, usually very cold and oppressive evenings in the ancient palazzo: then the halo died from around the furniture, and the things became things, lumps of matter that just stood there or hung there, *ad infinitum*, and said nothing; and Valerie and Erasmus almost hated them. The glow of beauty, like every other glow, dies down unless it is fed. The idealists still dearly loved their things. But they had got them. And the sad fact is, things that glow vividly while you're getting them, go almost quite cold after a year or two. Unless, of course, people envy them very much, and the museums are pining for them. And the Melvilles' 'things', though very good, were not quite so good as that.

So, the glow gradually went out of everything, out of Europe, out of Italy–'the Italians are *dears*'–even out of that marvellous apartment on the Arno. 'Why, if I had this apartment, I'd never, never even want to go out of doors! It's too lovely and perfect.' That was something, of course–to hear that.

And yet Valerie and Erasmus went out of doors; they even went to get away from its ancient, cold-floored, stone-heavy silence and dead dignity. 'We're living on the past, you know, Dick,' said Valerie to her husband. She called him Dick.

They were grimly hanging on. They did not like to give in. They did not like to own up that they were through. For twelve years, now, they had been 'free' people living a 'full and beautiful life'. And America for twelve years had been their anathema, the Sodom and Gomorrah of industrial materialism.

It wasn't easy to own that you were 'through'. They hated to admit that they wanted to go back. But at last, reluctantly, they decided to go, 'for the boy's sake'.–'We can't *bear* to leave Europe. But Peter is an American, so he had better look at America while he's young.' The Melvilles had an entirely English accent and manner, almost; a little Italian and French here and there.

They left Europe behind, but they took as much of it along with them as possible. Several van-loads, as a matter of fact. All those adorable and irreplaceable 'things'. And all arrived in New York, idealists, child, and the huge bulk of Europe they had lugged along.

Valerie had dreamed of a pleasant apartment, perhaps on Riverside Drive, where it was not so expensive as east of Fifth Avenue, and where all their wonderful things would look marvellous. She and Erasmus house-hunted.

But alas! their income was quite under three thousand dollars a year. They found—well, everybody knows what they found. Two small rooms and a kitchenette, and don't let us unpack a *thing*!

The chunk of Europe which they had bitten off went into a warehouse, at fifty dollars a month. And they sat in two small rooms and a kitchenette, and wondered why they'd done it.

Erasmus, of course, ought to get a job. This was what was written on the wall, and what they both pretended not to see. But it had been the strange, vague threat that the Statue of Liberty had always held over them: 'Thou shalt get a job!' Erasmus had the tickets, as they say. A scholastic career was still possible for him. He had taken his exams brilliantly at Yale, and had kept up his 'researches' all the time he had been in Europe.

But both he and Valerie shuddered. A scholastic career! The scholastic world! The *American* scholastic world! Shudder upon shudder! Give up their freedom, their full and beautiful life? Never! Never! Erasmus would be forty next birthday.

The 'things' remained in warehouse. Valerie went to look at them. It cost her a dollar an hour, and horrid pangs. The 'things', poor things, looked a bit shabby and wretched, in that warehouse.

However, New York was not all America. There was the great clean West. So the Melvilles went West, with Peter, but without the things. They tried living the simple life, in the mountains. But doing their own chores became almost a nightmare. 'Things' are all very well to look at, but it's awful handling them, even when they're beautiful. To be the slave of hideous things, to keep a stove going, cook meals, wash dishes, carry water and clean floors:

pure horror of sordid anti-life!

In the cabin on the mountains, Valerie dreamed of Florence, the lost apartment; and her Bologna cupboard and Louis-Quinze chairs, above all, her 'Chartres' curtains, stood in New York and costing fifty dollars a month.

A millionaire friend came to the rescue, offering them a cottage on the Californian coast—California! Where the new soul is to be born in man. With joy the idealists moved a little farther west, catching at new vine-props of hope.

And finding them straws! The millionaire cottage was perfectly equipped. It was perhaps as labour-savingly perfect as is possible: electric heating, and cooking, a white-and-pearl-enamelled kitchen, nothing to make dirt except the human being himself. In an hour or so the idealists had got through their chores. They were 'free'—free to hear the great Pacific pounding the coast, and to feel a new soul filling their bodies.

Alas! the Pacific pounded the coast with hideous brutality, brute force itself! And the new soul, instead of sweetly stealing into their bodies, seemed only meanly to gnaw the old soul out of their bodies. To feel you are under the fist of the most blind and crunching brute force; to feel that your cherished idealist's soul is being gnawed out of you, and only irritation left in place of it; well, it isn't good enough.

After about nine months, the idealists departed from the Californian West. It had been a great experience, they were glad to have had it. But, in the long run, the West was not the place for them, and they knew it. No, the people who wanted new souls had better get them. They, Valerie and Erasmus Melville, would like to develop the old soul a little further. Anyway, they had not felt any influx of new soul on the Californian coast. On the contrary.

So, with a slight hole in their material capital, they returned to Massachusetts and paid a visit to Valerie's parents, taking the boy along. The grandparents welcomed the child–poor expatriated boy–and were rather cold to Valerie, but really cold to Erasmus. Valerie's mother definitely said to Valerie, one day, that Erasmus ought to take a job, so that Valerie could live decently. Valerie haughtily reminded her mother of the beautiful apartment on the Arno, and the 'wonderful' things in store in New York, and of the 'marvellous and satisfying life' she and Erasmus had led. Valerie's mother said that she didn't think her daughter's life looked so very marvellous at present: homeless, with a husband idle at the age of forty, a child to educate, and a dwindling capital: looked the reverse of marvellous to *her*: Let Erasmus take some post in one of the universities.

'What post? What university?' interrupted Valerie.

'That could be found, considering your father's connections and Erasmus's qualifications,' replied Valerie's mother. 'And you could get all your valuable things out of store, and have a really lovely home, which everybody in America would be proud to visit. As it is, your furniture is eating up your income, and you are living like rats in a hole, with nowhere to go to.'

This was very true. Valerie was beginning to pine for a home, with her 'things'. Of course, she could have sold her furniture for a substantial sum. But nothing would have induced her to. Whatever else passed away, religions, cultures, continents, and hopes. Valeries would *never* part from the 'things' which she and Erasmus had collected with such passion. To these she was nailed.

But she and Erasmus still would not give up that freedom, that full and beautiful life they had so believed in. Erasmus cursed America. He did not *want* to earn a living. He panted for Europe.

Leaving the boy in charge of Valerie's parents, the two idealists once more set off for Europe. In New York they paid two dollars and looked for a brief, bitter hour at their 'things'. They sailed 'student class'–that is, third. Their income now was less than two thousand dollars instead of three. And they made straight for Paris–cheap Paris.

They found Europe, this time, a complete failure. 'We have returned like dogs to our vomit,' said Erasmus; 'but the vomit has staled in the meantime.' He found he couldn't stand Europe. It irritated every nerve in his body. He hated America too. But America at least was a darn sight better than this miserable, dirt-eating continent; which was by no means cheap any more, either.

Valerie, with her heart on her things–she had really burned to get them out of that warehouse, where they had stood now for three years, eating up two thousand dollars wrote to her mother she thought Erasmus would come back if he could get some suitable work in America. Erasmus, in a state of frustration bordering on rage and insanity, just went round Itay in a poverty-stricken fashion, his coat -cuffs frayed hating everything with intensity. And when a post was found for him in Cleveland University, to teach French, Italian, and Spanish literature, his eyes grew more beady, and his long, queer face grew sharper and more rat-like with utter baffled fury. He was forty, and the job was upon him.

'I think you'd better accept dear. You don't care for Europe any longer. As you say, it's dead and finished. They offer us a house on the college, lot, and mother says there's room in it for all our things. I think we'd better cable "Accept".'

He glowered at her like a cornered rat. One almost expected to see rat's whiskers twitching at the sides of the sharp nose.

'Shall I send the cablegram?' she asked.

'Send it!' he blurted.

And she went out and sent it.

He was a changed man, quieter, much less irritable. A load was off him. He was inside the cage.

But when he looked at the furnaces of Cleveland, vast and like the greatest of black forests, with red and white-hot cascades of gushing metal, and tiny gnomes of men, and terrific noises, gigantic, he said to Valerie:

'Say what you like, Valerie, this is the biggest thing the modern world has to show.'

And when they were in their up-to-date little house on the college lot of Cleveland University, and that woebegone débris of Europe: Bologna cupboard, Venice book-shelves, Ravenna bishop's chair, Louis-Quinze side-tables, 'Chartres' curtains, Siena bronze lamps, all were arrayed, and all looked perfectly out of keeping, and therefore very impressive; and when the idealists had had a bunch of gaping, people in, and Erasmus had showed off in his best European manner, but still quite cordial and American; and Valerie had been most ladylike, but for all that, 'we prefer America'; then Erasmus said, looking at her with queer, sharp eyes of a rat:

'Europe's the mayonnaise all right, but America supplies the good old lobster—what?'

'Every time!' she said, with satisfaction.

And he peered at her. He was in the cage: but it was safe inside. And she, evidently, was her real self at last. She had got the goods. Yet round his nose was a queer, evil scholastic look of pure scepticism. But he liked lobster.

ODOUR OF CHRYSANTHEMUMS

I

THE small locomotive engine, Number 4, came clanking, stumbling down from Selston with seven full wagons. It appeared round the corner with loud threats of speed, but the colt that it startled from among the gorse, which still flickered indistinctly in the raw afternoon, out-distanced it at a canter. A woman, walking up the railway line to Underwood, drew back into the hedge, held her basket aside, and watched the footplate of the engine advancing. The trucks thumped heavily past, one by one, with slow inevitable movements, as she stood insignificantly trapped between the jolting black wagons and the hedge; then they curved away towards the coppice where the withered oak leaves dropped noiselessly, while the birds, pulling at the scarlet hips beside the track, made off into the dusk that had already crept into the spinney. In the open, the smoke from the engine sank and cleaved to the rough grass. The fields were dreary and forsaken, and in the marshy strip that led to the whimsey, a reedy pit-pond, the fowls had already abandoned their run among the alders, to roost in the tarred fowl-house. The pit-bank looked up beyond the pond, flames like red sores licking its ashy sides, in the afternoon's stagnant light. Just beyond rose the tapering chimneys and the clumsy black headstocks of Brinsley Colliery. The two wheels were spinning fast up against the sky, and the winding engine rapped out its little spasms. The miners were being turned up.

The engine whistled as it came into the wide bay of railway lines beside the colliery, where rows of trucks stood in harbour.

Miners, single, trailing and in groups, passed like shadows diverging home. At the edge of the ribbed level of sidings squat a low cottage, three steps down from the cinder track. A large bony vine clutched at the house, as if to claw down the tiled roof. Round the bricked yard grew a few wintry primroses. Beyond, the long garden sloped down to a bush-covered brook course. There were some twiggy apple trees, winter-crack trees, and ragged cabbages. Beside the path hung dishevelled pink chrysanthemums, like pink cloths hung on bushes. A woman came stooping out of the felt-covered fowlhouse, half-way down the garden. She closed and padlocked the door, then drew herself erect, having brushed some bits from her white apron.

She was a tall woman of imperious mien, handsome, with definite black eyebrows. The smooth black hair was parted exactly. For a few moments she stood steadily watching the miners as they passed along the railway; then she turned towards the brook course. Her face was calm and set, her mouth was closed with disillusionment. After a moment she called:

'John!' There was no answer. She waited, and then said distinctly:

'Where are you?'

'Here!' replied a child's sulky voice from among the bushes. The woman looked piercingly through the dusk.

'Are you at that brook?' she asked sternly.

For answer the child showed himself before the

raspberry-canes that rose like whips. He was a small, sturdy boy of five. He stood quite still, defiantly.

'Oh!' said the mother, conciliated. 'I thought you were down at that wet brook—and you remember what I told you—'

The boy did not move or answer.

'Come, come on in,' she said more gently, 'it's getting dark. There's your grandfather's engine coming down the line!'

The lad advanced slowly, with resentful, taciturn movement. He was dressed in trousers and waistcoat of cloth that was too thick and hard for the size of the garments. They were evidently cut down from a man's clothes.

As they went slowly towards the house he tore at the ragged wisps of chrysanthemums and dropped the petals in handfuls along the path.

'Don't do that—it does look nasty,' said his mother. He refrained, and she, suddenly pitiful, broke off a twig with three or four wan flowers and held them against her face. When mother and son reached the yard her hand hesitated, and instead of laying the flower aside, she pushed it in her apron-band. The mother and son stood at the foot of the three steps looking across the bay of lines at the passing home of the miners. The trundle of the small train was imminent. Suddenly the engine loomed past the house and came a stop opposite the gate.

The engine-driver, a short man with round grey beard, leaned out of the cab high above the woman.

'Have you got a cup of tea?' he said in a cheery, hearty fashion.

It was her father. She went in, saying she would mash. Directly, she returned.

'I didn't come to see you on Sunday,' began the little grey-bearded man.

'I didn't expect you,' said his daughter.

The engine-driver winced; then, reassuming his cheery, airy manner, he said:

'Oh, have you heard then? Well, and what do you think—'

'I think it is soon enough,' she replied.

At her brief censure the little man made an impatient gesture, and said coaxingly, yet with dangerous coldness:

'Well, what's a man to do? It's no sort of life for a man of my years, to sit at my own hearth like a stranger. And if I'm going to marry again it may as well be soon as late—what does it matter to anybody?'

The woman did not reply, but turned and went into the house. The man in the engine-cab stood assertive, till she returned with a cup of tea and a piece of bread and butter on a plate. She went up the steps and stood near the footplate of the hissing engine.

'You needn't 'a' brought me bread an' butter,' said her father. 'But a cup of tea'—he sipped appreciatively—'it's very nice.' He sipped for a moment or two, then: 'I hear as Walter's got another bout on,' he said.

'When hasn't he?' said the woman bitterly.

'I heerd tell of him in the "Lord Nelson" braggin' as he was going to spend that b——afore he went: half a sovereign that was.'

'When?' asked the woman.

'A' Sat'day night—I know that's true.'

'Very likely,' she laughed bitterly. 'He gives me twenty-three shillings.'

'Aye, it's a nice thing, when a man can do nothing with his money but make a beast of himself!' said the grey-whiskered man. The woman turned her head away. Her father swallowed the last of his tea and handed her the cup.

'Aye,' he sighed, wiping his mouth. 'It's a settler, it is—'

He put his hand on the lever. The little engine strained and groaned, and the train rumbled towards the crossing. The woman again looked across the metals. Darkness was settling over the spaces of the railway and trucks; the miners, in grey sombre groups, were still passing home. The winding engine pulsed hurriedly, with brief pauses. Elizabeth Bates looked at the dreary flow of men, then she went indoors. Her husband did not come.

The kitchen was small and full of firelight; red coals piled glowing up the chimney mouth. All the life of the room seemed in the white, warm hearth and the steel fender reflecting the red fire. The cloth was laid for tea; cups glinted in the shadows. At the back, where the lowest stairs protruded into the room, the boy sat struggling with a knife and a piece of white wood. He was almost hidden in the shadow. It was half-past four. They had but to await the father's coming to begin tea. As the mother watched her son's sullen little struggle with the wood, she saw herself in his silence and pertinacity; she saw the father in her child's indifference to all but himself. She seemed to be occupied by her husband. He had probably gone past his home, slunk past his own door, to drink before he came in, while his dinner spoiled and wasted in waiting. She glanced at the clock, then took the potatoes to strain them in the yard. The garden and fields beyond the brook were closed in uncertain darkness. When she rose with the saucepan, leaving the drain steaming into the night behind her, she saw the yellow lamps were lit along the high road that went up the hill away beyond the space of the railway lines and the field.

Then again she watched the men trooping home, fewer now and fewer.

Indoors the fire was sinking and the room was dark red. The woman put her saucepan on the hob, and set a batter-pudding near the mouth of the oven. Then she stood unmoving. Directly, gratefully, came quick young steps to the door. Something hung on the latch a moment, then a little girl entered and began pulling off her outdoor things, dragging a mass of curls, just ripening from gold to brown, over her eyes with her hat.

Her mother chid her for coming late from school, and said she would have to keep her at home the dark winter days.

'Why, mother, it's hardly a bit dark yet. The lamp's not lighted, and my father's not home.'

'No, he isn't. But it's a quarter to five! Did you see anything of him?'

The child became serious. She looked at her mother with large, wistful blue eyes.

'No, mother, I've never seen him. Why? Has he come up an' gone past, to Old Brinsley? He hasn't, mother, 'cos I never saw him.'

'He'd watch that,' said the mother bitterly, 'he'd take care as you didn't see him. But you may depend upon it, he's seated in the "Prince o' Wales". He wouldn't be this late.'

The girl looked at her mother piteously.

'Let's have our teas, mother, should we?' said she.

The mother called John to table. She opened the door once more and looked out across the darkness of the lines. All was deserted; she could not hear the winding-engines.

'Perhaps,' she said to herself, 'he's stopped to get some ripping done.'

They sat down to tea. John, at the end of the table near the door, was almost lost in the darkness. Their faces were hidden from each other. The girl crouched against the fender slowly moving a thick piece of bread before the fire. The lad, his face a dusky mark on the shadow, sat watching her who was transfigured in the red glow.

'I do think it's beautiful to look in the fire,' said the child.

'Do you?' said her mother. 'Why?'

'It's so red, and full of little caves—and it feels so nice, and you can fair smell it.'

'It'll want mending directly,' replied her mother, 'and then if your father comes he'll carry on and say there never is a fire when a man comes home sweating from the pit. A public-house is always warm enough.'

There was silence till the boy said complainingly: 'Make haste, our Annie.'

'Well, I am doing! I can't make the fire do it no faster, can I?'

'She keeps wafflin' it about so's to make 'er slow', grumbled the boy.

'Don't have such an evil imagination, child,' replied the mother.

Soon the room was busy in the darkness with the crisp sound of crunching. The mother ate very little. She drank her tea determinedly, and sat thinking. When she rose her anger was evident in the stern unbending of her head. She looked at the pudding in the fender, and broke out:

'It is a scandalous thing as a man can't even come home to his dinner! If it's crozzled up to a cinder I don't see why I should care. Past his very door he goes to get to a public-house, and here I sit with his dinner waiting for him—'

She went out. As she dropped piece after piece of coal on the red fire, the shadows fell on the walls, till the room was almost in total darkness.

'I canna see,' grumbled the invisible John. In spite of herself, the mother laughed.

'You know the way to your mouth,' she said. She set the dust-pan outside the door. When she came again like a shadow on the hearth, the lad repeated, complaining sulkily:

'I canna see.'

'Good gracious!' cried the mother irritably, 'you're as bad as your father if it's a bit dusk!'

Nevertheless, she took a paper spill from a sheaf on the mantelpiece and proceeded to light the lamp that hung from the ceiling in the middle of the room. As she reached up, her figure displayed itself just rounding with maternity.

'Oh, mother—!' exclaimed the girl.

'What?' said the woman, suspended in the act of putting the lamp-glass over the flame. The copper reflector shone handsomely on her, as she stood with uplifted arm, turning to face her daughter.

'You've got a flower in your apron!' said the child, in a little rapture at this unusual event.

'Goodness me!' exclaimed the woman, relieved. 'One would think the house was afire.' She replaced the glass and waited a moment before turning up the wick. A pale shadow was seen floating vaguely on the floor.

'Let me smell!' said the child, still rapturously, coming forward and putting her face to her mother's waist.

'Go along, silly!' said the mother, turning up the lamp. The light revealed their suspense so that the woman felt it almost unbearable. Annie was still bending at her waist. Irritably, the mother took the flowers out from her apron-band.

'Oh, mother—don't take them out!' Annie cried catching her hand and trying to replace the sprig.

'Such nonsense!' said the mother, turning away. The child put the pale chrysanthemums to her lips, murmuring:

'Don't they smell beautiful!'

Her mother gave a short laugh.

'No,' she said, 'not to me. It was chrysanthemums when I married him, and crysanthemums when you were born, and the first time they ever brought him home drunk, he'd got brown crysanthemums in his button-hole.'

She looked at the children. Their eyes and their parted lips were wondering. The mother sat rocking in silence for some time. Then she looked at the clock.

'Twenty minutes to six!' In a tone of fine bitter carelessness she continued: 'Eh, he'll not come now till they bring him There he'll stick! But he needn't come rolling in here in his pit-dirt, for *I* won't wash him. He can lie on the floor——Eh, what a fool I've been, what a ' fool! And this is what I came here for, to this dirty hole, rats and all, for him to slink past his very door. Twice last week—he's begun now——' She silenced herself, and rose to clear the table.

While for an hour or more the children played, subduedly intent, fertile of imagination, united in fear of the mother's wrath, and in dread of their father's home-coming, Mrs. Bates sat in her rocking-chair making a 'singlet' of thick cream-coloured flannel, which gave a dull wounded sound as she tore off the grey edge. She worked at her sewing with energy, listening to the children, and her anger wearied itself, lay down to rest, opening its eyes from time to time and steadily watching, its ears raised to listen. Sometimes even her anger quailed and shrank, and the mother suspended her sewing, tracing the footsteps that thudded along the sleepers outside; she would lift her head sharply to bid the children 'hush', but she recovered herself in time, and the footsteps went past the gate, and the children were not flung out of their playworld.

But at last Annie sighed, and gave in. She glanced at her wagon of slippers, and loathed the game. She turned plaintively to her mother.

'Mother!'—but she was inarticulate.

John crept out like a frog from under the sofa. His mother glanced up.

'Yes,' she said, 'just look at those shirt-sleeves!'

The boy held them out to survey them, saying nothing. Then somebody called in a hoarse voice away down the line, and suspense bristled in the room, till two people had gone by outside, talking.

'It is time for bed,' said the mother.

'My father hasn't come,' wailed Annie plaintively. But her mother was primed with courage.

'Never mind. They'll bring him when he does come—like a log.' She meant there would be no scene. 'And he may sleep on the floor till he wakes himself. I know he'll not go to work to-morrow after this!'

The children had their hands and faces wiped with a flannel. They were very quiet. When they had put on their nightdresses, they said their prayers, the boy mumbling. The mother looked down at them, at the brown silken bush of interwining curls in the nape of the girl's neck, at the little black head of the lad, and her heart burst with anger at their father, who caused all three such distress. The children hid their face in her skirts for comfort.

When Mrs. Bates came down, the room was strangely empty, with a tension of expectancy. She took up her sewing and stitched for some time without raising her head. Meantime her anger was tinged with fear.

II

The clock struck eight and she rose suddenly, dropping her sewing on her chair. She went to the stair-foot door, opened it, listening. Then she went out, locking the door behind her.

Something scuffled in the yard, and she started, though she knew it was only the rats with which the place was over-run. The night was very dark. In the great bay of railway lines, bulked with trucks, there was no trace of light, only away back she could see a few yellow lamps at the pit-top, and the red smear of the burning pit-bank on the night. She hurried along the edge of the track, then, crossing the converging lines, came to the stile by the white gates, whence she emerged on the road. Then the fear which had led her shrank. People were walking up to New Brinsley; she saw the lights in the houses; twenty yards farther on were the broad windows of the 'Prince of Wales', very warm and bright, and the loud voices of men could be heard distinctly. What a fool she had been to imagine that anything had happened to him! He was merely drinking over there at the 'Prince of Wales'. She faltered. She had never yet been to fetch him, and she never would go. So she continued her walk towards the long straggling line of houses, standing back on the highway. She entered a passage between the dwellings.

'Mr. Rigley?—Yes! Did you want him? No, he's not in at this minute.'

The raw-boned woman leaned forward from her dark scullery and peered at the other, upon whom fell a dim light through the blind of the kitchen window.

'Is it Mrs. Bates?' She asked in a tone tinged with respect.

'Yes. I wondered if your Master was at home. Mine hasn't come yet.'

' 'Asn't e! Oh, Jack's been 'ome an' 'ad 'is dinner an' gone out. 'E's just gone for 'alf an hour afore bed-time. Did you call at the "Prince of Wales"?'

'No—'

'No, you didn't like—! It's not very nice.' The other woman was indulgent. There was an awkward pause. 'Jack never said nothink about—about your Master,' she said.

'No!—I expect he's stuck in there!'

Elizabeth Bates said this bitterly, and with recklessness. She knew that the woman across the yard was standing at her door listening, but she did not care. As she turned:

'Stop a minute! I'll just go an' ask Jack if 'e knows anythink,' said Mrs. Rigley.

'Oh no—I wouldn't like to put—!'

'Yes, I will, if you'll just step inside an' see as th' childer doesn't come downstairs and set theirselves afire.'

Elizabeth Bates, murmuring a remonstrance, stepped inside. The other woman apologised for the state of the room.

The kitchen needed apology. There were little frocks and trousers and childish undergarments on the squab and on the floor, and a litter of playthings everywhere. On the black American cloth of the table were pieces of bread and cake, crusts, slops, and a teapot with cold tea.

'Eh, ours is just as bad,' said Elizabeth Bates, looking at the woman, not at the house. Mrs. Rigley put a shawl over her head and hurried out, saying:

'I shanna be a minute.'

The other sat, nothing with faint disapproval the general untidiness of the room. Then she fell to counting the shoes of various sizes scattered over the floor. There were twelve. She sighed and said to herself: 'No wonder!'– glancing at the litter. There came the scratching of two pairs of feet on the yard, and the Rigleys entered. Elizabeth Bates rose. Rigley was a big man, with very large bones. His head looked particularly bony. Across his temple was a blue scar, caused by a wound got in the pit, a wound in which the coal-dust remained blue like tattooing.

' 'Asna 'e come whoam yit?' asked the man, without any form of greeting, but with deference and sympathy. 'I couldn't say wheer he is–'e's non ower theer!'–he jerked his head to signify the 'Prince of Wales.'

' 'E's 'appen gone up to th' "Yew",' said Mrs. Rigley.

There was another pause. Rigley had evidently something to get off his mind:

'Ah left 'im finishin' a stint,' he began. 'Loose-all 'ad bin gone about ten minutes when we com'n away, an' I shouted: "Are ter comin', Walt?" an' 'e said: "Go on, Ah shanna be but a'ef a minnit," so we com'n ter th' bottom, me an' Bowers, thinkin' as 'e wor just behint, an' 'ud come up i' the' next bantle—'

He stood perplexed, as if answering a charge of deserting his mate. Elizabeth Bates, now again certain of disaster, hastened to reassure him:

'I expect 'e's gone up to th' "Yew Tree", as you say. It's not the first time. I've fretted myself into a fever before now. He'll come home when they carry him.'

'Ay, isn't it too bad!' deplored the other woman.

'I'll just step up to Dick's an' see if 'e *is* there,' offered the man, afraid of appearing alarmed, afraid of taking liberties.

'Oh, I wouldn't think of bothering you that far,' said Elizabeth Bates, with emphasis, but he knew she was glad of his offer.

As they stumbled up the entry, Elizabeth Bates heard Rigley's wife run across the yard and open her neighbour's door. At this, suddenly the blood in her body seemed to switch away from her heart.

'Mind!' warned Rigley. 'Ah've said many a time as Ah'd fill up them ruts in this entry, sumb'dy 'll be breakin' their legs yit.'

She recovered herself and walked quickly along with the miner.

'I don't like leaving the children in bed, and nobody in the house,' she said.

'No, you dunna!' he replied courteously. They were soon at the gate of the cottage.

'Well, I shanna be many minnits. Dunna you be frettin' now, 'e'll be all right,' said the butty.

'Thank you very much, Mr. Rigley,' she replied.

'You're welcome!' he stammered, moving away. 'I shanna be many minnits.'

The house was quiet. Elizabeth Bates took off her hat and shawl, and rolled back the rug. When she had finished, she sat down. It was a few minutes past nine. She was startled by the rapid chuff of the winding-engine at the pit, and the sharp whirr of the brakes on the rope as it descended. Again she felt the painful sweep of her blood, and she put her hand to her side, saying aloud: 'Good gracious!—it's only the nine o'clock deputy going down,' rebuking herself.

She sat still, listening. Half an hour of this, and she was wearied out.

'What am I working myself up like this for?' she said pitiably to herself. 'I'll only be doing myself some damage.'

She took out her sewing again.

At a quarter to ten there were footsteps. One person! She watched for the door to open. It was an elderly woman, in a black bonnet and a black woollen shawl—his mother. She was about sixty years old, pale, with blue eyes, and her face all wrinkled and lamentable. She shut the door and turned to her daughter-in-law peevishly.

'Eh, Lizzie, whatever shall we do, whatever shall we do!' she cried.

Elizabeth drew back a little, sharply.

'What is it, mother?' she said.

The elder woman seated herself on the sofa.

'I don't know, child, I can't tell you!'—she shook her head slowly. Elizabeth sat watching her, anxious and vexed.

'I don't know,' replied the grandmother, sighing very deeply. 'There's no end to my troubles, there isn't. The things I've gone through, I'm sure it's enough—!' She wept without wiping her eyes, the tears running.

'But, mother,' interrupted Elizabeth, 'what do you mean? What is it?'

The grandmother slowly wiped her eyes. The fountains of her tears were stopped by Elizabeth's directness. She wiped her eyes slowly.

'Poor child! Eh, you poor thing!' she moaned. 'I don't know what we're gong to do, I don't—and you as you are—it's a thing, it is indeed!'

Elizabeth waited.

'Is he dead?' she asked, and at the words her heart swung violently, though she felt a slight flush of shame at the ultimate extravagance of the question. Her words sufficiently frightened the old lady, almost brought her to herself.

'Don't say so, Elizabeth! We'll hope it's not as bad as that; no, may the Lord spare us that, Elizabeth. Jack Rigley came just as I was sittin' down to a glass afore going to bed, an' 'e said: " 'Appen you'll go down th' line, Mrs. Bates. Walt's had an accident. 'Appen you'll go an' sit wi' 'er till we can get him home." I hadn't time to ask him a word afore he was gone. An' I put my bonnet on an' come straight down, Lizzie. I thought to myself: "Eh, that poor blessed child, if anybody should come an' tell her of a sudden, there's no knowin' what'll 'appen to 'er." You mustn't let it upset you, Lizzie—or you know what to expect. How long is it, six months—or is it five, Lizzie? Ay!'—the old woman shook her head—'time slips on, it slips on! Ay!'

Elizabeth's thoughts were busy elsewhere. If he was killed—would she be able to manage on the little pension and what she would earn?—she counted up rapidly. If he was hurt—they wouldn't take him to the hospital—how tiresome he would be to nurse!—but perhaps she'd be able to get him away from the drink and his hateful ways. She would—while he was ill. The tears offered to come to her eyes at the picture. But what sentimental luxury was this she was beginning? She turned to consider the children. At any rate she was absolutely necessary for them. They were her business.

'Ay!' repeated the old woman, 'it seems but a week or two since he brought me his first wages. Ay—he was a good lad, Elizabeth, he was, in his way. I don't know why he got to be such a trouble, I don't. He was a happy lad at home, only full of spirits. But there's no mistake he's been a handful of trouble, he has! I hope the Lord'll spare him to mend his ways. I hope so, I hope so. You've had a sight o' trouble with him, Elizabeth, you have indeed. But he was a jolly enough lad wi' me, he was, I can assure you. I don't know how it is. . . .'

The old woman continued to muse aloud, a monotonous irritating sound, while Elizabeth thought concentratedly, startled once, when she heard the winding-engine chuff quickly, and the brakes skirr with a shriek. Then she heard the engine more slowly, and the brakes made no sound. The old woman did not notice. Elizabeth waited in suspense. The mother-in-law talked, with lapses into silence.

'But he wasn't your son, Lizzie, an' it makes a difference. Whatever he was, I remember him when he was little, an' I learned to understand him and to make allowances. You've got to make allowances for them—'

It was half-past ten, and the old woman was saying: 'But it's trouble from beginning to end; you're never too old for trouble, never too old for that—' when the gate banged back, and there were heavy feet on the steps.

'I'll go, Lizzie, let me go,' cried the old woman, rising. But Elizabeth was at the door. It was a man in pit-clothes.

'They're bringin' 'im, Missis,' he said. Elizabeth's heart halted a moment. Then it surged on again, almost suffocating her.

'Is he—is it bad?' she asked.

The man turned away, looking at the darkness:

'The doctor says 'e'd been dead hours. 'E saw 'im i' th' lamp-cabin.'

The old woman, who stood just behind Elizabeth, dropped into a chair, and folded her hands crying: 'Oh, my boy, my boy!'.

'Hush!' said Elizabeth, with a sharp twitch of a frown. 'Be still, mother, don't waken th' children: I wouldn't have them down for anything!'

The old woman moaned softly, rocking herself. The man was drawing away. Elizabeth took a step forward.

'How was it?' she asked.

'Well, I couldn't say for sure,' the man replied, very ill at ease. ' 'E wor finishin' a stint an' th' butties 'ad gone, an' a lot o' stuff come down atop 'n 'im.'

'And crushed him?' cried the widow, with a shudder.

'No,' said the man, 'it fell at th' back of 'im. 'E wor under th' face, an' it niver touched 'im. It shut 'im in. It seems 'e wor smothered.'

Elizabeth shrank back. She heard the old woman behind her cry:

'What?—what did 'e say it was?'

The man replied, more loudly: ' 'E wor smothered!'

Then the old woman wailed aloud, and this relieved Elizabeth.

'Oh, mother,' she said, putting her hand on the old woman, 'don't waken th' children, don't waken the' children.'

She wept a little, unknowing, while the old mother rocked herself and moaned. Elizabeth remembered that they were bringing him home, and she must be ready. 'They'll lay him in the parlour,' she said to herself, standing a moment pale and perplexed.

Then she lighted a candle and went into the tiny room. The air was cold and damp, but she could not make a fire, there was no fireplace. She set down the candle and looked round. The candlelight glittered on the lustre-glasses, on two vases that held some of the pink crysanthemums, and on the dark mahogany. There was a cold, deathly smell of crysanthemums in the room. Elizabeth stood looking at the flowers. She turned away, and calculated whether there would be room to lay him on the floor, between the couch and the chiffonier. She pushed the chairs aside. There would be room to lay him down and to step round him. Then she fetched the old red tablecloth, and another old cloth, spreading them down to save her bit of carpet. She shivered on leaving the parlour; so, from the dresser drawer she took a clean shirt and put it at the fire to air. All the time her mother-in-law was rocking herself in the chair and moaning.

'You'll have to move from there, mother,' said Elizabeth. 'They'll be bringing him in. Come in the rocker.'

The old mother rose mechanically, and seated herself by the fire, continuing to lament. Elizabeth went into the pantry for another candle, and there, in the little penthouse under naked tiles, she heard them coming. She stood still in the pantry doorway, listening. She heard them pass the end of the house, and come awkwardly down the three steps, a jumble of shuffling footsteps and muttering voices. The old woman was silent. The men were in the yard.

Then Elizabeth heard Matthews, the manager of the pit, say: 'You go in first, Jim. Mind!'

The door came open, and the two women saw a collier backing into the room, holding one end of a stretcher, on which they could see the nailed pit-boots of the dead man. The two carriers halted, the man at the head stooping to the lintel of the door.

'Wheer will you have him?' asked the manager, a short,

white-bearded man.

Elizabeth roused herself and came from the pantry carrying the unlighted candle.

'In the parlour,' she said.

'In there, Jim!' pointed the manager, and the carriers backed round into the tiny room. The coat with which they had covered the body fell off as they awkwardly turned through the two doorways, and the women saw their man, naked to the waist, lying stripped for work. The old woman began to moan in a low voice of horror.

'Lay th' stretcher at th' side,' snapped the manager, 'an' put 'im on th' cloths. Mind now, mind! Look you now—!'

One of the men had knocked off a vase of chrysanthemums. He stared awkwardly, then they set down the stretcher. Elizabeth did not look at her husband. As soon as she could get in the room, she went and picked up the broken vase and the flowers.

'Wait a minute!' she said.

The three men waited in silence while she mopped up the water with a duster.

'Eh, what a job, what a job, to be sure!' the manager was saying, rubbing his brow with trouble and perplexity. 'Never knew such a thing in my life, never! He'd no businews to ha' been left. I never knew such a thing in my life! Fell over him clean as a whistle, an' shut him in. Not four foot of space, there wasn't—yet it scarce bruised him.'

He looked down at the dead man, lying prone, half naked, all grimed with coal-dust.

' " 'Sphyxiated," the doctor said. It *is* the most terrible job I've ever known. Seems as if it was done o' purpose. Clean over him, an' shut 'im in like mouse-trap'—he made a sharp, descending gesture with his hand.

The colliers standing by jerked aside their heads in hopeless comment.

The horror of the thing bristled upon them all.

Then they heard the girl's voice upstairs calling shrilly: 'Mother, mother—who is it? Mother, who is it?'

Elizabeth hurried to the foot of the stairs and opened the door:

'Go to sleep!' She commanded sharply. 'What are you shouting about? Go to sleep at once—there's nothing—'

Then she began to mount the stairs. They could hear her on the boards, and on the plaster floor of the little bedroom. They could hear her distinctly:

'What's the matter now?—what's the matter with you, silly thing?'—her voice was much agitated, with an unreal gentleness.

'I thought it was some men come,' said the plaintive voice of the child. 'Has he come?'

'Yes, they've brought him. There's nothing to make a fuss about. Go to sleep now, like a good child.'

They could hear her voice in the bedroom, they waited whilst she covered the children under the bedclothes.

'Is he drunk?' asked the girl, timidly, faintly.

'No! No—he's not! He's asleep.'

'Is he asleep downstairs?'

'Yes—and don't make a noise.'

There was silence for a moment, then the men heard the frightened child again:

'What's that noise?'

'It's nothing, I tell you, what are you bothering for?'

The noise was the grandmother moaning. She was oblivious of everything, sitting on her chair rocking and moaning. The manager put his hand on her arm and bade her 'Sh—sh!!'

The old woman opened her eyes and looked at him. She was shocked by this interruption, and seemed to wonder.

'What time is it?' the plaintive thin voice of the child, sinking back unhappily into sleep, asked this last question.

'Ten o'clock,' answered the mother more softly. Then she must have bent down and kissed the children.

Matthews beckoned to the men to come away. They put on their caps and took up the stretcher. Stepping over the body, they tiptoed out of the house. None of them spoke till they were far from the wakeful children.

When Elizabeth came down she found her mother alone on the parlour floor, leaning over the dead man, the tears dropping on him.

'We must lay him out,' the wife said. She put on the kettle, then returning knelt at the feet, and began to unfasten the knotted leather laces. The room was clammy and dim with only one candle, so that she had to bend her face almost to the floor. At last she got off the heavy boots and put them away.

'You must help me now,' she whispered to the old woman. Together they stripped the man.

When they arose, saw him lying in the naïve dignity of death, the women stood arrested in fear and respect. For a few moments they remained still, looking down, the old mother whimpering. Elizabeth felt countermanded. She saw him, how utterly inviolable he lay in himself. She had nothing to do with him. She could not accept it. Stooping, she laid her hand on him, in claim. He was still warm for the mine was hot where he had died. His mother had his face between her hands, and was murmuring incoherently. The old tears fell in succession as drops from wet leaves; the mother was not weeping, merely her tears flowed. Elizabeth embraced the body of her husband, with cheek and lips. She seemed to be listening, inquiring, trying to get some connection. But she could not. She was driven away. He was impregnable.

She rose, went into the kitchen, where she poured warm water into a bowl, brought soap and flannel and a soft towel.

'I must wash him,' she said.

Then the old mother rose stiffly, and watched Elizabeth as she carefully washed his face, carefully brushing the big blond moustache from his mouth with the flannel. She was afraid with a bottomless fear, so she ministered to him. The old woman, jealous, said:

'Let me wipe him!'—and she knelt on the other side drying slowly as Elizabeth washed, her big black bonnet sometimes brushing the dark head of her daughter-in-law. They worked thus in silence for a long time. They never forgot it was death, and the touch of the man's dead body gave them strange emotions, different in each of the women; a great dread possessed them both, the mother felt the lie was given to her womb, she was denied; the wife felt the utter isolation of the human soul, the child within her was a weight apart from her.

At last it was finished. He was a man of handsome body, and his face showed no traces of drink. He was blond, full-fleshed, with fine limbs. But he was dead.

'Bless him,' whispered his mother, looking always at his face, and speaking out of sheer terror. 'Dear lad—bless him!' She spoke in a faint, sibilant ecstasy of fear and mother love.

Elizabeth sank down again to the floor, and put her face against his neck, and trembled and shuddered. But she had to draw away again. He was dead, and her living flesh had no place against his. A great dread and weariness held her: she was so unavailing. Her life was gone like this.

'White as milk he is, clear as a twelve-month baby, bless him, the darling!' the old mother murmured to herself. 'Not a mark on him, clear and clean and white, beautiful as ever a child was made,' she murmured with pride. Elizabeth kept her face hidden.

'He went peaceful, Lizzie—peaceful as sleep. Isn't he beautiful, the lamb? Ay—he must ha' made his peace, Lizzie. 'Appen he made it all right, Lizzie, shut in there. He'd have time. He wouldn't look like this if he hadn't made his peace. The lamb, the dear lamb. Eh, but he had a hearty laugh. I loved to hear it. He had the heartiest laugh, Lizzie, as a lad—'

Elizabeth looked up. The man's mouth was fallen back, slightly open under the cover of the moustache. The eyes, half shut, did not show glazed in the obscurity. Life with its smoky burning gone from him, had left him apart and utterly alien to her. And she knew what a stranger he was to her. In her womb was ice of fear, because of this separate stranger with whom she had been living as one flesh. Was this what it all meant—utter, intact separateness, obscured by heat of living? In dread she turned her face away. The fact was too deadly. There had been nothing between them, and yet they had come together, exchanging their nakedness repeatedly. Each time he had taken her, they had been two isolated beings, far apart as now. He was no more responsible than she. The child was like ice in her womb. For as she looked at the dead man, her mind, cold and detached, said clearly: 'Who am I? What have I been doing? I have been fighting a husband who did not exist.

He existed all the time. What wrong have I done? What was that I have been living with? There lies the reality, this man.' And her soul died in her for fear; she knew she had never seen him, and he had never seen her, they had met in the dark and had fought in the dark, not knowing whom they met not whom they fought. And now she saw, and turned silent in seeing. For she had been wrong. She had said he was something he was not; she had felt familiar with him. Whereas he was apart all the while, living as she never lived, feeling as she never felt.

In fear and shame she looked at his naked body, that she had known falsely. And he was the father of her children. Her soul was torn from her body and stood apart. She looked at his naked body and was ashamed, as if she had denied it. After all, it was itself. It seemed awful to her. She looked at his face, and she turned her own face to the wall. For his look was other than hers, his way was not her way. She had denied him what he was—she saw it now. She had refused his as himself. And this had been her life, and his life. She was grateful to death, which restored the truth. And she knew she was not dead.

And all the while her heart was bursting with grief and pity for him. What had he suffered? What stretch of horror for this helpless man! She was rigid with agony. She had not been able to help him. He had been cruelly injured, this naked man, this other being, and she could make no reparation. There were the children—but the children belonged to life. This dead man had nothing to do with them. He and she were only channels through which life had flowed to issue in the children. She was a mother—but how awful she knew it now to have been a wife. And he, dead now, how awful he must have felt it to be a husband. She felt that in the next world he would be a stranger to her. If they met, there in the beyond, they would only be ashamed of what had been before. The children had come, for some mysterious reason, out of both of them. But the children did not unite them. Now he was dead, she knew how eternally he was apart from her, how eternally he had nothing more to do with her. She saw this episode of her life closed. They had denied each other in life. Now he had withdrawn. An anguish came over her. It was finished then; it had become hopeless between them long before he died. Yet he had been her husband. But how little!

'Have you got his shirt, 'Elizabeth?'

Elizabeth turned without answering, though she strove to weep and behave as her mother-in-law expected. But she could not, she was silenced. She went into the kitchen and returned with the garment.

'It is aired,' she said, grasping the cotton shirt here and there to try. She was almost ashamed to handle him; what right had she or anyone to lay hands on him; but her touch was humble on his body. It was hard work to cloth him. He was so heavy and inert. A terrible dread gripped her all the while: that he could be so heavy and utterly inert, unresponsive, apart. The horror of the distance between them was almost too much for her—it was so infinite a gap she must look across.

At last it was finished. They covered him with a sheet and left him lying, with his face bound. And she fastened the door of the little parlour, lest the children should see what was lying there. Then, with peace sunk heavy on her heart, she went about making tidy the kitchen. She knew she submitted to life, which was her immediate master. But from death, her ultimate master, she winced with fear and shame.

SECOND BEST

'OH, I'm tired!' Frances exclaimed petulantly, and in the same instant she dropped down on the turf, near the hedge-bottom. Anne stood a moment surprised, then, accustomed to the vagaries of her beloved Frances, said:

'Well, and aren't you always likely to be tired, after travelling that blessed long way from Liverpool yesterday?' and she plumped down beside her sister. Anne was a wise young body of fourteen, very buxom, brimming with common sense. Frances was much older, about twenty-three, and whimsical, spasmodic. She was the beauty and the clever child of the family. She plucked the goose-grass buttons from her dress in a nervous, desperate fashion. Her beautiful profile, looped above with black hair, warm with the dusky-and-scarlet complexion of a pear, was calm as a mask, her thin brown hand plucked nervously.

'It's not the journey,' she said, objecting to Anne's obtuseness. Anne looked inquiringly at her darling. The young girl, in her self-confident, practical way, proceeded to reckon up this whimsical creature. But suddenly she found herself full in the eyes of Frances; felt two dark, hectic eyes flaring challenge at her, and she shrank away. Frances was peculiar for these great, exposed looks, which disconcerted people by their violence and their suddenness.

'What's a matter, poor old duck?' asked Anne, as she folded the slight, wilful form of her sister in her arms. Frances laughed shakily, and nestled down for comfort on the budding breasts of the strong girl.

'Oh, I'm only a bit tired,' she murmured, on the point of tears.

'Well, of course you are, what do you expect?' soothed Anne. It was a joke to Frances that Anne should play elder, almost mother to her. But then, Anne was in her unvexed teens; men were like big dogs to her; while Frances, at twenty-three, suffered a good deal.

The country was intensely morning-still. On the common everything shone beside its shadow, and the hillside gave off heat in silence. The brown turf seemed in a low state of combustion, the leaves of the oaks were scorched brown. Among the blackish foliage in the distance shone the small red and orange of the village.

The willows in the brook-course at the foot of the common suddenly shook with a dazzling effect like diamonds. It was a puff of wind. Anne resumed her normal position. She spread her knees, and put in her lap a handful of hazel nuts, whity-green leafy things, whose one cheek was tanned between brown and pink. These she began to crack and eat. Frances, with bowed head, mused bitterly.

'Eh, you know Tom Smedley?' began the young girl, as she pulled a tight kernel out of its shell.

'I suppose so,' replied Frances sarcastically.

'Well, he gave me a wild rabbit what he'd caught, to keep with my tame one—and it's living.'

'That's a good thing,' said Frances, very detached and ironic.

'Well, it *is*! He reckoned he'd take me to Ollerton Feast, but he never did. Look here, he took a servant from the rectory; I saw him.'

'So he ought,' said Frances.

'No, he oughtn't! And I told him so. And I told him I

should tell you—an' I have done.'

Click and snap went a nut between her teeth. She sorted out the kernel, and chewed complacently.

'It doesn't make much difference,' said Frances.

'Well, 'appen in doesn't; but I was mad with him all the same.'

'Why?'

'Because I was; he's no right to go with a servant.'

'He's a perfect right,' persisted Frances, very just and cold.

'No, he hasn't, when he'd said he'd take me.'

Frances burst into a laugh of amusement and relief.

'Oh no; I'd forgot that,' she said, adding, 'and what did he say when you promised to tell me?'

'He laughed and said: "She won't fret her fat over that."'

'And she won't,' sniffed Frances.

There was silence. The common, with its sere, blonde-headed thistles, its heaps of silent bramble, its brown-husked gorse in the glare of sunshine, seemed visionary. Across the brook began the immense pattern of agriculture, white chequering of barley stubble, brown squares of wheat, khaki patches of pasture, red stripes of fallow, with the woodland and the tiny village dark like ornaments, leading away to the distance, right to the hills, where the check-pattern grew smaller and smaller, till, in the blackish haze of heat, far off, only the tiny white squares of barley stubble showed distinct.

'Eh, I say, here's a rabbit-hole!' cried Anne suddenly. 'Should we watch if one come out? You won't have to fidget, you know.'

The two girls sat perfectly still. Frances watched certain object in her surroundings; they had a peculiar, unfriendly look about them; the weight of greenish elderberries on their purpling stalks; the twinkling of the yellowing crab-apple that clustered high up in the hedge, against the sky; the exhausted, limp leaves of the primroses lying flat in the hedge-bottom; all looked strange to her. Then her eyes caught a movement. A mole was moving silently over the warm, red soil, nosing, shuffling hither and thither, flat, and dark as a shadow, shifting about, and as suddenly brisk, and as silent, like a very ghost of *joie de vivre*. Frances started, from habit was about to call on Anne to kill the little pest. But, to-day her lethargy of unhappiness was too much for her. She watched the little brute paddling, snuffing, touching things to discover them, running in blindness, delighted to ecstasy by the sunlight and the hot, strange things that caressed its belly and its nose. She felt a keen pity for the little creature.

'Eh, our Fran, look there! It's a mole.'

Anne was on her feet, standing watching the dark, unconscious beast. Frances frowned with anxiety.

'It doesn't run off, does it?' said the young girl softly. Then she stealthily approached the creature. The mole paddled fumblingly away. In an instant Anne put her foot upon it, not too heavily. Frances could see the struggling, swimming movement of the little pink hands of the brute, the twisting and twitching of its pointed nose, as it wrestled under the sole of the boot.

'It *does* wriggle!' said the bonny girl, knitting her brows in a frown at the eerie sensation. Then she bent down to look at her trap. Frances could now see, beyond the edge of the boot-sole, the heaving of the velvet shoulders, the pitiful turning of the sightless face, the frantic rowing of the flat, pink hands.

'Kill the thing,' she said, turning away her face.

'Oh—I'm not,' laughed Anne, shrinking. 'You can, if you like.'

'I *don't* like,' said Frances, with quiet intensity.

After several dabbing attempts, Anne succeeded in picking up the little animal by the scruff of its neck. It threw back its head, flung its long blind snout from side to side, the mouth open in a peculiar oblong, with tiny pinkish teeth at the edge. The blind, frantic mouth gaped and writhed. The body, heavy and clumsy, hung scarcely moving.

'Isn't it a snappy little thing,' observed Anne, twisting to avoid the teeth.

'What are you going to do with it?' asked Frances sharply.

'It's got to be killed—look at the damage they do. I s'll take it home and let dadda or somebody kill it. I'm not going to let it go.'

She swaddled the creature clumsily in her pocket handkerchief and sat down beside her sister. There was an interval of silence, during which Anne combated the efforts of the mole.

'You've not had much to say about Jimmy this time. Did you see him often in Liverpool?' Anne asked suddenly.

'Once or twice,' replied Frances, giving no sign of how the question troubled her.

'And aren't you sweet on him any more, then?'

'I should think I'm not, seeing that he's engaged.'

'Engaged? Jimmy Barrass! Well, of all things! I never thought *he'd* get engaged.'

'Why not, he's as much right as anybody else?' snapped Frances.

Anne was fumbling with the mole.

' 'Appen so,' she said at length; 'but I never thought

Jimmy would, though.'

'Why not?' snapped Frances.

'*I* don't know—this blessed mole, it'll not keep still!—who's he got engaged to?'

'How should I know?'

'I thought you'd ask him; you've known him long enough. I s'd think he thought he'd get engaged now he's a Doctor of Chemistry.'

Frances laughed in spite of herself.

'What's that got to do with it?' she asked.

'I'm sure it's got a bit. He'll want to feel *somebody* now, so he's got engaged. Hey, stop it; go in!'

But at this juncture the mole almost succeeded in wriggling clear. It wrestled and twisted frantically, waved its pointed blind head, its mouth standing open like a little shaft, its big, wrinkled hands spread out.

'Go in with you!' urged Anne, poking the little creature with her forefinger, trying to get it back into the handkerchief. Suddenly the mouth turned like a spark on her finger.

'Oh!' she cried, 'he's bit me.'

She dropped him to the floor. Dazed, the blind creature fumbled round. Frances felt like shrieking. She expected him to dart away in a flash, like a mouse, and there he remained groping; she wanted to cry to him to be gone. Anne, in a sudden decision of wrath, caught up her sister's walking-cane. With one blow the mole was dead. Frances was startled and shocked. One moment the little wretch was fussing in the heat, and the next it lay like a little bag, inert and black—not a struggle, scarce a quiver.

'It is dead!' Frances said breathlessly. Anne took her finger from her mouth, looked at the tiny pin-pricks, and said:

'Yes, he is, and I'm glad. They're vicious little nuisances, moles are.'

With which her wrath vanished. She picked up the dead animal.

'Hasn't it got a beautiful skin,' she mused, stroking the fur with her forefinger, then with her cheek.

'Mind,' said Frances sharply. 'You'll have the blood on your skirt!'

One ruby drop of blood hung on the small snout, ready to fall. Anne shook it off on to some harebells. Frances suddenly became calm; in that moment, grown-up.

'I suppose they have to be killed,' she said, and a certain rather dreary indifference succeeded to her grief. The twinkling crab-apples, the glitter of brilliant wilows now seemed to her trifling, scarcely worth the notice. Something had died in her, so that things lost their poignancy. She was calm, indifference overlying her quiet sadness. Rising, she walked down to the brook course.

'Here, wait for me,' cried Anne, coming tumbling after.

Frances stood on the bridge, looking at the red mud trodden into pockets by the feet of cattle. There was not a drain of water felt, but everything smelled green, succulent. Why did she care so little for Anne, who was so fond of her! she asked herself. Why did she care so little for anyone? She did not know, but she felt a rather stubborn pride in her isolation and indifference.

They entered a field where stooks of barley stood in rows, the straight, blonde tresses of the corn streaming on to the ground. The stubble was bleached by the intense summer, so that the expanse glared white. The next field was sweet and soft with a second crop of seeds; thin, straggling clover whose little pink knobs rested prettily in the dark green. The scent was faint and sickly. The girls came up in single file, Frances leading.

Near the gate a young man was mowing with the scythe some fodder for the afternoon feed of the cattle. As he saw the girls he left off working and waited in an aimless kind of way. Frances was dressed in white muslin, and she walked with dignity, detached and forgetful. Her lack of agitation, her simple, unheeding advance made him nervous. She had loved the far-off Jimmy for five years, having had in return his half-measures. This man only affected her slightly.

Tom was of medium stature, energetic in build. His smooth, fairskinned face was burned red, not brown, by the sun, and this ruddiness enhanced his appearance of good humour and easiness. Being an year older than Frances, he would have courted her long ago had she been so inclined. As it was, he had gone his uneventful way amiably, chatting with many a girl, but remaining unattached, free of trouble for the most part. Only he knew he wanted a woman. He hitched his trousers just a trifle self-consciously as the girls approached. Frances was a rare, delicate kind of being, whom he realised with a queer and delicious stimulation in his veins. She gave him a slight sense of suffocation. Somehow, this morning she affected him more than usual. She was dressed in white. He, however, being matter-of-fact in his mind, did not realise. His feeling had never become conscious, purposive.

Frances knew what she was about. Tom was ready to love her as soon as she would show him. Now that she could not have Jimmy, she did not poignantly care. Still, she would have something. If she could not have the best— Jimmy, whom she knew to be something of a snob—she would have the second best, Tom. She advanced rather indifferently.

'You are back, then!' said Tom. She marked the touch of uncertainty in his voice.

'No,' she laughed, 'I'm still in Liverpool,' and the undertone of intimacy made him burn.

'This isn't you, then?' he asked.

Her heart leapt up in approval. She looked in his eyes, and for a second was with him.

'Why, what do you think?' she laughed.

He lifted his hat from his head with a distracted little gesture. She liked him, his quaint ways, his humour, his ignorance, and his slow masculinity.

'Here, look here, Tom Smedley,' broke in Anne.

'A moudiwarp! Did you find it dead?' he asked.

'No, it bit me,' said Anne.

'Oh, aye! An' that got your rag out, did it?'

No, it didn't! Anne scolded sharply. 'Such language!'

'Oh, what's up wi' it?'

'I can't bear you to talk broad.'

'Can't you?'

He glanced at Frances.

'It isn't nice,' Frances said. She did not care, really. The vulgar speech jarred on her as a rule; Jimmy was a gentleman. But Tom's manner of speech did not matter to her.

'I like you to talk *nicely*,' she added.

'Do you,' he replied, tilting his hat, stirred.

'And generally you *do*, you know,' she smiled.

'I s'll have to have a try,' he said, rather tensely gallant.

'What?' she asked brightly.

'To talk nice to you,' he said. Frances coloured furiously, bent her head for a moment, then laughed gaily, as if she liked this clumsy hint.

'Eh now, you mind what you're saying,' cried Anne, giving the young man an admonitory pat.

'You wouldn't have to give yon mole many knocks like that,' he teased, relieved to get on safe ground, rubbing his arm.

'No, indeed, it died in one blow,' said Frances, with a flippancy that was hateful to her.

'You're not so good at knockin' 'em?' he said, turning to her.

'I don't know, if I'm cross,' she said decisively.

'No?' he replied, with alert attentiveness.

'I could,' she added, harder, 'if it was necessary.'

He was slow to feel her difference.

'And don't you consider it *is* necessary?' he asked, with misgiving.

'W—ell—is it?' she said, looking at him steadily, coldly.

'I reckon it is,' he replied, looking away, but standing stubborn.

She laughed quickly.

'But it isn't necessary for *me*,' said, with slight contempt.

'Yes, that's quite true,' he answered.

She laughed in a shaky fashion.

'*I know it is*,' she said; and there was an awkward pause.

'Why, would you *like* me to kill mole then?' she asked tentatively, after a while.

'They do us a lot of damage,' he said, standing firm on his own ground, angered.

'Well, I'll see the next time I come across one,' she promised defiantly. Their eyes met, and she sank before him, her pride troubled. He felt uneasy and triumphant and baffled, as if fate had gripped him. She smiled as she departed.

'Well,' said Anne, as the sisters went through the wheat stubble; 'I don't know what you two's been jawing about, I'm sure.'

'Don't you?' laughed Frances significantly.

'No, I don't. But, at any rate, Tom Smedley's a good deal better to my thinking than Jimmy, so there—and nicer.'

'Perhaps he is,' said Frances coldly.

And the next day, after a secret, persistent hunt, she found another mole playing in the heat. She killed it, and in the evening, when Tom came to the gate to smoke his pipe after supper, she took him the dead creature.

'Here you are then!' she said.

'Did you catch it?' he replied, taking the velvet corpse into his fingers and examining it minutely. This was to hide his trepidation.

'Did you think I couldn't?' she asked, her face very near his.

'Nay, I didn't know.'

She laughed in his face, a strange little laugh that caught her breath, all agitation, and tears, and recklessness of desire. He looked frightened and upset. She put her hand to his arm.

'Shall you go out wi' me?' he asked, in a difficult, troubled tone.

She turned her face away, with a shaky laugh. The blood came up in him, strong, overmastering. He resisted it. But it drove him down, and he was carried away. Seeing the winsome, frail nape of her neck, fierce love came upon him for her, and tenderness.

'We s'll 'ave to tell your mother,' he said. And he stood, suffering, resisting his passion for her.

'Yes,' she replied, in a dead voice. But there was a thrill of pleasure in this death.

SAMSON AND DELILAH

A MAN got down from the mother-omnibus that runs from Penzance to St. Just-in-Penwith, and turned northwards, uphill towards the Pole-star. It was only half-past six, but already the stars were out, a cold little wind was blowing from the sea, and the crystalline, three-pulse flash of the lighthouse below the cliffs beat rhythmically in the first darkness.

The man was alone. He went his way unhesitating, but looked from side to side with cautious curiosity. Tall, ruined power-houses of tinmines loomed in the darkness from time to time, like remnants of some by-gone civilisation. The lights of many miners' cottages scattered on the hilly darkness twinkled desolate in their disorder, yet twinkled with the lonely homeliness of the Celtic night.

He tramped steadily on, always watchful with curiosity. He was a tall, well-built man, apparently in the prime of life. His shoulders were square and rather stiff, he leaned forward a little as he went, from the hips, like a man who must stoop to lower his height. But he did not stoop his shoulders; he bent his straight back from the hips.

Now and again short, stumpy, thick-legged figures of Cornish miners passed him, and he invariably gave them good-night, as if to insist that he was on his own ground. He spoke with the West Cornish intonation. And as he went along the dreary road, looking now at the lights of the dwellings on land, now at the lights away to sea, vessels veering round in sight of the Longships Lighthouse, the whole of the Atlantic Ocean in darkness and space between him and America, he seemed a little excited and pleased with himself, watchful, thrilled, veering along in a sense of mastery and of power in conflict.

The houses began to close on the road, he was entering the straggling, formless, desolate mining village, that he knew of old. On the left was a little space set back from the road, and cosy lights of an inn. There it was. He peered up at the sign: 'The Tinners' Rest'. But he could not make out the name of the proprietor. He listened. There was excited talking and laughing, a woman's voice laughing shrilly among the men's.

Stooping a little, he entered the warmly-lit bar. The lamp was burning, a buxom woman rose from the white-scrubbed deal table where the black and white and red cards were scattered, and several men, miners, lifted their faces from the game.

The stranger went to the counter, averting his face. His cap was pulled down over his brow.

'Good evening!' said the landlady, in her rather ingratiating voice.

'Good evening. A glass of ale.'

'A glass of ale,' repeated the landlady suavely. 'Cold night—but bright.'

'Yes,' the man assented, laconically. Then he added, when nobody expected him to say any more: 'Seasonable weather.'

'Quite seasonable, quite,' said the landlady. 'Thank you.'

The man lifted his glass straight to his lips, and emptied it. He put it down again on the zinc counter with a click.

'Let's have another,' he said.

The woman drew the beer, and the man went away

with his glass to the second table, near the fire. The woman, after a moment's hesitation, took her seat again at the table with the card-players. She had noticed the man: a big fine fellow, well dressed, a stranger.

But he spoke with that Cornish–Yankee accent she accepted as the natural twang among the miners.

The stranger put his foot on the fender and looked into the fire. He was handsome, well coloured, with well-drawn Cornish eyebrows, and the usual dark, bright, mindless Cornish eyes. He seemed abstracted in thought. Then he watched the card-party.

The woman was buxom and healthy, with dark hair and small, quick brown eyes. She was bursting with life and vigour, the energy she threw into the game of cards excited all the men, they shouted, and laughed, and the woman held her breast, shrieking with laughter.

'Oh, my, it'll be the death o' me,' she panted. 'Now, come on, Mr. Trevorrow, play fair. Play fair, I say, or I s'll put the cards down.'

'Play fair! Why, who's played unfair?' ejaculated Mr. Trevorrow. 'Do you mean t'accuse me, as I haven't played fair, Mrs. Nankervis?'

'I do. I say it, and I mean it. Haven't you got the Queen of Spades? Now, come on, no dodging round me. *I* know you've got that Queen, as well as I know my name's Alice.'

'Well—if your name's Alice, you'll have to have it—'

'Ay, now—what did I say? Did ever you see such a man? My word, but your missus must be easy took in, by the looks of things.'

And off she went into peals of laughter. She was interrupted by the entrance of four men in khaki, a short, stumpy sergeant of middle age, a young corporal, and two young privates. The woman leaned back in her chair.

'Oh, my!' she cried. 'If there isn't the boys back: looking perished, I believe—'

'Perished, Ma!' exclaimed the sergeant. 'Not yet.'

'Near enough,' said a young private uncouthly.

The woman got up.

'I'm sure you are, my dears. You'll be wanting your suppers, I'll be bound.'

'We could do with 'em.'

'Let's have a wet first,' said the sergeant.

The woman bustled about getting the drinks. The soldiers moved to the fire, spreading out their hands.

'Have your suppers in here, will you?' she said. 'Or in the kitchen?'

'Let's have it here,' said the sergeant. 'More cosier—*if* you don't mind.'

'You shall have it where you like, boys, where you like.'

She disappeared. In a minute a girl of about sixteen came in. She was tall and fresh, with dark, young, expressionless eyes, and welldrawn brows, and the immature softness and mindlessness of the sensous Celtic type.

'Ho, Maryann! Evenin,' Maryann! How's Maryann, now?' came the multiple greeting.

She replied to everybody in a soft voice, a strange, soft aplomb that was very attractive. And she moved round with rather mechanical, attractive movements, as if her thoughts were elsewhere. But she had always this dim far-awayness in her bearing: a sort of modesty. The strange man by the fire watched her curiously. There was an alert, inquisitive, mindless curiosity on his well-coloured face.

'I'll have a bit of supper with you, if I might,' he said.

She looked at him with her clear, unreasoning eyes, just like the eyes of some non-human creature.

'I'll ask mother,' she said. Her voice was soft-breathing, gently sing-song.

When she came in again:

'Yes,' she said, almost whispering. 'What will you have?'

'What have you got?' he said, looking up into her face.

'There's cold meat—'

'That's for me, then.'

The stranger sat at the end of the table, and ate with the tired, quiet soldiers. Now the landlady was interested in him. Her brow was knit rather tense, there was a look of panic in her large, healthy face, but her small brown eyes were fixed most dangerously. She was a big woman, but her eyes were small and tense. She drew near the stranger. She wore a rather loud-patterned flannelette blouse and a dark skirt.

'What will you have to drink with your supper?' she asked, and there was a new, dangerous note in her voice.

He moved uneasily.

'Oh, I'll go on with ale.'

She drew him another glass. Then she sat down on the bench at the table with him and the soldiers, and fixed him with her attention.

'You've come from St. Just, have you?' she said.

He looked at her with those clear, dark, inscrutable Cornish eyes, and answered at length:

'No, from Penzance.'

'Penzance!—but you're not thinking of going back there to-night?'

'No—no.'

He still looked at her with those wide, clear eyes that

seemed like very bright agate. Her anger began to rise. It was seen on her brow. Yet her voice was still suave and deprecating.

'I *thought* not—but you're not living in these parts, are you?'

'No—no, I'm not living here.' He was always slow in answering, as if something intervened between him and any outside question.

'Oh, I see,' she said. 'You've got relations down here.'

Again he looked straight into her eyes, as if looking her into silence.

'Yes,' he said.

He did not say any more. She rose with a flounce. The anger was tight on her brow. There was no more laughing and card-playing that evening, though she kept up her motherly, suave, good-humoured way with the men. But they knew her, they were all afraid of her.

The supper was finished, the table cleared, the stranger did not go. Two of the young soldiers went off to bed, with their cheery:

'Good-night, Ma. Good-night, Maryann.'

The stranger talked a little to the sergeant about the war, which was in its first year, about the new army, a fragment of which was quartered in this district, about America.

The landlady darted looks at him from her small eyes, minute by minute the electric storm welled in her bosom, as still he did not go. She was quivering with suppressed, violent passion, something frightening and abnormal. She could not sit still for a moment. Her heavy form seemed to flash with sudden, involuntary movements as the minutes passed by, and still he sat there, and the tension on her heart grew unbearable. She watched the hands of the clock move on. Three of the soldiers had gone to bed, only the crop-headed, terrier-like old sergeant remained.

The landlady sat behind the bar fidgeting spasmodically with the newspaper. She looked again at the clock. At last it was five minutes to ten.

'Gentlemen—the enemy!' she said in her diminished, furious voice. 'Time, please. Time, my dears. And good-night, all!'

The men began to drop out, with a brief good-night. It was a minute to ten. The landlady rose.

'Come,' she said. 'I'm shutting the door.'

The last of the miners passed out. She stood, stout and menacing, holding the door. Still the stranger sat on by the fire, his black overcoat opened, smoking.

'We're closed now, sir,' came the perilous, narrrowed voice of the landlady.

The little, dog-like, hard-headed sergeant touched the arm of the stranger.

'Closing time,' he said.

The stranger turned round in his seat, and his quick-moving, dark, jewel-like eyes went from the sergeant to the landlady.

'I'm stopping here to-night,' he said, in his laconic Cornish–Yankee accent.

The landlady seemed to tower. Her eyes lifted strangely, frightening.

'Oh, indeed!' she cried. 'Oh, indeed! And whose orders are those, may I ask?'

He looked at her again.

'My orders,' he said.

Involuntarily she shut the door, and advanced like a great, dangerous bird. Her voice rose, there was a touch of hoarseness in it.

'And what might *your* orders be, if you please?' she cried. 'Who might *you* be, to give orders, in the house?'

He sat still, watching her.

'You know who I am,' he said. 'At least, I know who you are.'

'Oh, do you? Oh, do you? And who am *I* then, if you'll be so good as to tell me?'

He stared at her with his bright, dark eyes.

'You're my Missis, you are,' he said. 'And you know it, as well as I do.'

She started as if something had exploded in her.

Her eyes lifted and flared madly.

'*Do* I know it, indeed!' she cried. 'I know no such thing! I know no such thing! Do you think a man's going to walk into this bar, and tell me off-hand I'm his Missis, and I'm going to believe him? I say to you, whoever you may be, you're mistaken. I know myself for no Missis of yours, and I'll thank you to go out of this house, this minute, before I get those that will put you out.'

The man rose to his feet, stretching his head towards her a little. He was a handsomely built Cornishman in the prime of life.

'What you say, eh? You don't know me?' he said in his sing-song voice, emotionless, but rather smothered and pressing: it reminded one of the girl's. 'I should know you anywhere, you see. I should! I shouldn't have to look twice to know you, you see. You see, now, don't you?'

The woman was baffled.

'So you may say,' she replied, staccato. 'So you may say. That's easy enough. My name's known, and respected, by most people for ten miles round. But I don't know *you*.'

Her voice ran to sarcasm. 'I can't say I know *you*.

You're a *perfect* stranger to me, and I don't believe I've ever set eyes on you before tonight.'

Her voice was very flexible and sarcastic.

'Yes, you have,' replied the man, in his reasonable way. 'Yes, you have. Your name's my name, and that girl Maryann is my girl; she's my daughter. You're my Missis right enough. As sure as I'm Willie Nankervis.'

He spoke as if it were an accepted fact. His face was handsome, with a strange, watchful alertness and a fundamental fixity of intention that maddened her.

'You villain!' she cried. 'You villain, to come to this house and dare to speak to me. You villain, you downright rascal!'

He looked at her.

'Ay,' he said, unmoved. 'All that.' He was uneasy before her. Only he was not afraid of her. There was something impenetrable about him, like his eyes, which were as bright as agate.

She towered, and drew near to him menacingly.

'You're going out of this house, aren't you?' She stamped her foot in sudden madness. '*This minute!*'

He watched her. He knew she wanted to strike him.

'No,' he said, with suppressed emphasis. 'I've told you, I'm stopping here.'

He was afraid of her personality, but it did not alter him. She wavered. Her small, tawny-brown eyes concentrated in a point of vivid, sightless fury, like a tiger's. The man was wincing, but he stood his ground. Then she bethought herself. She would gather her forces.

'We'll see whether you're stopping here,' she said. And she turned, with a curious, frightening lifting of her eyes, and surged out of the room. The man, listening, heard her go upstairs, heard her tapping at a bedroom door, heard her saying: 'Do you mind coming down a minute, boys? I want you. I'm in trouble.'

The man in the bar took off his cap and his black overcoat, and threw them on the seat behind him. His black hair was short and touched with grey at the temples. He wore a well-cut, well-fitting suit of dark grey, American in style, and a turn-down collar. He looked well-to-do, a fine, solid figure of a man. The rather rigid look of the shoulders came from his having had his collar-bone twice broken in the mines.

The little terrier of a sergeant, in dirty khaki, looked at him furtively.

'She's your Missis?' he asked, jerking his head in the direction of the departed woman.

'Yes, she is,' barked the man. 'She's that, sure enough.'

'Not seen her for a long time, haven't ye?'

'Sixteen years come March month.'

'Hm!'

And the sergeant laconically resumed his smoking.

The landlady was coming back, followed by the three young soldiers, who entered rather sheepishly, in trousers and shirt and stocking-feet. The woman stood histrionically at the end of the bar, and exclaimed:

'That man refuses to leave the house, claims he's stopping the night here. You know very well I have no bed, don't you? And this house doesn't accommodate travellers. Yet he's going to stop in spite of all! But not while I've a drop of blood in my body, that I declare with my dying breath. And not if you men are worth the name of men, and will help a woman as has no one to help her.'

Her eyes sparkled, her face was flushed pink. She was drawn up like an Amazon.

The young soldiers looked on in delight, the sergeant

smoked, looked at the man, they looked at the sergeant, one of them looked down and fastened his braces on the second button.

'What say, sergeant?' asked one whose face twinkled for a little devilment.

'Man says he's husband to Mrs. Nankervis,' said the sergeant.

'He's no husband of mine. I declare I never set eyes on him before this night. it's a dirty trick, nothing else, it's a dirty trick.'

'Why, you're a liar, saying you never set eyes on me before,' barked the man near the hearth. 'You're married to me, and that girl Maryann you had by me—well enough you know it.'

The young soldiers looked on in delight, the sergeant smoked imperturbed.

'Yes,' sang the landlady, slowly shaking her head in supreme sarcasm, 'it sounds very pretty, doesn't it? But you see we don't believe a word of it, and *how* are you going to prove it?' she smiled nastily.

The man watched in silence for a moment, then he said:

'It wants no proof.'

'Oh, yes, but it does! Oh, yes, but it does, sir, it wants a lot of proving!' sang the lady's sarcasm. 'We're not such gulls as all that, to swallow your words whole.'

But he stood unmoved near the fire. She stood with one hand resting on the zinc-covered bar, the sergeant sat with legs crossed, smoking, on the seat half-way between them, the three young soldiers in their shirts and braces stood wavering in the gloom behind the bar. There was silence.

'Do you know anything of the whereabouts of your

husband, Mrs. Nankervis? Is he still living?' asked the sergeant, in his judicious fashion.

Suddenly the landlady began to cry, great scalding tears, that left the young men aghast.

'I know nothing of him,' she sobbed, feeling for her pocket handkerchief. 'He left me when Maryann was a baby, went mining to America, and after about six months never wrote a line nor sent me a penny bit. I can't say whether he's alive or dead, the villain. All I've heard of him's the bad—and I've heard nothing for years an' all, now.' She sobbed violently.

The golden-skinned, handsome man near the fire watched her as she wept. He was frightened, he was troubled, he was bewildered, but none of his emotions altered him underneath.

There was no sound in the room but the violent sobbing of the landlady. The men, one and all, were overcome.

'Don't you think as you'd better go, for to-night?' said the sergeant to the man, with sweet reasonableness. 'You'd better leave it a bit, and arrange something between you. You can't have much claim on a woman, I should imagine, if it's how she says. And you've come down on her a bit too sudden-like.'

The landlady sobbed heart-brokenly. The man watched her large breasts shaken. They seemed to cast a spell over his mind.

'How I've treated her, that's no matter,' he replied. 'I've come back, and I'm going to stop in my own home— for a bit, anyhow. There you've got it.'

'A dirty action,' said the sergeant, his face flushing dark. 'A dirty action, to come, after deserting a woman for that number of years, and want to force yourself on her! A dirty action—as isn't allowed by the law.'

The landlady wiped her eyes.

'Never you mind about law or nothing,' cried the man, in a strange, strong voice. 'I'm not moving out of this public to-night.'

The woman turned to the soldiers behind her, and said in a wheeding, sarcastic tone:

'Are we going to stand it, boys? Are we going to be done like this, Sergeant Thomas, by a scoundrel and a bully as has led a life beyond *mention* in those American mining-camps, and then wants to come back and make havoc of a poor woman's life and savings, after having left her with a baby in arms to struggle as best she might? It's a crying shame if nobody will stand up for me—a crying shame—!'

The soldiers and the little sergeant were bristling. The woman stooped and rummaged under the counter for a minute. Then, unseen to the man away near the fire, she threw out a plaited grass rope, such as is used for binding bales, and left it lying near the feet of the young soldiers, in the gloom at the back of the bar.

Then she rose and fronted the situation.

'Come now,' she said to the man, in a reasonable, coldly-coaxing tone, 'put your coat on and leave us alone. Be a man, and not worse than a brute of a German. You can get a bed easy enough in St. Just, and if you've nothing to pay for it, sergeant would lend you a couple of shillings, I'm sure he would.'

All eyes were fixed on the man. He was looking down at the woman like a creature spell-bound or possessed by some devil's own intention.

'I've got money of my own,' he said. 'Don't you be frightened for your money, I've plenty of that, for the time.'

'Well, then,' she coaxed, in a cold, almost sneering, propitiation, 'put your coat on and go where you're wanted—be a *man*, not a brute of a German.'

She had drawn quite near to him, in her challenging coaxing intentness. He looked down at her with his bewitched face.

'No, I shan't,' he said. 'I shan't do no such thing. *You'll* put me up for to-night.'

'Shall I?' she cried. And suddenly she flung her arms round him, hung on to him with all her powerful weight, calling to the soldiers: 'Get the rope, boys, and fasten him up. Alfred—John, quick now—'

The man reared, looked round with maddened eyes, and heaved his powerful body. But the woman was powerful also, and very heavy, and was clenched with the determination of death. Her face, with its exulting, horribly vindictive look, was turned up to him from his own breast; he reached back his head frantically, to get away from it. Meanwhile the young soldiers, after having watched this frightful Laocoon swaying for a moment, stirred, and the malicious one darted swiftly with the rope. It was tangled a little.

'Give me the end here,' cried the sergeant.

Meanwhile the big man heaved and struggled, swung the woman round against the seat and the table, in his convulsive effort to get free. But she pinned down his arms like a cuttle-fish wreathed heavily upon him. And he heaved and swayed, and they thrashed about the room, the soldiers hopping, the furniture bumping.

The young soldier had got the rope once round, the brisk sergeant helping him. The woman sank heavily lower, they got the rope round several times. In the struggle the victim fell over against the table. The ropes tightened till they cut his arms. The woman clung to his knees. Another soldier ran in a flash of genius, and fastened the strange man's feet with the pair of braces. Seats had crashed over, the table was thrown against the wall, but the man was bound, his arms pinned against his sides, his feet tied. He lay half-fallen, sunk against the table, still for a moment.

The woman rose, and sank, faint, on to the seat against the wall. Her breast heaved, she could not speak, she thought she was going to die. The bound man lay against the overturned table, his coat all twisted and pulled up beneath the ropes, leaving the loins exposed. The soldiers stood around, a little dazed, but excited with the row.

The man began to struggle again, heaving instinctively against the ropes, taking great, deep breaths. His face, with its golden skin, flushed dark and surcharged. He heaved again. The great veins in his neck stood out. But it was no good, he went relaxed. Then again, suddenly, he jerked his feet.

'Another pair of braces, William,' cried the excited soldier. He threw himself on the legs of the bound man, and managed to fasten the knees. Then again there was stillness. They could hear the clock tick.

The woman looked at the prostrate figure, the strong, straight limbs, the strong back bound in subjection, the wide-eyed face that reminded her of a calf tied in a sack in a cart, only its head stretched dumbly backwards. And she triumphed.

The bound-up body began to struggle again. She watched fascinated the muscles working, the shoulders, the hips, the large, clean thighs. Even now he might break the ropes. She was afraid. But the lively young soldier sat on the shoulders of the bound man, and after a few perilous moments, there was stillness again.

'Now,' said the judicious sergeant to the bound man, 'if we untie you, will you promise to go off and make no more trouble?'

'You'll not untie him in here,' cried the woman. 'I wouldn't trust him as far as I could blow him.'

There was silence.

'We might carry him outside, and undo him there,' said the soldier. 'Then we could get the policeman, if he made any more bother.'

'Yes,' said the sergeant. 'We could do that.' Then again, in an altered, almost severe tone, to the prisoner: 'If we undo you outside, will you take your coat and go without creating any more disturbance?'

But the prisoner would not answer, he only lay with wide, dark, bright eyes, like a bound animal. There was a space of perplexed silence.

'Well, then, do as you say,' said the woman irritably. 'Carry him out amongst you, and let us shut up the house.'

They did so. Picking up the bound man, the four soldiers staggered clumsily into the silent square in front of the inn, the woman following with the cap and the overcoat. The young soldiers quickly unfastened the braces from the prisoner's legs, and they hopped indoors. They were in their stocking-feet, and outside the stars flashed cold. They stood in the doorway watching. The man lay quite still on the cold ground.

'Now,' said the sergeant, in a subdued voice, 'I'll loosen the knot, and he can work himself free, if you go in, Missis.'

She gave a last look at the dishevelled, bound man, as he sat on the ground. Then she went indoors, followed quickly by the sergeant. Then they were heard locking and barring the door.

The man seated on the ground outside worked and strained at the rope. But it was not so easy to undo himself even now. So, with hands bound, making an effort, he got on his feet, and went and worked the cord against the rough edge of an old wall. The rope, being of a kind of plaited grass, soon frayed and broke, and he freed himself. He had various contusions. His arms were hurt and bruised from the bonds. He rubbed them slowly. Then he pulled his clothes straight, stooped, put on his cap, struggled into his overcoat, and walked away.

The stars were very brilliant. Clear as crystal, the beam from the lighthouse under the cliffs struck rhythmically on the night. Dazed, the man walked along the road past the churchyard. Then he stood leaning up against a wall, for a long time.

He was roused because his feet were so cold. So he pulled himself together, and turned again in the silent night, back towards the inn.

The bar was in darkness. But there was a light in the kitchen. He hesitated. Then very quietly he tried the door.

He was surprised to find it open. He entered, and quietly closed it behind him. Then he went down the step past the bar-counter, and through to the lighted doorway of the kitchen. There sat his wife, planted in front of the range, where a furze fire was burning. She sat in a chair full in front of the range, her knees wide apart on the fender. She looked over her shoulder at him as he entered, but she did not speak. Then she stared in the fire again.

It was a small, narrow kitchen. He dropped his cap on the table that was covered with yellowish American cloth, and took a seat with his back to the wall, near the oven. His wife still sat with her knees apart, her feet on the steel fender and stared into the fire, motionless. Her skin was smooth and rosy in the firelight. Everything in the house was very clean and bright. The man sat silent, too, his head dropped. And thus they remained.

It was a question who would speak first. The woman leaned forward and poked the ends of the sticks in between the bars of the range. He lifted his head and looked at her.

'Others gone to bed, have they?' he asked.

But she remained closed in silence.

' "S a cold night, out,' he said, as if to himself.

And he laid his large, yet well-shapen workman's hand on the top of the stove, that was polished black and smooth as velvet. She would not look at him, yet she glanced out of the corners of her eyes.

His eyes were fixed brightly on her, the pupils large and electric like those of a cat.

'I should have picked you out among thousands,' he said. 'Though you're bigger than I'd have believed. Fine flesh you've made.'

She was silent for some time. Then she turned in her chair upon him.

'What do you think of yourself,' she said, 'coming back on me like this after over fifteen year? You don't think I've not heard of you, neither, in Butte City and elsewhere?'

He was watching her with his clear, translucent, unchallenged eyes.

'Yes,' he said. 'Chaps comes an' goes—I've heard tell of you from time to time.'

She drew herself up.

'And what lies have you heard about *me*?' she demanded superbly.

'I dunno as I've heard any lies at all—'cept as you was

getting on very well, like.'

His voice ran warily and detached. Her anger stirred again in her violently. But she subdued it, because of the danger there was in him, and more, perhaps, because of the beauty of his head and his level drawn brows, which she could not bear to forfeit.

'That's more than I can say of *you*,' she said. 'I've heard more harm than good about *you*.'

'Ay, I dessay,' he said looking in the fire. It was a long time since he had seen the furze burning, he said to himself. There was a silence, during which she watched his face.

'Do you call yourself a *man*?' she said, more in contemptuous reproach than in anger. 'Leave a woman as you've left me, you don't care to what!– and then to turn up in *this* fashion, without a word to say for yourself.'

He stirred in his chair, planted his feet apart, and resting his arms on his knees, looked steadily into the fire without answering. So near to her was his head, and the close black hair, she could scarcely refrain from starting away, as if it would bite her.

'Do you call that the action of a *man*?' she repeated.

'No,' he said, reaching and poking the bits of wood into the fire with his fingers. 'I didn't call it anything, as I know of. It's no good calling things by any names whatsoever, as I know of.'

She watched him in his actions. There was a longer and longer pause between each speech, though neither knew it.

'I *wonder* what you think of yourself!' she exclaimed, with vexed emphasis. 'I *wonder* what sort of fellow you take yourself to be!' She was really perplexed as well as angry.

'Well,' he said, lifting his head to look at her, 'I guess I'ill answer for my own faults, if everybody else'll answer for theirs.'

Her heart beat fiery hot as he lifted his face to her. She breathed heavily, averting her face, almost losing her self-control.

'And what do you take *me* to be?' she cried, in real helplessness.

His face was lifted, watching her soft, averted face. And the softly heaving mass of her breasts.

'I take you,' he said, with that laconic truthfulness which exercised such power over her, 'to be the deuce of a fine woman—darn me if you're not as fine a built woman as I've seen, handsome with it as well. I shouldn't have expected you to put on such handsome flesh: 'struth I shouldn't.'

Her heart beat fiery hot, as he watched her with those bright agate eyes, fixedly.

'Been very handsome to *you*, for fifteen years, my sakes!' she replied.

He made no answer to this, but sat with his bright, quick eyes upon her.

There he rose. She started involuntarily. But he only said, in his laconic, measured way:

'It's warm in here now.'

And he pulled off his overcoat throwing it on the table. She sat as it slightly cowed, whilst he did so.

'Them ropes has given my arms something, by Ga-ard,' he drawled, feeling his arms with his hands.

Still she sat in her chair before him, slightly cowed.

'You was sharp, wasn't you, to catch me like that, eh?' he smiled slowly. 'By Ga-ard, you had me fixed proper, proper you had. Darn me, you fixed me up proper—proper, you did.'

He leaned forward in his chair towards her.

'I don't think no worse of you for it, no, darned if I do. Fine pluck in a woman's what I admire. That I do, indeed.'

She only gazed into the fire.

'We fet from the start, we did. And, my word, you begin again quick the minute you see me, you did. Darn me, you was too sharp for me. A darn fine woman, puts up a darn good fight. Darn me if I could find a fine woman you be, truth to say, at this minute.'

She only sat glowering into the fire.

'As grand a pluck as a man could wish to find in a woman, ture as I'm here,' he said, reaching forward his hand and tentatively touching her between her full, warm breasts, quietly.

She started, and seemed to shudder. But his hand insinuated itself between her breasts, as she continued to gaze in the fire.

'And don't you think I've come back here a-begging,' he said. 'I've more than *one* thousand pounds to my name, I have. And a bit of a fight for a how-de-do pleases me, that it do. But that doesn't mean as you're going to deny as you're my Missis . . .'

SUN

I

'Take her away, into the sun,' the doctors said.

She herself was sceptical of the sun, but she permitted herself to be carried away, with her child, and a nurse, and her mother, over the sea.

The ship sailed at midnight. And for two hours her husband stayed with her, while the child was put to bed, and the passengers came on board. It was a black night, the Hudson swayed with heavy blackness, shaken over with spilled dribbles of light. She leaned on the rail, and looking down thought: This is the sea; it is deeper than one imagines, and fuller of memories. At that moment the sea seemed to heave like the serpent of chaos that had lived for ever.

'These partings are no good, you know,' her husband was saying, at her side. 'They're no good. I don't like them.'

His tone was full of apprehension, misgiving, and there was a certain note of clinging to the last straw of hope.

'No, neither do I,' she responded in a flat voice.

She remembered how bitterly they had wanted to get away from one another, he and she. The emotion of parting gave a slight tug at her emotions, but only caused the iron that had gone into her soul to gore deeper.

So, they looked at their sleeping son, and the father's eyes were wet. But it is not the wetting of the eyes which counts, it is the deep iron rhythm of habit, the year-long, life-long habits; the deep-set stroke of power.

And in their two lives the stroke of power was hostile, his and hers. Like two engines running at variance, they shattered one another.

'All ashore! All ashore!'

'Maurice, you must go!'

And she thought to herself: For him it is *All Ashore!* For me it is *Out to sea!*

Well, he waved his hanky on the midnight dreariness of the pier as the boat inched away; one among the crowd. One among a crowd! *C'est ça!*

The ferry-boats, like great dishes piled with rows of lights, were still slanting across the Hudson. That black mouth must be the Lackawanna Station.

The ship ebbed on, the Hudson seemed interminable. But at last they were round the bend, and there was the poor harvest of lights at the Battery. Liberty flung up her torch in a tantrum. There was the wash of the sea.

And though the Atlantic was grey as lava, she did come at last into the sun. Even she had a house above the bluest of seas, with a vast garden, or vineyard, all vines and olives steeply, terrace after terrace, to the strip of coast-plain; and the garden full of secret places, deep groves of lemon far down in the cleft of the earth, and hidden, pure green reservoirs of water; then a spring issuing out of a little cavern, where the old Sicules had drunk before the Greeks came; and a grey goat bleating, stabled in an ancient tomb, with all the niches empty. There was the scent of mimosa, and beyond the snow of the volcano.

She saw it all, and in a measure it was soothing. But it was all external. She didn't really care about it. She was herself, just the same, with all her anger and frustration inside her, and her incapacity to feel anything real. The child irritated her, and preyed on her peace of mind. She felt so horribly, ghastly responsible for him; as if she must be responsible for every breath he drew. And that was torture to her, to the child, and to everybody else concerned.

'You know, Juliet, the doctor told you to lie in the sun, without your clothes. Why don't you?' said the mother.

'When I am fit to do so, I will. Do you want to kill me?' Juliet flew at her.

'To kill you, no! Only to do you good.'

'For God's sake, leave off wanting to do me good.'

The mother at last was so hurt and incensed, she departed. The sea went white—and then invisible. Pouring rain fell. It was cold, in the house built for the sun.

Again a morning when the sun lifted himself naked and molten, sparkling over the sea's rim. The house faced south-west. Juliet lay in her bed and watched him rise. It was as if she had never seen the sun rise before. She had never seen the naked sun stand up pure upon the sea-line, shaking the night off himself.

So the desire sprang secretly in her to go naked in the sun. She cherished her desire like a secret.

But she wanted to go away from the house—away from people. And it is not easy, in a country where every olive tree has eyes, and every slope is seen from afar, to go hidden.

But she found a place: a rocky bluff, shoved out to the sea and sun and overgrown with large cactus, the flat-leaved cactus called prickly pear. Out of this blue-grey knoll of cactus rose one cypress tree, with a pallid, thick trunk, and a tip that leaned over, flexible, up in the blue. It stood like a guardian looking to sea; or a low, silvery

candle whose huge flame was darkness against light: eart'
sending up her proud tongue of gloom.

Juliet sat down by the cypress trees and took off her clothes. The contorted cactus made a forest, hideous yet fascinating, about her. She sat and offered her bosom to the sun, sighing, even now, with a certain hard pain, against the cruelty of having to give herself.

But the sun marched in blue heaven and sent down his rays as he went. She felt the soft air of the sea on her breasts, that seemed as if they would never ripen. But she hardly felt the sun. Fruits that would wither and not mature, her breasts.

Soon, however, she felt the sun inside them, warmer than ever love had been, warmer than milk or the hands of her baby. At last, at last her breasts were like long white grapes in the hot sun.

She slide off all her clothes and lay naked in the sun, and as she lay she looked up through her fingers at the central sun, his blue pulsing roundness, whose outer edges streamed brilliance. Pulsing with marvellous blue, and alive, and streaming white fire from his edges, the sun! He faced down to her with his look of blue fire, and enveloped her breasts and her face, her throat, her tired belly, her knees, her thighs and her feet.

She lay with shut eyes, the colour of rosy flame through her lids. It was too much. She reached and put leaves over her eyes. Then she lay again, like a long white gourd in the sun, that must ripen to gold.

She could feel the sun penetrating even into her bones; nay, farther, even into her emotions and her thoughts. The dark tensions of her emotion began to give way, the cold dark clots of her thoughts began to dissolve. She was beginning to feel warm right through. Turning over, she let her shoulders dissolve in the sun, her loins, the backs of her things, even her heels. And she lay half stunned with wonder at the thing that was happening to her. Her weary, chilled heart was melting, and, in melting, evaporating.

When she was dressed again she lay once more and looked up at the cypress tree, whose crest, a flexible filament, fell this way and that in the breeze. Meanwhile, she was conscious of the great sun roaming in heaven.

So, dazed, she went home, only half-seeing, sun-blinded and sun-dazed. And her blindness was like a richness to her, and her dim, warm, heavy half-consciousness was like wealth.

'Mummy! Mummy!' her child came running towards her, calling in that peculiar bird-like little anguish of want, always wanting her. She was surprised that her drowsed heart for once felt none of the anxious love-anguish in return. She caught the child up in her arms, but she thought: He should not be such a lump! If he were in the sun, he would spring up.

She resented, rather, his little hands clutching at her, especially at her neck. She pulled her throat away. She did not want to be touched. She put the child gently down.

'Run!' she said. 'Run in the sun!'

And there and then she took off his clothes and set him naked on the warm terrace.

'Play in the sun!' she said.

He was frightened and wanted to cry. But she, in the warm indolence of her body, and the complete indifference of her heart, rolled him an orange across the red tiles, and with his soft, unformed little body he toddled after it. Then immediately he had it, he dropped it because it felt strange against his flesh. And he looked back at her, querulous, wrinkling his face to cry, frightened because he was stark.

'Bring me the orange,' she said, amazed at her own deep indifference to his trepidation. 'Bring Mummy the orange.'

'He shall not grow up like his father,' she said to herself. 'Like a worm that the sun has never seen.'

II

She had had the child so much on her mind, in a torment of responsibility, as if, having borne him, she had to answer for his whole existence. Even if his nose were running, it had been repulsive and a goad in her vitals, as if she must say to herself: Look at the thing you brought forth!

Now a change took place. She was no longer vitally interested in the child, she took the strain of her anxiety and her will from off him. And he thrived all the more for it.

She was thinking inside herself, of the sun in his splendour, and her mating with him. Her life was now a whole ritual. She lay always awake, before dawn, watching for the grey to colour to pale gold, to know if cloud lay on the sea's edge. Her joy was when he rose all molten in his nakedness, and threw off blue-white fire, into the tender heaven.

But sometimes he came ruddy, like a big, shy creature. And sometimes slow and crimson red, with a look of anger, slowly pushing and shouldering. Sometimes again she could not see him, only the level cloud threw down gold and scarlet from above, as he moved behind the wall.

She was fortunate. Weeks went by, and though the

dawn was sometimes clouded, and afternoon was sometimes grey, never a day passed sunless, and most days, winter though it was, streamed radiant. Then thin little wild crocuses came up mauve and stripped, the wild narcissi hung their winter stars.

Every day she went down to the cypress tree, among the cactus grove on the knoll with yellowish cliffs at the foot. She was wiser and subtler now, wearing only a dove-grey wrapper, and sandals. So that in an instant, in any hidden niche, she was naked to the sun. And the moment she was covered again she was grey and invisible.

Every day, in the morning towards noon, she lay at the foot of the powerful, silver-pawed cypress tree, while the sun rode jovial in heaven. By now she knew the sun in every thread of her body, there was not a cold shadow left. And her heart, that anxious, straining heart, had disappeared altogether, like a flower that falls in the sun, and leaves only a ripe seed-case.

She knew the sun in heaven, blue-molten with his white fire edges, throwing off fire. And though he shone on all the world, when she lay unclothed he focussed on her. It was one of the wonders of the sun, he could shine on a million people and still be the radiant, splendid, unique sun, focussed on her alone.

With her knowledge of the sun, and her conviction that the sun *knew* her, in the cosmic carnal sense of the word, came over her a feeling of detachment from people, and a certain contempt for human beings altogether. They were so un-elemental, so unsunned. They were so like graveyard worms.

Even the peasants passing up the rocky, ancient little road with their donkeys, sun-blackened as they were, were not sunned right through. There was a little soft white core of fear, like a snail in a shell, where the soul of the men cowered in fear of death, and in fear of the natural blaze of life. He dared not quite emerge: always innerly cowed. All men were like that.

Why admit men!

With her indifference to people, to men, she was not now so cautious about being unseen. She had told Marinina, who went shopping for her in the village, that the doctor had ordered sun-baths. Let that suffice.

Marinina was a woman over sixty, tall, thin, erect, with curling dark grey hair, and dark grey eyes that had the shrewdness of thousands of years in them, with the laugh that underlies all long experience. Tragedy is lack of experience.

'It must be beautiful to go unclothed in the sun,' said Marinina, with a shrewd laugh in her eyes, as she looked keenly at the other woman. Juliet's fair, bobbed hair curled in a little cloud at her temple. Marinina was a woman of magna Græcia, and had far memories. She looked again at Juliet. 'But you have to be beautiful yourself, if you're not going to give offence to the sun? Isn't it so?' she added, with that queer, breathless little laugh of the women of the past.

'Who knows if I am beautiful?' said Juliet.

But beautiful or not, she felt that by the sun she was appreciated. Which is the same.

When, out of the sun at noon, sometimes she stole down over the rocks and past the stiff-edge, down to the deep gully where the lemons hung in cool eternal shadow, and in the silence slipped off her wrapper to wash herself quickly at one of the deep, clear green basins, she would notice, in the bare green twilight under the lemon leaves, that all her body was another person.

So she remembered that the Greeks had said, a white, unsunned body was fishy and unhealthy.

And she would rub a little olive oil in her skin, and wander a moment in the dark underworld of the lemons, balancing a lemon flower in her navel, laughing to herself. There was just a chance some peasant might see her. But if he did he would be more afraid of her than she of him. She knew the white core of fear in the clothed bodies of men.

She knew it even in her little son. How he mistrusted her, now that she laughed at him, with the sun in her face! She insisted on his toddling naked in the sunshine every day. And now his litle body was pink, too, his blond hair was pushed thick from his brow, his cheeks had a pomegranate scarlet, in the delicate gold of the sunny skin. He was bonny and healthy, and the servants, loving his red and gold and blue, called him an angel from heaven.

But he mistrusted his mother: she laughed at him. And she saw in his wide blue eyes, under the little frown, that centre of fear, misgiving, which she believed was at the centre of all male eyes now. She called it fear of the sun.

'He fears the sun,' she would say to herself, looking down into the eyes of the child.

And as she watched him toddling, swaying, tumbling in the sunshine, making his little, bird-like noises, she saw that he held himself tight and hidden from the sun, inside himself. His spirit was like a snail in a shell, in a damp, cold crevice inside himself. It made her think of his father. She wished she could make him come forth, break out in a gesture of recklessness and salutation.

She determined to take him with her, down to the cypress tree among the cactus. She would have to watch him, because of the thorns. But surely in that place he would come forth from that little shell, deep inside him. That little civilised tension would disappear off his brow.

She spread a rug for him and sat him down. Then she slid off her wrapper and lay down herself, watching a hawk high in the blue, and the tip of the cypress hanging over.

The boy played with stones on the rug. When he got up to toddle away, she sat up too. He turned and looked at her. Almost, from his blue eyes, it was the challenging, warm look of the true male. And he was handsome, with the scarlet in the golden blond of his skin. He was not really white. His skin was gold-dusky.

'Mind the thorns, darling,' she said.

'Thorns!' re-echoed the child, in a birdy chirp, still looking at her over his shoulder, like some naked cherub in a picture, doubtful.

'Nasty prickly thorns.'

' 'Ickly thorns!'

He staggered in his little sandals over the stones, pulling at the dry, wild mint. She was quick as a serpent, leaping to him, when he was going to fall against the prickles. It surprised even herself. 'What a wild cat I am, really!' she said to herself.

She brought him every day, when the sun shone, to the cypress tree.

'Come!' she said. 'Let us go to the cypress tree.'

And if there was a cloudy day, with the tramontana blowing, so that she could not go down, the child would chirp incessantly: 'Cypress tree! Cypress tree!'

He missed it as much as she did.

It was not just taking sunbaths. It was much more than that. Something deep inside her unfolded and relaxed, and she was given. By some mysterious power inside her, deeper than her known consciousness and will, she was put into connection with the sun, and the stream flowed of itself, from her womb. She herself, her conscious self, was secondary, a secondary person, almost an onlooker. The true Juliet was this dark flow from her deep body to the sun.

She had always been mistress of herself, aware of what she was doing, and held tense for her own power. Now she felt inside her quite another sort of power, something greater than herself, flowing by itself. Now she was vague, but she had a power beyond herself.

III

The end of February was suddenly very hot. Almond blossom was falling like pink snow, in the touch of the smallest breeze. The mauve, silky little anemonies were out, the asphodels tall in bud, and the sea was cornflower blue.

Juliet had ceased to trouble about anything. Now, most of the day, she and the child were naked in the sun, and it was all she wanted. Sometimes she went down to the sea to bathe; often she wandered in the gullies where the sun shone in, and she was out of sight. Sometimes she saw a peasant with an ass, and he saw her. But she went so simply and quietly with her child; and the fame of the sun's healing power, for the soul as well as for the body, had already spread among the people; so that there was no excitement.

The child and she were now both tanned with a rosy-golden tan all over. 'I am another being!' she said to herself, as she looked at her redgold breasts and thighs.

The child, too, was another creature, with a peculiar, quiet, sun-darkened absorption. Now he played by himself in silence, and she hardly need notice him. He seemed no longer to know when he was alone.

There was a breeze, and the sea was ultramarine. She sat by the great silver paw of the cypress tree, drowsed in the sun, but her breasts alert, full of sap. She was becoming aware that an activity was rousing in her, an activity which would carry her into a new way of life. Still she did not want to be aware. She knew well enough the vast cold apparatus of civilisation, so difficult to evade.

The child had gone a few yards down the rocky path, round the great sprawling of a cactus. She had seen him, a real gold-brown infant of the winds, with burnt gold hair and red cheeks, collecting the speckled pitcher-flowers and laying them in rows. He could balance now, and was quick for his own emergencies, like an absorbed young animal playing silent.

Suddenly she heard him speaking: '*Look, Mummy! Mummy, look!*' A note in his bird-like voice made her lean forward sharply.

Her heart stood still. He was looking over his naked little shoulder at her, and pointing with a loose little hand at a snake which had reared itself up a yard away from him, and was opening its mouth so that its forked, soft tongue flickered black like a shadow, uttering a short hiss.

'Look, Mummy!'

'Yes, darling, it's a snake!' came the slow, deep voice.

He looked at her, his wide blue eyes uncertain whether to be afraid or not. Some stillness of the sun in her reassured him.

'Snake!' he chirped.

'Yes, darling! Don't touch it, it can bite.'

The snake had sunk down, and was reaching away from the coils in which it had been basking asleep, and slowly was easing its long, gold-brown body into the rocks, with slow curves. The boy turned and watched it in silence out of sight.

'Snake gone back,' he said.

'Yes, it's gone back. Come to Mummy a moment.'

He came and sat with his plump, naked little body on her naked lap, and she smoothed his burnt, bright hair. She said nothing, feeling that everything was passed. The curious soothing power of the sun filled her, filled the whole place like a charm, and the snake was part of the place, along with her and the child.

Another day, in the dry stone wall of one of the olive terraces, she saw a black snake horizontally creeping.

'Marinina,' she said, 'I saw a black snake. Are they harmful?'

'Ah, the black snakes, no! But the yellow ones, yes! If the yellow ones bite you, you die. But they frighten me, they frighten me, even the black ones, when I see one.'

Juliet still went to the cypress tree with the child. But she always looked carefully round before she sat down, examining everywhere where the child might go. Then she would lie and turn to the sun again, her tanned, pear-shaped breasts pointing up. She would take no thought for the morrow. She refused to think outside her garden, and she could not write letters. She would tell the nurse to write.

IV

It was March, and the sun was growing very powerful. In the hot hours she would lie in the shade of the trees, or she would even go down to the depths of the cool lemon grove. The child ran in the distance, like a young animal absorbed in life.

One day she was sitting in the sun on the steep slope of the gully, having bathed in one of the great tanks. Below, under the lemons, the child was wading among the yellow oxalis flowers of the shadow, gathering fallen lemons, passing with his tanned little body into flecks of light, moving all dappled.

Suddenly, high over the land's edge, against the full-lit pale blue sky, Marinina appeared, a black cloth tied round her head, calling quietly: '*Signora! Signora Giulietta!*'

Juliet faced round, standing up. Marinina paused a moment, seeing the naked woman standing alert, her sun-faded fair hair in a little cloud. Then the swift old woman came on down the slant of the steep track.

She stood a few steps, erect, in front of the sun-coloured woman, and eyed her shrewdly.

'But how beautiful you are, you!' she said coolly, almost cynically. 'There is your husband.'

'My husband!' cried Juliet.

The old woman gave a shrewd bark of a little laugh, the mockery of the women of the past.

'Haven't you got one, a husband, you?' she taunted.

'But where is he?' cried Juliet.

The old woman glanced over her shoulder.

'He was following me,' she said. 'But he will not have found the path.' And she gave another little bark of a laugh.

The paths were all grown high with grass and flowers and nepitella, till they were like bird-trails in an eternally wild place. Strange, the vivid wildness of the old places of civilisation, a wildness that is not gaunt.

Juliet looked at her serving-woman with meditating eyes.

'Oh, very well!' she said at last. 'Let him come.'

'Let him come here? Now?' asked Marinina, her laughing, smoke-grey eyes looking with mockery into Juliet's. Then she gave a little jerk of her shoulders.

'All right, as you wish. But for him it is a rare one!'

She opened her mouth in a laugh of noiseless joy. Then she pointed down to the child, who was heaping lemons against his little chest. 'Look how beautiful the child is! That, certainly, will please him, poor thing. Then I'll bring him.'

'Bring him,' said Juliet.

The old woman scrambled rapidly up the track again. Maurice was standing grey-faced, in his grey felt hat and his dark grey suit, at a loss among the vine terraces. He looked pathetically out of place, in that resplendent sunshine and the grace of the old Greek world; like a blot of ink on the pale, sun-glowing slope.

'Come!' said Marinina to him. 'She is down here.'

And swiftly she led the way, striding with a rapid stride, making her way through the grasses. Suddenly she stopped on the brow of the slope. The tops of the lemon trees were dark, away below.

'You, you go down here,' she said to him, and he thanked her, looking up at her swiftly.

He was a man of forty, clean-shaven, grey-faced, very quiet and really shy. He managed his own business carefully, without startling success, but efficiently. And he confided in nobody. The old woman of Magna Græcia saw him at a glance: he is good, she said to herself, but not a man, poor thing.

'Down there is the Signora!' said Marinina, pointing like one of the Fates.

And again he said. 'Thank you! Than you!' without a twinkle, and stepped carefully into the track. Marinina lifted her chin with a joyful wickedness. Then she strode off towards the house.

Maurice was watching his step through the tangle of Mediterranean herbage, so he did not catch sight of his wife till he came round a little bend, quite near her. She was standing erect and nude by the jutting rock, glistening with the sun and with warm life. Her breasts seemed to be lifting up, alert, to listen, her thighs looked brown and fleet. Her glance on him, as he came like ink on blotting paper, was swift and nervous.

Maurice, poor fellow, hesitated, and glanced away from her. He turned his face aside.

'Hello, Julie!' he said, with a little nervous cough— 'Splendid! Splendid!'

He advanced with his face averted, shooting further glances at her, as she stood with the peculiar satiny gleam of the sun on her tanned skin. Somehow she did not seem so terribly naked. It was the golden-rose tan of the sun that clothed her.

'Hello, Maurice!' she said, hanging back from him. 'I wasn't expecting you so soon.'

'No,' he said. 'No! I managed to slip away a little earlier.'

And again he coughed awkwardly.

They stood several yards away from one another, and there was silence.

'Well!' he said, 'er—this is splendid, splendid! You are— er—splendid! Where is the boy?'

'There he is,' she said, pointing down to where a naked urchin in the deep shade was piling fallen lemons together.

The father gave an odd little laugh.

'Ah, yes, there he is! So there's the little man! Fine!' he said. He really was thrilled in his suppressed nervous soul. 'Hello, Johnny!' he called, and it sounded rather feeble. 'Hello, Johnny!'

The child looked up, spilling lemons from his chubby arms, but did not respond.

'I guess we'll go down to him,' said Juliet, as she turned and went striding down the path. Her husband followed, watching the rosy, fleet-looking lifting and sinking of her quick hips, as she swayed a little in the socket of her waist. He was dazed with admiration, but also, at a deadly loss. What should he do with himself? He was utterly out of the picture, in his dark grey suit and pale grey hat, and his grey, monastic face of a shy business man.

'He looks all right, doesn't he,' said Juliet, as they came through the deep sea of yellow-flowering oxalis, under the lemon trees.

'Ah!–yes! yes! Splendid! Splendid! Hello, Johnny! Do you know Daddy? Do you know Daddy? Do you know Daddy, Johnny?'

He crouched down and held out his hands.

'Lemons!' said the child, birdily chirping. 'Two lemons!'

'Two lemons!' replied the father. 'Lots of lemons.'

The infant came and put a lemon in each of his father's open hands. Then he stood back to look.

'Two lemons!' repeated the father. 'Come, Johnny! Come and say "Hello" to Daddy.'

'Daddy going back?' said the child.

'Going back? Well–well–not to-day.'

And he gathered his son in his arms.

'Take a coat off! Daddy take a coat off!' said the boy,

squirming debonair away from the cloth.

'All right, son! Daddy take a coat off!'

He took off his coat and laid it carefully aside, then again took his son in his arms. The naked woman looked down at the naked infant in the arms of the man in his shirt-sleeves. The boy had pulled off the father's hat, and Juliet looked at the sleek, black-and-grey hair of her husband, not a hair out of place. And utterly, utterly indoors. She was silent for a long time, while the father talked to the child, who was fond of his Daddy.

'What are you going to do about it, Maurice?' she said suddenly.

He looked at her swiftly, sideways.

'Er—about what, Julie?'

'Oh, everything! About this! I can't go back into East Forty-Seventh.'

'Er—' he hesitated, 'no, I suppose not—not just now at least.'

'Never,' she said, and there was a silence.

'Well—er—I don't know,' he said.

'Do you think you can come out here?' she said.

'Yes, I can stay for a month. I think I can manage a month,' he hesitated. Then he ventured a complicated, shy peep at her, and hid his face again.

She looked down at him, her alert breasts lifted with a sigh, as if a breeze of impatience shook them.

'I can't go back,' she said slowly. 'I can't go back on this sun. If you can't come here—'

She ended on an open note. He glanced at her again and again, furtively, but with growing admiration and lessening confusion.

'No!' he said. 'This kind of thing suits you. You are splendid! No, I don't think you can go back.'

He was thinking of her in the New York flat, pale, silent, oppressing him terrible. He was the soul of gentle timidity, in his human relations, and her silent, awful hostility after the baby was born, had frightened him deeply. Because he had realised she couldn't help it. Women were like that. Their feelings took a reverse direction, even against their own selves, and it was awful—awful! Awful, awful to live in the house with a woman like that, whose feelings were reversed even against herself! He had felt himself ground down under the millstone of her helpless enmity. She had ground even herself down to the quick, and the child as well. No, anything rather than that.

'But what about *you*?' she asked.

'I? Oh, I! I can carry on the business, and—er—come over here for the holidays—as long as you like to stay. You stay as long as you wish.' He looked a long time down at the earth, then glanced up at her with a touch of supplication in his uneasy eyes.

'Even for ever?'

'Well—er—yes, if you like. For ever is a long time. One can't set a date.'

'And I can do anything I like?' She looked him straight in the eyes, challenging. And he was powerless against her rosy, wind-hardened nakedness.

'Er—yes! I suppose so! So long as you don't make yourself unhappy—or the boy.'

Again he looked up at her with a complicated, uneasy appeal—thinking of the child, but hoping for himself.

'I won't,' she said quickly.

'No!' he said. 'No! I don't think you will.'

There was a pause. The bells of the village were hastily clanging midday. That meant lunch.

She slipped into her grey crêpe kimono, and fastened a broad green sash round her waist. Then she slipped a little blue shirt over the boy's head, and they went up to the house.

At table she watched her husband, his grey city face, his fixed, black-grey hair, his very precise table manners, and his extreme moderation in eating and drinking. Sometimes he glanced at her, furtively, from under his black lashes. He had the gold-grey eyes of an animal that has been caught young, and reared completely in captivity.

They went on to the balcony for coffee. Below, beyond, on the next podere across the steep little gully, a peasant and his wife were sitting under an almond tree, near the green wheat, eating their midday meal from a little white cloth spread on the ground. There was a huge piece of bread, and glasses with dark wine.

Juliet put her husband with his back to this picture she sat facing. Because, the moment she and Maurice had come out on the balcony, the peasant had glanced up.

She knew him, in the distance, perfectly. He was a rather fat, very broad fellow of about thirty-five, and he chewed large mouthfuls of bread, His wife was stiff and dark-faced, handsome, sombre. They had no children. So much Juliet had learned.

The peasant worked a great deal alone, on the opposite podere. His clothes were always very clean and cared-for, white trousers and a coloured shirt, and an old straw hat. Both he and his wife had that air of quiet superiority which belongs to individuals, not to a class.

His attraction was in his vitality, the peculiar quick energy which gave a charm to his movements, stout and broad as he was. In the early days before she took to the sun, Juliet had met him suddenly, among the rocks, when she had scrambled over to the next podere. He had been aware of her before she saw him, so that when she did look up, he took off his hat, gazing at her with shyness and pride, from his big blue eyes. His face was broad, sunburnt, he had cropped brown moustache, and thick brown eyebrows, nearly as thick as his moustache, meeting under his low, wide brow.

'Oh!' she said. 'Can I walk here?'

'Surely!' he replied with that peculiar hot haste which characterised his movement. 'My padrone would wish you to walk wherever you like on his land.'

And he pressed back his head in the quick, vivid, shy generosity of his nature. She had gone on quickly. But instantly she had recognised the violent generosity of his blood, and the equally violent *farouche* shyness.

Since then she had seen him in the distance every day, and she came to realise that he was one who lived a good deal to himself, like a quick animal, and that his wife loved him intensely, with a jealousy that was almost hate; because, probably, he wanted to give himself still, still further, beyond where she could take him.

One day, when a group of peasants sat under a tree, she had seen him dancing quick and gay with a child—his wife watching darkly.

Gradually Juliet and he had become intimate, across the distance. They were aware of one another. She knew, in the morning, the moment he arrived with his ass. And the moment she went out on the balcony he turned to look. But they never saluted. Yet she missed him when he did not come to work on the podere.

Once, in the hot morning when she had been walking naked, deep in the gully between the two estates, she had came upon him, as he was bending down, with his powerful shoulders, picking up wood to pile on his motionless, waiting donkey. He saw her as he lifted his flushed face, and she was backing away. A flame went over his eyes, and a flame flew over her body, melting her bones. But she backed away behind the bushes, silently, and retreated whence she had come. And she wondered a little resentfully over the silence in which he could work, hidden in the bushy places. He had that wild animal faculty.

Since then there had been a definite pain of consciousness in the body of each of them, though neither would admit it, and they gave no sign of recognition. But the man's wife was instinctively aware.

And Juliet had thought: Why shouldn't I meet this man for an hour, and bear his child? Why should I have to identify my life with a man's life? Why not meet him for an hour, as long as the desire lasts, and no more? There is already the spark between us.

But she had never made any sign. And now she saw him looking up, from where he sat by the white cloth, opposite his black-clad wife, looking up at Maurice. The wife turned and looked, too, saturnine.

And Juliet felt a grudge come over her. She would have to bear Maurice's child again. She had seen it in her husband's eyes. And she knew it from his answer, when she spoke to him.

'Will you walk about in the sun, too, without your clothes?' she asked him.

'Why–er–yes! Yes, I should like to, while I'm here–I suppose it's quite private?'

There was a gleam in his eyes, a desperate kind of courage of his desire, and a glance at the alert lifting of her breasts in her wrapped. In this way, he was man, too, he faced the world and was not entirely quenched in his male courage. He would dare to walk in the sun, even ridiculously.

But he smelled of the world, and all its fetters and its mongrel cowering. He was banded with the brand that is not a hall-mark.

Ripe now, and brown-rosy all over with the sun, and with a heart like a fallen rose, she had wanted to go down to the hot, shy peasant and bear his child. Her sentiments had fallen like petals. She had seen the flushed blood in the burnt face, and the flame in the southern blue eyes, and the answer in her had been a gush of fire. He would have been a procreative sun-bath to her, and she wanted it.

Nevertheless, her next child would be Maurice's. The fatal chain of continuity would cause it.

Rupa-73
२२।६।५